SLAY IT
WITH A
DIAMOND

SLAY IT
WITH A
DIAMOND

THE DIAMOND DISTRICT MYSTERY SERIES, BOOK THREE

ROB BATES

Kenmore, WA

CAMEL
PRESS

A Camel Press book published by Epicenter Press

Epicenter Press
6524 NE 181st St.
Suite 2
Kenmore, WA 98028

For more information go to:
www.Camelpress.com
www.Coffeetownpress.com
www.Epicenterpress.com
www.robbatesauthor.com

This is a work of fiction. Names, characters, places, brands, media, and incidents are the product of the author's imagination or are used fictitiously.

Cover and interior design by Scott Book and Melissa Vail Coffman

Slay It With a Diamond
Copyright © 2023 by Rob Bates

Library of Congress Control Number: 2022936022

ISBN: 978-1-68492-045-7 (Trade Paper)
ISBN: 978-1-68492-046-4 (eBook)

Printed in the United States of America

To Susan and Mikey. Rock on.

ACKNOWLEDGEMENTS

THANK YOU TO MY EDITOR, Jennifer McCord of Coffeetown Press, for making this book better, and my agent, Dawn Dowdle, for making it happen.

Thank you to my writing group for all your excellent feedback.

Thank you to all the industry folk who have informed the writing of this book (and the prior two), and for all your patience and camaraderie over the years. And thanks to my co-workers at *JCK* and elsewhere.

As always, I give my sincere thanks and deepest love to my family, for your patience, support, and general awesomeness. Also, my friends. You're great, too.

And, of course, thank you to everyone who is reading this, especially if you've read the first two books. It means more than I can say.

CHAPTER ONE

Mimi Rosen had long been jealous of Rosalyn Lowery. She never liked to admit it, but she was.

Mimi didn't like being competitive. It made her feel small and petty. Besides, Mimi couldn't compete with Rosalyn Lowery. Rosalyn was too far ahead of her.

Her former newspaper colleague had just been promoted to deputy editor at *The Look*, the widely followed—and feared—"fashion Bible." Rosalyn's husband was the CEO of Lowery, the world-renowned, century-old, ultra-high-end jeweler.

Rosalyn had money, a husband, and a prestigious job. Mimi had none of those things.

So, when Rosalyn said she wanted to stop by Mimi's father's office to sell a diamond, Mimi flew into a panic.

The Max Rosen Diamond Company was a rundown mess. The office hadn't gotten any TLC since Mimi's mom died a few years ago. The carpet was frayed. Its brown wood-paneled walls were aged and peeling. Every desk was drowning in papers. Mimi cringed thinking how it must compare to the digs at Lowery or *The Look*. It wasn't even as nice as their old newspaper.

In the two years Mimi had worked at her father's office, she'd always wanted to fix up the place, but had never found the time, and her father was dead-set against it.

"When you're in the diamond business," Max would say, "you don't want your place to look too nice, because then people will think you have a lot of money, and they'll try and take you."

Since then, Mimi had seen plenty of well-maintained diamond offices. Her father just kept his a mess because that was how he had always done it, which was why he did most things.

With Rosalyn on her way, Mimi hurriedly grabbed stacks of paper from the desktops and dropped them into drawers—which wasn't easy, since most of the drawers were already filled to the brim.

"Be careful with that stuff!" Max yelled, adjusting the *yarmulke* on his bald head. He was dressed in his standard outfit—a white button-down shirt and brown wool pants. "There could be important things in there. I need to go through it all."

"If they're so important, why are they lying around?" Mimi asked.

Max ignored this. "What's with this sudden urge to clean up? Who are you expecting? Royalty?"

When Mimi said it was a member of the Lowery family, Max's mouth formed a circle, then he sprang from his chair and helped with the cleaning. There weren't that many jewelry names that impressed Max, but Lowery was one of them.

Lowery wasn't just any century-old jeweler. It was an institution. Magazines called it the store "everyone dreams of entering," and its salespeople were so notorious for being stuffy, it was nicknamed "Glowery." Its Fifty-Seventh Street flagship resembled a creamy limestone castle, complete with Lowery flag on top, marking its territory.

As they frantically tidied up, Mimi told her father, "Rosalyn and I used to work together at *The West Jersey Metro*. She's now the deputy editor of *The Look*. I'm hoping she'll give me some freelance work.

"She's coming over to sell a diamond. I'm asking you, please, be open-minded about what she has to offer. Obviously, you have to do what's right for your business, but if she has something nice for sale, I hope that you—" She flapped her hands. "Consider buying it."

Max stopped cleaning and stared at his daughter. "Basically, you're asking me to buy whatever she's selling, so she'll give you work."

"No!" Mimi said. "I would never—"

Max cut her off. "It's fine. I'll look at what she has, as I would with any private." He pinched his forehead. "But this seems strange to me. Why is she trying to sell me a diamond, when her husband's the head of a major jeweler?"

That was something Mimi wondered about, too. It was a good question.

ROSALYN SWEPT INTO THE OFFICE TWENTY minutes later, wearing a clingy orange dress topped with a leather jacket. It was an expertly calibrated mix of hip and elegant, perfect for a cool fall day. Her hair was a buttery brown, not the bleach-blonde Mimi remembered. A thick gold chain hung around her neck. While Rosalyn was close to Mimi's height—five foot, four—she wore glitzy heels that made her look taller; Mimi was impressed with how she walked without wobbling.

Mimi's outfit, on the other hand, consisted of nondescript flats and a plain brown dress she'd bought at Kohl's because her father insisted everyone wear "business attire" around the office. This was the first time she felt grateful for that policy. Mimi had cut her brown hair short, after months of growing it long. It looked fine. Rosalyn's looked better.

Rosalyn gave Mimi a perfunctory hug, said it was great to see her, and suggested that they should "do lunch" sometime—none of which Mimi took seriously. Mimi sat her on a chair facing her father's cluttered desk. Rosalyn didn't place her Birkin bag on the floor, but clutched it to her side.

"So," Max said, "my daughter said you work at the fashion Bible. I guess that means you work for God."

Mimi wanted to scream. Her dad was making dad jokes.

"I work directly under Eloise," Rosalyn said. She used the famed editor's first name as if the whole world would recognize it.

Mimi knew who she was. Her father just nodded.

"Mimi also said you're part of the Lowery family. They've built a sensational business over there."

"Yes," Rosalyn said. "My husband's grandfather founded the company." As Rosalyn talked, Mimi could hear her old New Jersey accent bubble up occasionally, only to be quickly submerged.

Mimi couldn't stop staring at her shoes. They appeared purple—or maybe pink, or mauve, or some weird blend of all three. Mimi spotted something shiny on their bottoms. Was it a gemstone? Even someone connected to the Lowery jewelry empire wouldn't have gemstones under their shoes; would they?

Rosalyn apparently sensed Mimi's interest. She crossed and uncrossed her legs and swung her shoes back and forth, continually bringing them into view. They were probably some Italian brand whose name Mimi couldn't pronounce, though she made a mental note to hunt for knockoffs on eBay.

Then came the question Mimi dreaded. "So, Mimi," Rosalyn asked, "what have you been up to?"

Mimi stammered a bit. "For the past two years, I've worked here. You know how it is with editorial jobs these days." Mimi hoped that would be a hint, since she'd reached out to Rosalyn, looking for work.

Rosalyn didn't react.

"I'm working on this cool new project," Mimi continued. "We're responsibly sourcing diamonds from the African Democratic Republic."

"Sounds great," Rosalyn responded, without much conviction. "And how's your husband?"

"We divorced three years ago." Mimi thought she'd told Rosalyn that in an old Facebook exchange, but *The Look's* deputy editor can't be expected to remember everything. "I'm now dating a police detective."

"Really?" Rosalyn re-crossed her legs. "How'd you meet him?"

"It just kind of happened. I was investigating this murder and—"

"Hold it." Rosalyn squinted. "You investigated a murder?"

"Well, yeah. I've investigated two."

"As a reporter?" Rosalyn asked.

"No. On my own." Mimi never liked mentioning she'd solved two murders. Nobody ever believed her. "It's a long story."

"We definitely need to get together and catch up. Anyway—" Rosalyn's voice became businesslike. "Let's discuss my diamond."

She reached into her purse and pulled out a yellow velour gold-trimmed box, with the "Lowery" logo embossed on top. She lifted the cover to reveal a heart-shaped brooch, which held a black diamond.

Max's brow knitted. "A black diamond, huh? In the trade, they're called carbonados. They're what we dealers call a specialty item. That means no one wants to buy them.

"Not that they're ugly, necessarily. But they're brittle, and a lot of them don't reflect light very well. Only the real nice ones are desirable."

"This is a nice one," Rosalyn declared. "A really nice one." She removed the diamond from the brooch. It was a pear shape, though it looked more like a dark teardrop.

When Max angled the diamond's table under his viewing lamp, light burst from its surface, and it gleamed like the outside of a Porsche.

"It *is* nice," Max said. As he examined it, his hands trembled slightly; even after decades in the industry, he still got excited by nice diamonds. "It has a good make," he said, meaning the diamond was well-cut.

"How much is it worth?" Rosalyn asked.

"It's hard to say," Max said, peering at it through a jeweler's loupe. "Has it been treated? That means: has any irradiation been done to improve its color?"

"Yes, I know what that means," Rosalyn said. "Remember, I'm a Lowery. I hear about this stuff all day. No, it hasn't been treated.

Here's its cert." She reached into her pocketbook and pulled out a yellowed grading report.

"Impressive," Max said, scanning the paper through his spectacles. "It says it's three carats and internally flawless."

"That's one of Lowery's mottos. 'Never less than flawless.'" Rosalyn said. "Every stone must be perfect clarity." She glanced around the room, then leaned in conspiratorially. "Though lately, the company's been selling VVS1s."

"Sorry to hear you're slumming," Max said.

He turned his attention to the gold heart-shaped brooch which held the diamond. "What's this?"

Rosalyn covered it with her hand. "Don't worry about the brooch. I'm having it melted down for scrap."

"What's it supposed to be?" Max said.

"A stylized heart," Rosalyn said.

Max shrugged. "Looks like a *tuchus*."

Mimi was mortified. Her father had just compared Rosalyn's brooch to a butt. She hoped that he'd buy the diamond. Otherwise, she could kiss getting an assignment from *The Look* goodbye.

Max spent another minute examining both the diamond and the report, then swiveled his chair toward his computer. "I'll check the biggest trading website for similar stones."

A sea of numbers, letters, and values appeared on screen. Mimi and Rosalyn watched as Max narrowed down list after list.

He angled the screen toward them. "This kind of item is super-rare. I can't find any comparable sales for a black stone of this quality. The closest was a five carater that sold for about thirty-two thousand dollars a year ago, and while that was a larger stone, it had a weaker color." He thought a bit. "How does twenty thousand dollars sound?"

"From everything I hear about this type of stone, color matters as much as size," said Rosalyn. "I think thirty thousand is a much fairer price."

Max looked startled by this sudden burst of negotiating savvy. His glasses bumped up and down on his nose. "Let's meet in the middle," he said. "Twenty-five."

"Fine."

"Before we shake on a deal here, I need to ask you something," Max said, his forehead suddenly full of lines. "Your husband is the head of Lowery. That's a big company. Doesn't he have trade contacts he can sell this to?"

Rosalyn's features tightened. "My husband doesn't know I am selling this."

Max peered at her. "Do you mind if I ask why?"

Rosalyn fidgeted in her chair. The conversation was clearly wandering into uncomfortable territory. Her polish was cracking. "Remember how Mimi just called something a long story? This is even longer."

Max put the diamond back on the papers and pushed them away. "I'll be honest, you seem like a perfectly nice person, but I find this strange. It seems like you want to get rid of this stone very quickly. Normally, that's a red flag, and I would cancel the sale immediately. But since you come from a good family, and you're a friend of Mimi's, I'll give you a chance to explain why you're so anxious to unload this thing."

Mimi reddened. *Why did her father have to be so blunt all the time?* Though, she had to admit, he had a point.

Rosalyn was quiet for a second. "I do have a reason, but you may not believe it." She slumped on the chair and her fancy shoes clomped on the floor. "The diamond is cursed."

Max hunched forward. "You're joking, right?"

Rosalyn shook her head. She wasn't.

CHAPTER TWO

Rosalyn calling her diamond "cursed" was strange. But it was strange that she'd come to Mimi's office at all.

Mimi had known Rosalyn Lowery before she was a Lowery, before she called herself Rosalyn. Fifteen years ago, when Roz Ghinkert was Mimi's co-worker on *The West Jersey Metro* night shift, she was a brash, fun Jersey girl, more interested in doing shots than doing lunch.

The late shift was usually slow and consisted mostly of monitoring the police scanner and wire services in case something exciting happened, which it rarely did. Even though Roz and Mimi tried to adjust their systems to the last-night schedule, they were almost always tired, prone to three a.m. giggle fits and pre-dawn confessionals.

They became close friends, though they were from very different backgrounds. Mimi was raised in an Orthodox Jewish family in Queens—though, by the time she'd joined the newspaper, she was thoroughly secular. Roz hailed from Short Hills, a ritzy Jersey suburb.

One night at the newspaper, when things were especially quiet, Mimi and Roz were sitting at one of the two tables beside the newsroom vending machine—which the higher-ups called the "cafeteria"—gobbling sugary snacks to keep their energy up, and Mimi mentioned Roz had a "privileged" background.

Her companion's face fell. "Don't idealize it. It was terrible."

Yes, Rosalyn said, her father was a high-ranking corporate executive—when he had a job. But he could never hold on to one. Far too often, he'd cut corners, and, when his employers found out, they'd cut him. He was always beset by problems, both legal and financial.

"I spent half my childhood worried we'd lose our house," Roz said. "We were never secure. At one point, both my parents' cars were repossessed. You know how humiliating that is, to have everyone on the block watch them take our cars away?" Another time, the family lost its electricity. "We spent two days in the dark, with no refrigerator, no anything. We had to use candles and hope we didn't burn the place down."

When she was fourteen years old, Roz went to a party with her mother, who had just developed the drinking problem that would one day kill her. By night's end, mom was too drunk to get home, so Roz—who had no license or ability to drive—took the wheel and steered the car home, her mother passed out and snoring in the next seat.

In college, Roz enjoyed the rebellious adolescence she'd always wanted but was too busy playing adult to have. She drank. She smoked pot. Strapped for cash, she developed a shoplifting habit, and engaged in what she called "light B and E"—though Mimi never understood how that differed from standard breaking-and-entering.

Roz eventually "got help" and put those days behind her. Yet, when she'd tell stories about her old adventures, she made being a petty criminal sound so glamorous and exciting, Mimi was tempted to give it a shot.

"That's why I like being a reporter," Roz said. "It lets me get my aggressions out. You can stick it to people, and not get in trouble for it."

Mimi grinned. "I knew there was a reason I liked you."

Like Mimi, Roz struggled with the newspaper's low wages, and worked weekends as a waitress, which left her exhausted. After a few years, Roz ditched both gigs, and "went over to the dark side," taking a better-paying job at a PR firm. There, she met and began to date Archibald Lowery.

After a year, they got married in the South of France, at the Lowery family chateau. Mimi was invited to the wedding but couldn't afford the airfare. And so Roz Ghinkert became Rosalyn Lowery. Roz always swore she'd never change her name if she got married, but that was before she had the chance to use *this* name.

Shortly after Rosalyn got married, she started working at *The Look*, thanks, no doubt, to her Lowery connections. She flourished there, rising quickly through the ranks. Perhaps she hadn't lost her Jersey-girl hustle, even if it was hidden under layers of Lowery polish.

As Rosalyn embraced her new lifestyle, she and Mimi drifted apart. Every now and then Facebook would show Mimi a "memory"—usually a drunken bar selfie—that reminded her of how close they had been. On occasion, they'd trade messages, and promise to meet up. They never did. After a while, Mimi gave up, assuming that they'd never see each other again.

WHICH WOULD HAVE BEEN THE CASE, if Rosalyn hadn't posted about her new promotion on Facebook.

"I'm humbled to announce I've been appointed deputy editor of *The Look*," she wrote, drawing a long stream of congratulations.

Mimi gave it the obligatory virtual thumbs-up, but she couldn't help feeling truly humbled that her one-time comrade had nabbed a top job at a prestigious publication, while she worked for her father at his diamond office.

"I feel like I'm stuck," Mimi told her boyfriend, Michael—the gruff policeman she used to call Detective Matthews. "I'm forty-one, and I don't know what I'm doing with my life."

Michael rubbed his rock-like forehead. His plus-sized frame sank into the stuffed chair at his modest home in Brooklyn.

"Your life isn't so bad," Michael said. He swung his arm around her. "You're happy with me, aren't you?" At that moment, he looked less like the barrel-chested cop Mimi had been dating for a year, and more like an overgrown little boy.

Which Mimi found adorable. "Of course I am," she said, giving him a kiss.

That was true. She and Michael had a lot in common: books, old movies, crossword puzzles. He had an unfortunate bias against foreign films—"I don't like reading when I go to the movies," he'd say—but Mimi figured he'd get over that. She enjoyed his often-pointed sense of humor. They could talk for hours about subjects, both silly and serious.

She also relished his occasional bursts of goofiness, like when he'd geek out over the clarinet—he performed every month in a jazz band—or make faces at his dog, a brown Maltese named Louie. Mimi took an instant liking to the excitable little fellow, who always greeted her with a generous amount of face licks.

Her main complaint with Michael was that she didn't see him enough. Every other weekend, Michael had custody of his fourteen-year-old daughter, Catherine. Mimi hadn't met her, much to her chagrin. She also hadn't met Michael's mom. Mimi didn't press him on either; she figured it would happen eventually.

His job also meant he spent a lot of nights working. Occasionally, he'd muse about retiring. He'd just completed his twenty-second year as a New York City police officer, so he was guaranteed a full pension and half his annual salary for life. Mimi couldn't imagine Michael giving up his job, which he was both fascinated by and committed to.

Yet, while Mimi was happy with Michael, she was never quite sure where things were headed. Michael had told her he loved her, but it was clearly a word he felt uncomfortable saying, and parceled out stingily.

And sometimes, like this night, he struggled to understand where she was coming from.

"So you're upset about your career?" Michael said. "I thought you liked working for your dad."

"I do," Mimi said, as she curled up in his arms. "It's fun. But who knows how long my father will keep his company going? He's seventy-five, well past retirement age."

The week before, Max's friend Sol had announced he was leaving the business and moving to Miami. "I'm seventy and Jewish, Maxie. I have to retire in Florida. It's like a law."

Mimi didn't believe her father was ready to retire. Though, in the end, it was his call. And if he did hang it up, what would she do?

"How about your responsible diamond project?" Michael asked. "I thought you said that could become a full-time job."

"I did," Mimi said. "Until I started doing it."

It had taken Mimi an absurd amount of time to set up her project to responsibly source diamonds from the African Diamond Republic. First, she needed a government-issued mining license, which, she found out—to her shock—cost two hundred thousand dollars. That was why the local industry was controlled by a small group of dealers, who paid miners far less than they deserved. She reached out to the local consulate, which got that knocked down to a more reasonable five thousand.

Then, she had to hire local monitors, to ensure all the miners were well treated and fairly paid.

All this took months, particularly since she was doing it from several continents away. She considered traveling to the ADR, but there weren't many flights there, and their fares made going to France look cheap.

By the time she'd jumped through all those hoops, it was the ADR's rainy season, which put the project on hold yet again.

Digging finally began one year after the project was conceived, which should have been cause for celebration, but a more serious problem popped up: no diamonds. Since Mimi and Max didn't have a lot of money to put behind the project, the government allocated them a small patch of land—where locals had been digging for diamonds for decades. Almost every gem there had already been found.

Every week, Mimi would write her contact there, and ask if they'd found anything. And every week, he'd text back, "regrettably, no."

"I had such high hopes for that project," Mimi lamented. "It's not going anywhere."

"I don't know if I can help you there," Michael said. "But regarding this thing you saw on Facebook, I have two suggestions. First, delete your social media accounts. Between this, the baby pictures, and the stupid political rants, you get depressed every time you go on there."

Mimi knew that was sound counsel, which she probably wouldn't follow. "What else?"

"Send Rosalyn a message that you'd like to work for her. You've always said you want to start writing again. That sounds like a good place to start."

Mimi gulped. "I couldn't do that! Rosalyn was my co-worker. She was junior to me."

Michael clicked his tongue. "That was years ago. It doesn't matter now. Call her. What have you got to lose? Even if you embarrass yourself, it won't be the first time."

Mimi groaned; sometimes Michael's jokes were a little too pointed.

"You know what I'm saying. Just reach out. It's like my dad used to say when I was too nervous to ask out a girl: 'What's the worst that could happen? You lose a little pride. You'll get it back.'"

"Your father said that?"

"He was a strange man," Michael said. "Send Rosalyn a note."

He had a point. Except Mimi hated networking, especially when it involved friends. It made her feel fake. She never quite knew how to do it.

For instance, how should she approach Rosalyn? Her old friend might ignore an email. A phone call might feel intrusive. Mimi finally decided she'd reach out via Facebook, a happy medium between the two.

She started her message on a casual, friendly note. "Hey, Rosalyn," she began.

After that, she got stuck.

First, she wrote, "hope you're doing well," but that felt cliché.

For this to work, it had to be personal. She added, "it sure seems like it," but worried that might come across as too eager. She changed that to "hope you're doing fantastic," but that sounded worse. She finally reverted to "hope you're doing well." After all her fretting, she'd settled for the phrase that adorns ninety percent of all emails.

The next sentence proved another challenge. Mimi wrote she was "putting out feelers" about freelance work, and would "be excited if you knew of any freelance opportunities at *The Look*."

God that's stupid, she thought. *Of course, Rosalyn knows about freelance opportunities at* The Look. *She's the deputy editor.*

But she couldn't think of any better way to phrase that, so she moved on to the next, equally precarious, sentence. "I am especially equipped to write about jewelry, as I'm working for my father's diamond company."

That last part was risky. It marked her as a subject matter expert—setting her apart from the other folks rapping on Rosalyn's door—but it was also an admission she was no longer working full-time in journalism. Rosalyn might see her as another person with their nose pressed against the window.

Mimi repeatedly interrupted Michael's Sunday football viewing to show him draft after draft. Finally, he lost patience. "Why are you so stressed about this?"

Mimi pulled away, wounded. "I'm not a natural networker."

"I'm not either." Michael turned down the TV volume. "Most people aren't. But you know how to talk to people. That's the only skill you need."

"But I'm not good at acting fake!"

"Then, don't! When I worked at police headquarters, it was incredibly political. My co-workers would spend most of their day jockeying for position, and maybe twenty minutes doing their jobs. I'd see these games played constantly.

"Here's what I noticed. The best networkers didn't try to B.S. people. They didn't hide their ambition. They didn't do this passive-aggressive 'maybe you can help me, if you don't mind' crap.

They asked for what they wanted, straight up. They had no shame. They were born without the shame gene."

"That doesn't help me!" Mimi protested. "I have that gene!"

"I get that. But look at it this way. This woman will either have something for you, or she won't. There's no magic phrase that will create work when none exists. So don't drive yourself nuts. Just let her know you're interested. Whatever you've written, just send it. It'll be fine."

Mimi wasn't so sure. Part of her wanted to keep honing her pitch, but she didn't want to spend her whole night fiddling with a Facebook message.

"All right," she said. "Though I have to proofread it first."

After some quick edits—and minor tweaks she didn't tell Michael about—Mimi took a deep breath and hit "send." By then, the football game was over, so she and Michael walked the dog, then went out to dinner. Later, Mimi fell asleep in Michael's arms, and forgot everything she'd spent the day worrying about.

ROSALYN RESPONDED TO MIMI'S OUTREACH the next morning. "Great hearing from you Mimi!" she wrote. "As far as freelance, we're currently booked for the next six months, but we may be able to assign you something down the road. I'll get back to you if and when something opens up."

Rosalyn closed with, "Hope you're doing well!"—which she undoubtedly stressed over less than Mimi did.

That felt like a blow-off, though Rosalyn did add a smile emoticon.

A few hours later, Rosalyn sent another message. "Hi, Mimi. One more thing. You said that you work for a diamond company. I have a beautiful old diamond I am looking to sell. Would you be interested in buying it?"

Mimi didn't respond right away—and when she did, her answer was just as noncommittal as Rosalyn's.

"My father handles the diamond buying for the company," Mimi wrote. "I am not sure what he needs. But if you're near the

Diamond District, you can stop by our office. It's right on Forty-Seventh Street."

"Great," came the surprisingly quick reply. "How about I come over in an hour?"

Mimi was shocked. That was soon. But she said, "sure." It would be nice to see Rosalyn again, and Mimi would get another chance to plug her services.

"I'm happy she's coming over," Mimi told Michael on the phone. "But it's weird that she wants to sell my dad a diamond. Her husband heads a major jeweler. Why would she sell it to us?"

"I find that strange, too," Michael said. "Maybe there's a perfectly rational explanation why she's doing this. But when I look at the fact pattern here—she's linked to a major jewelry company, and wants to quickly pawn a diamond—it sure sounds like she's selling a stolen stone."

CHAPTER THREE

ROSALYN *DID* HAVE AN EXPLANATION for wanting to sell her diamond so quickly. It just wasn't "perfectly rational."

"I don't believe in curses," Rosalyn said, her face pink. "But this diamond is part of the Prince Corthoff. Ever heard of it?"

"Yeah," Max said. "Wasn't that a big stone?"

"It was, originally," Rosalyn said. "One hundred-and-twenty-eight carats. Then the Lowerys cut it into three pieces. They sold the other two parts, and kept this smaller bit."

"But why is it considered cursed?" Mimi asked.

"It's from this old legend," Rosalyn sighed. "The Prince Corthoff was supposedly mounted in the eye of a holy statue in India. A British soldier stole it during that whole colonialism thing. Which, let me say, I completely condemn.

"When the Lowerys bought it, they cut it into three pieces, so the curse might not pass on to you. Though I can't guarantee anything. I don't know how curses work."

"I'll explain to you how they work," Max said. "They don't. Curses don't exist."

"I know that." Rosalyn stiffened. "But you never know, right?"

"I guess not," Max said. "But I'm more concerned with why you're offering me this diamond. You said the Lowery family owns it. Are you selling it on their behalf?"

"No." Rosalyn smoothed her skirt. "A few years ago, my brother-in-law, Shepherd, had a dispute with my husband over the business. He received this brooch as part of the settlement. And right before he died, he sent it to me."

"Your brother-in-law just gave you this diamond?" Mimi asked. "Why?"

Rosalyn let out a long sigh. "Shepherd and I had a history. I'll leave it at that. We hadn't spoken in a while. A few weeks ago, I heard he killed himself. Or so they say."

Mimi did a double-take. Did Rosalyn just imply that her brother-in-law was murdered? And when Rosalyn said she "had a history" with Shepherd—what did that mean? Mimi was tempted to ask, but her father would have a fit. He was dead-set against her getting involved in any more investigations.

"As I said, it's a long story," Rosalyn said. "You don't want to hear it."

Mimi almost blurted, "I do!"

Max arched his eyebrow. "You haven't explained why your brother-in-law left it to you. Especially if it's cursed."

"I believe he gave me the diamond—" Her face grew pinched and she brought her chin to her chest. "To hurt me."

Max's head jerked back. He was becoming wary of Rosalyn, and he didn't even know about the "light B & E."

"Okay, hold it," Max said. "I have tremendous respect for the Lowery family. But you come in here with this *verkakte* story. I'd like to see proof that you own this diamond. You do know that, under New York City second-hand dealer laws, I have to get your I.D. and report this purchase to the police?"

"I'm happy to provide those, Mr. Rosen. And I didn't steal this diamond, if that's what you're suggesting." Rosalyn reached into her handbag. "I have a letter from the attorney handling Shepherd Lowery's estate which shows I have legal title to this brooch."

Rosalyn plucked the piece of paper from her purse, and handed it to Mimi. It came from one of those elite law firms that have six names on their masthead and another twenty down the side. It backed up Rosalyn's claim that her late brother-in-law, Shepherd Lowery, had sent her a "3.2 carat black diamond set in an 18-karat gold heart-shaped brooch." The letter was issued three days prior, which showed how eager Rosalyn was to sell that diamond.

Mimi didn't know how to judge the letter, but it looked fine to her. She passed it to her father, who glanced at it and put it down. It apparently looked fine to him, too.

The three of them sat in awkward silence.

Rosalyn checked her watch. "We agreed on a price of twenty-five thousand dollars. Do we have a deal? I don't wish to be rude, but I have an important meeting to get to."

Mimi always liked Roz, but was growing less-than-fond of Rosalyn. Roz was down-to-earth and had an easy smile; Rosalyn was rigid and a bit of a show-off. And now that Mimi had gotten a good look at her shoes, they appeared mighty uncomfortable.

"I have to decide right now?" Max asked.

"I'd prefer that," Rosalyn said coolly. "I don't have a lot of time to shop this around. I'd rather not bring this to an auction house, because certain members of my family might find out, and I'd like to keep this quiet."

"All right," Max said. "When you say things like that, I get suspicious."

"Mr. Rosen, there's no reason for you to feel that way. I just showed you evidence the diamond wasn't stolen. You don't believe it's cursed. And you'll likely make money on it. Is there any reason why you won't buy it?"

Max leaned over his desk and stared intently at the diamond, hunting for a way out of this strange situation. "I'll admit, I am not usually offered diamonds like this, even when they're cursed. This is a pretty big purchase for me."

Max had just received a new credit line from his bank, so he was flusher than usual. But it had been a long time since he'd bought such an expensive gem. He once told Mimi: "I don't care how rich you are, every time you make a major business, you feel it in your *kishkes*." Mimi knew her father was checking his *kishkes*.

Just when Mimi had become resigned that her father would not buy the diamond—and that she'd never get a byline in *The Look*—Max declared they had a deal.

"I've figured out what I'm going to do with it," he said, with surprising enthusiasm. "If twenty-five thousand is good with you, we'll say *Mazal*."

Mazal was the magic word in the diamond business. Once it was uttered, you had a deal. There were no take-backs.

"*Mazal*," Rosalyn said.

They shook hands, and she placed the diamond back in the Lowery box. For the first time that afternoon, Rosalyn flashed what looked like a genuine smile.

"If you want," Max said, "you can give me that *tuchus* thing, and I'll have it melted down. I can probably get you about two hundred dollars for it."

"The brooch?" Rosalyn said. "Sure." She slid it toward him.

Max brought out his checkbook, which was the length of a slide rule, and signed a check in his chicken-scrawl.

Rosalyn rose from her chair and gave Mimi a hug even more half-hearted than her first. "I was just thinking," she told her, "maybe I *can* assign you a piece or two. As long as you don't tell people who you got this diamond from." That was her not-so-subtle way of conditioning one on the other.

As Rosalyn left, she said, "It was lovely seeing you again, Mimi. It seems like you're doing really well."

Yeah, whatever, Rosalyn. Mimi thought. *I know I'm not doing as well as you. You don't need to rub it in.* Mimi forced a smile and gave her a cursory wave goodbye.

"I'll be honest," Max said, dropping his voice, "I wasn't sure if I should buy that stone. I don't want something that'll just sit in my safe. I'm not running a museum here.

"Then I figured out what I'd do with it. For the last few days, I've been talking with Zeke. He's proposing to Channah tonight. It's the one-year anniversary of their first date."

Channah Morgenstern was Max's longtime receptionist, and

Mimi's close friend. Channah and Zeke had been dating for a year without getting married, a long time in their religious community. Zeke had wanted to wed Channah from the moment they met, but Channah—still reeling from the death of her first fiancé—always put him off.

"So, Channah's finally ready?" Mimi asked.

"That's what he tells me," Max said. "He called me this weekend, asking if I can get him a diamond. I've been trying all day to find him the right stone. I'd like to get Channah something really special, but his budget is just seven thousand dollars, which doesn't get you much in today's market. I thought these computer guys made a lot of money. Leave it to Channah to find a poor one.

"I found him something perfectly nice. But it's not a 'wow.' And Channah deserves a 'wow.' This stone is perfect for her. She always dresses in black."

"Won't you be taking a little loss?" Mimi asked.

"Not a little loss," Max said. "A huge loss! An eighteen-thousand dollar loss. They'll probably take away my diamond dealer's license for this. But we haven't had such a bad year. And Channah's worth it."

Mimi sighed. That was her father's problem. When business was good, he did favors for friends, and didn't keep track of who owed what. Then, people would be slow to pay, he'd run low on cash, and have to tighten up. Until his coffers filled again, and the cycle would begin anew. Yet, as character flaws went, there were worse ones than being too generous.

"Besides," Max said, "whenever I have a computer problem, I call Zeke and he comes and fixes it right away. And he never accepts a penny."

That was true. Max would summon Zeke to his office for even mundane problems—like his Internet being slow—and Zeke would instantly leave his job and rush over. Mimi suspected Zeke did that to spend extra time with Channah.

Mimi was more concerned about something else. "What about the—you know—" Mimi didn't want to say it.

"Second-hand dealer laws?" Max responded. "The way they work is, I can't sell anything I buy off the street for five days afterward. But this isn't considered a sale, since I'm giving it to Channah as a gift. If there's any problem, she can just give it back."

"No, I mean the, you know—" Mimi grew frustrated. Her father wasn't helping. "The curse."

"Don't tell me you believe that *bubbe-meise*," Max said.

"No, of course not. But Channah might."

Max ground his teeth. "Yeah, you're right. She is *meshuga* enough to believe something like that. Whatever you do, don't tell her."

Max phoned Zeke. "I have wonderful news. I have a beautiful stone for you, it's very rare. Channah's gonna love it."

Mimi could hear Zeke ask him a long list of questions.

"Yes, I'm taking a loss," Max said. "You're getting a deal. Isn't that what everyone wants? A deal?" Max was trying to get the perpetually long-winded Zeke off the phone. "Don't worry about it. You don't have to pay me more later. Just consider it my engagement gift."

After he hung up, Max put the diamond in a ring prong and dropped it in the Lowery box. "Unfortunately," he told Mimi, "you'll have to play messenger." Normally, when there was a diamond delivery, Channah would call a courier. That wouldn't work here.

"Zeke is waiting by the subway station at the end of the block," Max said. "Just hurry up and get this to him. He and Channah are going for dinner at six. That's in—" He checked his watch. "Ten minutes.

"But be discreet." He wagged his finger. "I'm just having you do this because it's a rush. I don't like you carrying goods. You don't know who's out there."

"Yes, Dad," Mimi said. "I'll be careful." She dropped the Lowery box in her purse and zipped it tight.

On her way out, Mimi passed Channah, who was perched at her usual spot at the reception desk.

"Who was that snotty girl who just came in here?" Channah asked.

"Oh, you mean Rosalyn?" Mimi asked, amused. "She's an old friend."

Channah's eyes became circles. "Oh, I'm sorry, Mimi. I didn't realize she was a friend of yours."

"It's fine," Mimi said. "Why'd you think she was snotty?"

"I don't know," Channah shrugged. "She was kind of stiff. Not warm. Like she had an edge."

"I can see that." Mimi eyed the door. "Let's talk later. I have to run an errand."

"Can you wait?" Channah said. "In ten minutes, I'm meeting Zeke and we're going out to dinner. I think he's going to ask me to marry him tonight." A smile appeared on her round freckled face.

Mimi tried to act surprised. "That's great!"

"I'm really happy. I mean, it's not a big deal he's proposing. He's already done it five times." Channah chuckled. "Now I'm the one sounding snotty. Anyway, I let him know, this time, it'll take."

Mimi laughed. "What made you finally decide?"

Channah shook her curly locks. "It's strange. For a long time, I was reluctant, because of, you know, what happened to Yosef, *olaf v'shalom*." Channah never liked to say that her fiancé had been murdered.

"That makes sense," Mimi said.

"I thought so. But nobody understood. And Mimi, I give you credit, you never said anything. You have no idea how much that meant to me."

Channah had been under tremendous pressure from her parents to marry Zeke. Because of that, Mimi kept her feelings to herself—though she was pulling for their marriage as much as anyone.

"Lately, everyone seems to have given up," Channah continued. "Even my parents got tired of arguing with me. Which was good. Without everyone *hocking* me, I could think about whether I was really ready.

"And the other day, I woke up, and decided it was time, that this was something I really wanted to do. I mean, part of me is still scared, but I'm also super-happy. I love Zeke so much. I can't wait to spend the rest of my life with him."

Mimi got choked up, and they hugged again. She checked the clock on the wall. "I have to run this errand so I can't talk now. But call me after dinner. I want to hear everything."

Channah promised she would. Mimi raced to the elevator, thrilled that Channah and Zeke were finally tying the knot, and that she was playing a small role in making it happen.

Outside, it was a crisp fall evening—a lovely night to get engaged. The sun was setting, the sky was getting dark, and the street-level retailers were bringing down the gates on their shops.

Even so, Forty-Seventh Street was full of people. Mimi walked quickly, trying to hide the fact she was carrying a twenty-five-thousand-dollar diamond in her purse.

Outside her building, she noticed three muscular guys, wearing leather jackets and ratty sweaters, all standing in a circle. She could have sworn one pointed at her.

As she headed down the street, she noticed the three men walking behind her. Mimi told herself not to get paranoid. But she couldn't shake the feeling they were following her.

CHAPTER FOUR

MIMI HURRIED TOWARD THE END OF THE STREET, where she saw Zeke standing by the subway entrance, a smile peeking out under his beard.

When Mimi first met Zeke, she didn't know what to make of him. He was short and pudgy and kept lapsing into tech monologues so long and detailed they even tried the patience of good-humored Channah. Mimi often asked him to use "plain English," but soon learned that was fruitless, as even his simple explanations confused her.

But Mimi had become quite fond of Zeke, even charmed by him. She enjoyed his sincere excitement about new technology, even if she rarely understood what he was talking about. He was also extremely smart, and could do four-digit multiplication problems in his head. He considered that no big deal, saying, "obviously, the credit belongs to *Hashem*." But it was quite the party trick.

Most importantly, he loved Channah, and Channah loved him. He'd waited patiently while Channah sorted out her issues, which made Mimi like him even more. Mimi always believed that the two of them would get engaged someday, and she was glad that day had finally come.

"Your father said he's giving me an incredible diamond," Zeke said, his face glowing in the night.

"Yes." Mimi tried to discreetly hand him the bright yellow Lowery box. Instead of putting it away, Zeke stood and examined it, a big grin on his face. "Ooh, Lowery. Fancy."

He opened the box, took out his phone, and shone it on the diamond. "Wow, the color on this is amazing. Do you know if black diamonds reflect light like regular ones? It wasn't clear from the information I saw online."

Mimi glanced around nervously. "I don't know, but Zeke, please, don't be so conspicuous. There could be crooks here."

Mimi spun around to see if the three men were following her. She thought she saw them, but it was dark, and Forty-Seventh Street was so crowded she couldn't be sure, and she didn't know what to do even if they were. Should she call the cops? Were they even doing anything illegal? The only thing she was sure of was that Zeke needed to put that box away. But the diamond held him rapt.

"I can't wait to read more about black diamonds online," Zeke exclaimed. "Apparently, they don't find them in regular mines. Some people think they come from asteroids. Where did they find this one?"

"I don't know." Mimi was getting impatient. "My friend Rosalyn said it was stolen from a statue in India during that whole colonialism thing."

Zeke scratched his beard. "When she said, 'during that whole colonialism thing,' what did she mean? The history of colonialism in India is long and complex."

"I don't know. Please, Zeke. Put the box away."

"Okay," he said, and stuffed it in his pocket.

Mimi kept sneaking glances over her shoulder. She thought she saw one of the men hovering nearby. She told Zeke to wait a second, and craned her neck to get a better look at him. Whoever it was, walked away. Mimi turned back to Zeke, who'd removed a folded piece of paper from his pocket.

"I've been reading online about how to propose," he said. "I've narrowed it down to three options. Tell me what you think of these."

"Zeke, you shouldn't just repeat something you found on the

Internet," Mimi said. "Say what's in your heart."

"I don't trust myself to do that." Zeke nervously fiddled with his *yarmulke.* "I have the tendency to drone on. Or so people tell me."

"I'm sure Channah's used to it." Mimi chuckled. "In fact, I know she is."

"Right. But I've already proposed a bunch of times, and she never accepted. Now, she says she's ready, but I'm worried I'm going to blow it. What if I say the wrong thing? Channah is the most wonderful woman in the world. I want to marry her more than anything."

"You know what, Zeke?" Mimi smiled. "Just say that. You'll be fine." Mimi checked the time. "I gotta go. Channah will be here any second and I don't want to spoil the surprise. Good luck."

She wanted to give Zeke a hug, but she knew he wouldn't do it for religious reasons. She waved goodbye, and hurried across the street, continually looking behind her to see if she was being followed. She wasn't.

From her vantage point across the street, she looked for the three men, but didn't see them—only Zeke clutching the box in his pocket, hopping from one foot to the other as he waited for Channah. When she arrived, they greeted each other with broad smiles, then walked down the subway steps, talking and laughing and ready to start their new life.

Mimi couldn't stop thinking about the three guys who followed her. She wondered if they'd returned to her building, but when she got back there, they were nowhere to be found.

She did spot the "hawker" who stood in front of her building, continually asking passersby if they wanted to sell their gold, hoping to lure them into a nearby jeweler. He asked Mimi this every day, even though she always ignored him, except for the one time she snapped and called him "human spam." The landlord had repeatedly tried to get him removed—to no avail.

Sure enough, when Mimi passed him that night, he asked if she wanted to sell her gold. Except this time, instead of ignoring him, Mimi stopped and said, "can I ask you something?"

This so unnerved the hawker, he inched backward. "Do you want to sell your gold?" he repeated.

"No, but I have a question," Mimi said. "Did you see three guys standing right in front of the building?"

His eyes narrowed to slits. "You mean the men that were following you?"

"Yes!" Mimi said. "I knew that wasn't my imagination. They were following me. Do you know who they were?"

"No."

"And do you know why they followed me?" Mimi asked.

"No, but this afternoon, I saw them follow a blonde woman to your building."

"A blonde woman?" Mimi searched for a picture of Rosalyn on her phone, and when she found one, she showed it to him. "Is this her?"

The hawker pursed his lips. "I think so."

"And they followed her to my building?"

"Yes, and one of the guys trailed her inside, and then came out and waited with the others," said the hawker. "Then, when the woman left, they started following her again."

"Did she see them?"

"Definitely. She even yelled at them to stop following her. But they didn't. She screamed that she didn't have what they wanted, she'd just sold it. She looked very scared. I was thinking maybe I should do something. But then the car came."

"The car?" Mimi asked.

"Yes, it might have been an Uber or something. She seemed surprised when it stopped for her. She said something to the driver, and he said something back, and she got in. Then, the guys went back to standing outside your building."

Mimi wished she had a reporter's notebook. "Did they follow anyone else besides the blonde and me?"

"I don't think so."

"And what happened after they followed me?"

The hawker shook his head. "I don't know. I haven't seen them since."

"Me neither," Mimi said. "I'm impressed you noticed so much."

"You stand outside here every day, you notice things. This job is very boring. So when something different happens, you remember. Like, one time, you called me 'human spam.'"

Mimi felt a stab of shame. "Yeah, sorry about that."

He shrugged it off. "Don't be. I've been called worse."

Mimi now grasped the reality of this man's situation: he stood outside all day in the cold, badgering pedestrians. What a horrible way to make a living.

"I understand you're just doing a job," Mimi said. "But you have to admit, it can be kind of annoying."

He nodded ruefully. "People tell me that. Every day."

"Sorry. I'll be nicer from now on. Thanks for your help. If you see those guys again, let me know."

"I will. And if you're ever looking to sell your gold—"

Mimi smiled at him. "Of course."

WHILE MIMI WAITED IN HER BUILDING LOBBY for the elevator, she called Rosalyn. No one picked up, so Mimi left a message, saying she'd heard that Rosalyn had been followed, and wanted to make sure everything was okay.

Just as Mimi was finishing the message, a call came in from an unlisted number. Mimi picked up, hoping it was Rosalyn. It wasn't.

"Is this Mimi Rosen?" asked an angry, insistent voice. He didn't wait for an answer.

"My name is George Morton. I'm a private investigator working for the estate of the late Josephine Tomaso, the designer who created the Heartbrooch. I understand that Rosalyn Lowery just sold it to you."

"The what?"

"The Heartbrooch. The famous brooch, shaped like a heart, designed by Josephine Tomaso. Did Rosalyn Lowery just sell that to you?"

"I'm sorry, I am not allowed to discuss that." Mimi didn't expect she'd have to worry about violating Rosalyn's confidence so soon. "And I don't know how you got this number. It's unlisted."

"I got it because I'm a private detective," said Morton. "Uncovering information is my job. And I've discovered that Rosalyn Lowery sold you that brooch, even though she had no right to."

"What are you talking about?"

"That brooch was designed by Josephine Tomaso. It belongs to the Tomaso estate. And Rosalyn Lowery, who wasn't even a member of the Lowery corporation, had no right to sell it."

"Actually," Mimi countered, "Rosalyn showed us proof of ownership."

"Give me a break!" shouted Morton. "Any proof she showed you was a fraud, just like she was a fraud. Were you aware that, a few months ago, Rosalyn Lowery was busted for shoplifting?"

"No," Mimi said. She had no reason to believe this guy, but given Rosalyn's history, that was not out of the question.

"Well, she was. And her husband got her off. She was a dishonest lowdown thief. And you're an accessory to her crimes."

"Look," Mimi said. "I have no idea if what you're saying about Rosalyn is true. But you have not proved to me that the brooch was stolen."

"Please. Common sense should have told you it was stolen. Its rightful owners want it back. I'll give you a post office box to send it to."

Mimi almost laughed at this. "I am not sending you anything. If you think the piece is stolen, call the police."

"The Tomaso family doesn't work like that," said Morton. "We prefer to handle things our own way. I don't know if you're aware of the connections the Tomaso family has in Italy, but trust me, they are not people you want to mess with. They don't take thefts of their possessions lightly."

"Hey, listen," Mimi said sharply. "I don't appreciate threats."

"Don't worry. The Tomaso family doesn't threaten. They act. And they'll act very harshly when someone robs them of a five-million-dollar piece of jewelry."

"What are you talking about?" Mimi snapped. "That piece isn't worth five million dollars."

"Listen, lady, I'm not stupid. Five million is a *conservative* estimate. That brooch could probably get ten million at auction."

"What are you talking about?" Mimi asked. "Why would that brooch be so valuable?"

"Because it's the last piece Josephine Tomaso ever designed. It's a major collector's item. You can read about it online if you don't believe me."

"I will! And don't call me again!" Mimi hung up.

At first, Mimi planned to wait until she returned to her father's office before doing her research. But curiosity overcame her.

It didn't take long to discover the caller was right: the piece they'd bought was indeed called the "Heartbrooch," and it was the last item Josephine Tomaso ever designed. One site estimated its value as "priceless." Another said if it was ever sold, it would fetch seven million dollars—"easy."

Mimi stared at her phone. What had Rosalyn gotten her into?

CHAPTER FIVE

"**T**HAT PIECE IS WORTH *MILLIONS*?" Max exclaimed after Mimi tried to explain everything. "Wow. I really *did* get a deal." He leaned back on his chair. "What kind of *schmuck* am I, giving that stone to Zeke?"

"That's what this private investigator told me on the phone," Mimi said, trying to catch her breath. "He said it's this famous piece, the Heartbrooch."

"It can't be that famous if I've never heard of it," Max said.

Mimi hadn't either, but after some frantic Googling, she'd received a crash course. The Heartbrooch was historically important not just because it contained a famous, supposedly cursed diamond. It was created by Josephine Tomaso, the Italian jewelry designer who was a fixture of New York's fashion scene in the seventies.

Tomaso's work was emotional and hyper-romantic, and stood in contrast to the then-dominant "cool" aesthetic. That made her a perfect fit for Lowery, which called itself the "Kingdom of Love." The Heartbrooch was designed with Wyllis Lowery, the son of the store's founder. It was billed as the first in a series of collaborations. Instead, it was the last piece Tomaso produced before she dropped out of sight.

"Tomaso aficionados consider the Heartbrooch one of her most startling works," said one website. "Its innovative design—a twisted heart holding a black diamond that was supposedly 'cursed'—both evokes love and serves as a sardonic commentary on its pitfalls. The piece suggested a new direction for Tomaso's artistry, where her designs would communicate a deeper textual meaning.

"The real-life events that occurred following its creation—particularly Tomaso's subsequent disappearance from the design world—have only heightened the piece's mystery and power to fascinate."

"But why would that diamond be so valuable?" Max asked. "It's just a carbonado."

"It's not the diamond that's valuable," Mimi said. "It's the brooch."

"The brooch?" Max asked. "The *tuchus*?"

"Yes. That's what I've been trying to tell you. It's a rare and valuable work of art."

Max scratched his head. "I was going to melt that thing for scrap."

Mimi rose from her chair. "Don't!"

"All right." Max held out his hands. "Calm down. I haven't sent it out yet." He bent over and picked up the blue plastic tub underneath his desk, filled with scattered pieces of gold. "It should be in here somewhere."

He sifted through the box, then held up the brooch. "This is it, right?"

"Yes!" Mimi ran to his desk and snatched it from him. She compared it to the Heartbrooch pictures she'd found online. It had the same design, and was inscribed with the initials of the two jewelry notables who created it—"JT," for Josephine Tomaso, and "WL," for Wyllis Lowery, Archibald's father. It was stamped with the renowned "Lowery" hallmark—a cursive "L."

"If that brooch is worth so much," Max asked, "why'd your friend sell it to me to melt for scrap?"

"I have no idea." Mimi felt tension grow in her gut. "But the private investigator said the brooch was stolen, and that the Tomasos had connections back in Italy and we didn't want to mess with them."

"Connections to who?"

"I don't know. The Mob, I guess." Just uttering those words, was enough to make Mimi shudder.

Max shrugged dismissively. "Whoever the guy is, he sounds like a nut. He's probably running some kind of scam, trying to steal the piece himself."

"Yes, but he knew exactly what the piece was, and who designed it. Maybe it *is* stolen."

"Then we'll give it back," Max said. "We didn't do anything wrong. Your friend showed us proof she owned it. We followed all the rules. We have only the word of one guy it was stolen, and he's probably a crazy person. Just call your friend Rosalyn and tell her what happened. Double check if everything's kosher."

Mimi drew a breath. She'd already texted and phoned Rosalyn several times, and hadn't heard back. She called her again—and again, there was no answer.

"Why don't you call your friend Michael?" Max said.

"Good idea!" Mimi said, while noting her father had called Michael her "friend," as he was less than thrilled she was again dating a non-Jew.

Mimi tried Michael, but he didn't pick up. A minute later, he sent her a text, saying he couldn't talk just then, he was dealing with a "late-breaking homicide."

"You know who you should call?" Max said. "Zeke."

"Right!" Mimi said. She tried Zeke, but he didn't answer either.

"My God. Where is everybody?" Mimi raised her hand to her forehead. "Zeke and Channah have probably just arrived at the restaurant. Zeke could be proposing right now. Maybe he just gave her the diamond. What if the diamond turns out to be stolen, and we have to give it back? What if Channah loves it, and can't bear to part with it?" She clutched her desk. "I hope she hates it."

"Would you relax?" Max said. "Right now, we don't have to give anything back to anyone. Worse comes to worst, in the morning, we'll call Rabinowitz." He scowled. "Though I hate dealing with that guy. He charges a fortune."

Max's longtime lawyer, Elliot Rabinowitz, did not actually charge a fortune. That was why Max, and many others in the diamond business, used him, despite the widespread perception that he was past his prime.

Rosalyn's number appeared on Mimi's phone. She breathed a sigh of relief and picked up.

But it wasn't Rosalyn on the line. It was a gruff voice. And not just any gruff voice—Michael's.

"Hold it," he said. "Who's this?"

"Michael, it's me! Something must be wrong with my phone. It says this call came from my friend Rosalyn."

"It came from who?" Michael asked.

"My friend Rosalyn."

"Huh," Michael grunted. "I am at this homicide scene and found this phone on the victim. I saw someone kept calling so I decided to call back. I thought this was your number! For a minute there, I was worried I was going nuts."

Mimi froze. "Hold it, if you have Rosalyn's phone, does that mean—?"

Michael breathed out, loud enough for Mimi to hear. "I'm sorry."

Rosalyn Lowery was Michael's late-breaking homicide.

CHAPTER SIX

Mimi sat stunned. She felt dizzy. Acid rose in her throat. For a second, she thought she might throw up.

"So, Rosalyn is—" Mimi didn't even want to say the word. "My God. How did that happen?"

"The victim appears to have been strangled, possibly with the necklace she was wearing." Michael was in terse professional mode. Mimi could hear his footsteps on the sidewalk. "Her body was found at a construction site. It was probably tossed from a car."

"That's crazy. She was just in our office a few hours ago."

"Hold it." Michael sounded incredulous. "This victim is the same person you wrote to on Facebook? The editor that wanted to sell you the diamond?"

"Yes. Rosalyn Lowery. Married to the head of the famous jewelry company. This is her phone. Didn't you recognize the name?"

"No! She hasn't been positively IDed. I just got here and saw her phone ringing. This is definitely her?"

"What does she look like?" Mimi asked.

"She has brownish hair, looks over five feet tall. Pretty."

Mimi almost chastised Michael for calling Rosalyn "pretty," but figured it was silly to be jealous of a dead woman.

"She's wearing an orange dress," he continued.

"Yes. That's what she wore to our office. And a leather jacket."

"Right. Plus she has really nice shoes. Kind of purple."

"Yes!" Mimi said. "But also, pink."

"Yeah. And I think there's something on their bottoms. It looks like a gemstone." Michael walked a bit. "Wow. Those are really nice. And I'm not usually into shoes."

"I know!" Mimi exclaimed.

"So this is the woman who wanted to sell you a diamond?"

"Yes."

"So what happened with that?"

"She came to our office, and sold us this black diamond. But she also gave us this brooch to melt for scrap. And the brooch may be worth millions."

"Hold it," Michael said. "If the brooch is worth millions, why'd she give it to you for scrap?"

"I don't know!" Mimi's hands turned into claws. "The whole thing is crazy!"

"Remember I said it was suspicious she wanted to get rid of that diamond so fast? Did she give you a reason for that?"

"She said the diamond was cursed," Mimi said.

"Seriously?" Michael's footsteps stopped. "*That* was her reason?"

"That's what she said."

"That's the craziest thing I ever heard," Michael said.

"I know, but I looked it up online, and the diamond seems to have had an actual curse on it. I mean, it's not an actual curse, because curses don't exist." Mimi paused. "You agree with that, right? Curses don't exist? Right?"

"Of course, they don't!" Michael grumbled. "Your friend probably stole it, and used that as an excuse."

"She had a letter from a lawyer saying she owned it."

"Do you have a copy of that document?" Michael asked.

"Yes."

"Okay. Make sure you don't lose that. And you're one hundred percent sure the brooch wasn't stolen?"

Mimi's palms grew clammy. "Well, no."

Michael groaned. "Why not?"

"This private investigator called me and said the diamond belonged to the family of Josephine Tomaso. And then he implied they're connected to the Mob!"

"Hold it. The Mob? How did they get involved in this?"

Mimi flashed back to her days nervously trying to explain things to the imposing policeman she then called Detective Matthews. Even though they'd been dating for a year, his barrage of questions still unnerved her.

"It's a long story. We couldn't have a messenger deliver the diamond to Zeke, so I had to do it. And when I was walking on Forty-Seventh Street, I thought these guys were following me. This hawker thought so, too."

"And those guys were connected to the Mafia?"

"No. The Mafia came later. When I got a call from the private investigator."

"You know what?" Michael cut her off. "You have me totally confused. Just write down everything you remember that occurred with Rosalyn Lowery. And make sure the items she sold you and any documents you received are securely locked up. I need to get back to inspecting this crime scene."

"Is there any kind of physical evidence?"

"Well, there's—" Michael's voice gained an edge. "Okay, Mimi. Let me be clear. I understand you were once friends with the victim. But I do not want you playing Nancy Drew again. Last time you did, you nearly got yourself killed."

"I wasn't planning on it, Detective!" Mimi called Michael "Detective" when she was mad at him. Mimi had told him over and over that she had no desire to get involved with any more investigations, but he never believed her. It was a minor point of contention between them that threatened to become a major one.

"All I did was ask a question," she continued. "A friend of mine, who was just in my office a couple of hours ago, was murdered. I'm pretty shaken up by that. Can't I have a normal human reaction?"

"Of course, you can," Michael said. "But I've been doing this a long time, and I can tell you, a normal human reaction to a friend's death does not involve asking about physical evidence."

"Then tell me this, Detective, how normal is it to have an argument with your girlfriend when you're standing next to a corpse?"

For once, Michael had no comeback. Mimi could see his craggy face slink down his neck. "My God. You're right. What the hell am I doing?" He grunted. "Let's talk later. And just so you know, I'll probably be taken off this case, since you're a likely witness."

"I am?"

"Of course," Michael said. "You were one of the last people to see her alive. That's a conflict, and we try to avoid those. You'll probably get a call from another detective tomorrow. And if you think I'm difficult, wait till you deal with some of the other guys." He laughed.

This so irked Mimi, she hung up.

The minute she smacked the phone down on her desk, Max asked, "What was that about?"

"That was Michael. Rosalyn, the woman who was here this afternoon, was just murdered."

"My God, that's terrible." Max turned white. "Do they have any idea why?"

"No, but—" Mimi felt a chill. "Do you think it was because of the diamond? Since it's—"

"Valuable?"

"No, not that it's valuable. It's also—" She lowered her voice. Her father was again not helping. "You know. Cursed."

Max scowled. "Oh please, don't tell me you believe that *narishkeit*?"

"No. But you have to admit, it's kind of weird, Rosalyn owned a cursed diamond, and then she gets killed. Though she sold it before that happened. But maybe the curse stayed with her. Who knows how these things work?"

"What are you talking about?" Max screamed. "Curses don't work! They don't exist!" He calmed down. "I'm sorry. I shouldn't yell at you. I know you just had a big shock. How are you feeling?"

Mimi was processing everything. "I'm okay. I should probably go home."

Max shut down his computer and rose from his desk. He dropped a few items in his canvas bag, and switched off his desk lamp. "I agree. It's been a crazy day. If you need to take some time off, please do."

"Thanks," Mimi half-smiled.

Max put on his hat and jacket. "Go home and relax. And don't worry about a stupid curse. Zeke has that diamond now. And nothing's happened to him, right?"

"No," Mimi said, her voice trailing off.

She didn't tell her father, but she'd been calling Zeke repeatedly for the last twenty minutes, and he hadn't phoned back. She was starting to worry about him, too.

MIMI'S MIND REELED ON THE TRAIN HOME to New Jersey. When she finally arrived at her cramped one-bedroom apartment, she poured herself a glass of wine, stretched out on her favorite recliner, put on Edith Piaf—her thinking music of choice—and took stock of this very strange day.

Her friend Rosalyn had been murdered. It was a sad, ugly ending for someone who had been through so much, yet had accomplished a lot. Today was the first time Mimi had seen Rosalyn in years. It would also be the last.

Mimi went to Rosalyn's Facebook page, and clicked on the nine-year-old pictures of her wedding in Tuscany. Rosalyn, her gown, the seaside setting, all looked stunning. One thing was missing: photos of the groom. According to Rosalyn, ever since Archibald's father, Wyllis, was killed in a robbery, the family's insurance policy mandated they never be photographed. That apparently extended to wedding shots on Facebook.

Rosalyn, however, posted tons of pictures, including her headshot from *The Look*. Her friends left comments calling it "incredible," "beautiful," and "super-hot."

There was also a comment from Shepherd Lowery—her

brother-in-law, who gave her the Heartbrooch—angrily asking for his calls to be returned. Rosalyn's response: "Blocked." Those two *definitely* had a history.

Mimi clicked over to Shepherd Lowery's Facebook page. Rosalyn's now-deceased brother-in-law apparently shared his family's fear of self-portraits. His page had no pictures and very little personal information, except that his "life events" included his marriage seven years ago to Valerie Lowery, though his relationship status was listed as "separated."

Shepherd's postings were mostly ads for his jewelry brand, which he'd launched with huge fanfare three years ago—and closed, with great bitterness, thirty months later.

"As many of you know," he wrote, "after a long power struggle with my mother and brother, I decided to leave my family business. I sold my shares for far less than they were worth. I was excited to launch my new jewelry line, and make it on my own.

"I am not the type of person who ever gives up. But certain events with my family made it no longer possible for this business to continue. My family has always been toxic. I will never escape their poisonous influence.

"Closing this company breaks my heart. I put everything I had into it. Now I have nothing left."

A little while later, his timeline was filled with shocked posts, wondering why Shepherd Lowery had driven his car off a cliff.

At around nine-thirty, Channah called. With all that had happened, Mimi had forgotten her friend was getting engaged. She picked up, eager for good news.

"Hey there!" Mimi said, trying to sound upbeat. "Are you an official fiancé?"

"No," Channah sounded near tears.

"What's the matter? Didn't Zeke propose?"

"He couldn't. We were on our way to the restaurant, when these three guys came up behind us, grabbed Zeke by the neck, and demanded he hand over the brooch. Zeke said he didn't have a brooch, only a diamond, and he wasn't going to give it to them, because it was special and meant for me. So, they threw him to the ground and one guy started hitting him. Luckily, the restaurant owner saw what was happening, and screamed and drove them off. But Zeke was seriously hurt."

Mimi's hands flew to her mouth. "Oh my God. Is he okay?"

"Not really," Channah said. "He's in the hospital. That's where I am now. They're making him stay overnight."

"Oh, Channah, I'm so sorry." Something occurred to her. "The guys who attacked Zeke, were they big muscular guys, wearing leather jackets and sweaters?"

"Yes! How did you know?"

"I think I saw them on Forty-Seventh Street. They followed me when I gave the diamond to Zeke."

"But why?" Channah asked. "The diamond wasn't *that* expensive, was it?"

"No," Mimi said. "But the brooch it came with is famous. And the diamond's well-known because it's supposed to be—"

Mimi stopped herself. She didn't want to tell Channah her diamond was supposedly cursed. That would only upset her more. Mimi was also starting to worry it was true.

CHAPTER SEVEN

Mimi didn't sleep much that night. She awoke early the next morning, around six-thirty. She sent a quick text to Channah: "Call me when you're up."

Channah phoned right away. She hadn't slept much either.

"Zeke is okay," Channah said, her voice raw. "But his arm is fractured. The doctors say he'll be fine, when his arm heals."

"Are you with him now?"

"I was at the hospital until about eleven last night, when they made me go home. But now I'm headed back."

"Okay," Mimi said. "I'll meet you."

Mimi took an early train into New York, then a subway to the Kings County Medical Center in Brooklyn. Exiting the station, Mimi passed a newsstand, and there, on the front page of the *New York Post*, was Rosalyn. Mimi was startled to see her dead friend's face looking up at her; it was like bumping into a ghost. She nearly burst into tears, right there on the sidewalk.

Mimi bent over and studied the photo. Rosalyn looked determined and glamorous, like she belonged on a newspaper cover. Mimi felt weirdly proud of her. She'd come a long way from the night shift.

But Mimi hated the headline. "'The Look' of Death," it said. "Police probe murder of fashionista, jeweler's wife." She knew

Rosalyn was more than those two things—though they were probably how she'd want to be remembered.

Mimi purchased a copy of the paper, with a lump in her throat.

Inside, a picture showed Archibald Lowery—Rosalyn's now-widower—trying to evade the paparazzi by holding a briefcase over his face. While that likely stemmed from the Lowery family's longstanding photo-phobia, it sure made him look guilty.

Mimi couldn't decide what to do with the newspaper after she read it. It had her dead friend's picture on it, so she didn't want to toss it in the garbage. But it wasn't the kind of thing she'd keep as a souvenir.

WHEN MIMI ARRIVED AT ZEKE'S HOSPITAL ROOM, she found the mood surprisingly upbeat. Zeke had just proposed to Channah from his hospital bed, and they were both mooning over the black diamond on her finger. Mimi gave her a congratulatory hug.

Zeke and Channah both looked happy, and at the same time, terrible: Channah's face was haggard and drawn, while Zeke's was dotted with scars and his arm was in a sling.

"How are you feeling, Zeke?" Mimi asked.

"Well, I'm happy I just got engaged." Zeke grabbed the bedrail with his good arm and pulled himself up, his hospital gown falling around him. "Otherwise, I've been better.

"Thank your father for the diamond, Mimi," he added. "It really is an incredible stone. I had to fight for it, but I'm glad I did."

"It's lovely," Channah whispered. She held out her arm, and pointed the diamond at the fluorescent bulb on the ceiling, and watched, transfixed, as light swam along its inky surface.

Just then, Mimi remembered the prior night's call from the private investigator, claiming the brooch was stolen. Until now, that had slipped her mind—which surprised her, considering how much it shook her up. But it was just one more crazy moment in a day full of them.

What if the private investigator was telling the truth? Channah might have to return the diamond. Zeke would have gotten beat up for nothing.

Mimi couldn't worry about that now. Too much had happened since.

"I had always hoped for a unique proposal," said Zeke, a smile forming on his swollen lips. "Not this unique."

"It was a beautiful proposal, Zeke," said Channah, standing by his bed. "You've made me very happy."

Zeke let loose a wide grin that, for a brief moment, blotted out his bruises.

A little later, a doctor arrived to examine Zeke. That was Mimi and Channah's cue to leave for a "celebratory lunch," though given everything that happened, they wouldn't be doing much celebrating.

CHANNAH AND MIMI SAT, BUNDLED IN LIGHT OVERCOATS, on a park bench on the Brooklyn promenade. The day was sunny but gray, and a cool fall breeze periodically blew in from the water.

They organized their lunch neatly on the bench. Channah bought a banana and box of Special K from the hospital commissary—two items she was sure were kosher. Mimi got a tuna sandwich, which she considered eating over the newspaper with Rosalyn's picture on it, but decided that was disrespectful.

The conversation mostly centered on the upcoming wedding, until Channah spied the newspaper.

"Oh my God," she said. "Is that the woman who came in the office yesterday?"

"Yes," Mimi said. "My friend Rosalyn. She was murdered last night. That was the other crazy news yesterday."

Channah grabbed the paper and started leafing through it, her eyes like saucers. "That's so awful. That poor girl. I feel so sorry for her."

Channah laid the newspaper down and pointed to an article titled "The Lowery family has history of violence, tragedy."

"Did you see this?" Channah asked.

Mimi hadn't, but once Channah started reading it aloud, Mimi wished she had.

"In 1982," Channah read out loud, "designer Josephine Tomaso and Wyllis Lowery, son of the store's founder, created a piece they called the Heartbrooch. The mysterious and intricate 18-karat gold heart-shaped pin featured a jet-black diamond cut from the famed Prince Corthoff.

"The legendary Corthoff diamond was supposedly cursed after it was stolen from the eye of an Indian statue in the 1800s. Its fabled hex reportedly wreaked havoc on several generations of Russian royals.

"Lowery's purchase of the gem in the 1980s coincided with a string of tragedies for the glitzy jeweler. Within months, Wyllis was killed in a robbery, and his father—company founder Nicholas— died soon after. Tomaso, considered one of the major talents of the seventies design scene, suffered what friends called a nervous breakdown. She returned to her native Italy and never designed again."

Channah pointed to the picture of the Heartbrooch. "That black diamond, is that the one I'm wearing?"

Mimi nodded and averted her eyes.

"Did that Rosalyn woman sell it to you?"

"Yes," Mimi murmured.

Channah became alarmed. "And did she tell you it was cursed?"

"It came up," Mimi said stiffly.

"But if you knew it was cursed, why'd you give it to Zeke?"

"It was my father's idea." Mimi didn't want to throw her dad under the bus, but she had no choice. "He thought the diamond was so beautiful, he wanted you to have it. He doesn't believe in curses."

"I don't either," Channah said. "But you never know, right? Your friend was murdered, and Zeke was attacked. And the newspaper says terrible things happened to the Lowery family after they bought it. How do you explain all that?"

"It's a coincidence." Mimi tugged her jacket close to her chest.

SLAY IT WITH A DIAMOND

"Yes, probably." Channah's hands balled into fists. "But what if it isn't? Would you want to be proposed to with a cursed diamond?"

"I don't know. It's never come up." Mimi touched Channah's arm. "If it's a problem, we can always get you another diamond. You can even get engaged without one. There's no law or anything."

Channah wasn't listening; she was staring, stone-faced, at the river, watching the water get roiled by the wind. Finally, she spoke, her voice quiet but determined. "I'm calling the engagement off."

Mimi wasn't sure what she just heard. Channah wasn't the type to say something like that if she didn't mean it. Mimi searched her friend's face for a sign that was a joke. She didn't find any: Channah was crying.

"Oh, come on," Mimi said. "Don't say that."

"I have no choice," Channah said. The tears were flowing now. "If Zeke proposed with a cursed diamond, maybe our marriage is cursed."

It was cold out, but Mimi was starting to sweat. "How can your marriage be cursed? Zeke loves you. And you love him."

"I know that!" Channah stamped her foot on the concrete. "I just don't want to see him get hurt—or should I say, hurt more." Channah rummaged through her purse, and pulled out a tissue.

"Come on, Channah. Be logical. Yes, some bad things happened. But we both know curses don't exist. Everybody says so."

"Like who?"

"Everybody. Michael. My father."

"That's two people!" Channah loudly blew her nose. "Look, today in the hospital room, it was all smiles, but last night was scary. Zeke was badly beat up. For a second, I thought he was dead. What if this is just the start of what the curse does? What if he gets hurt again?"

"But come on. You can't cancel the engagement. You already said yes. You can't back out now."

"I said yes twenty minutes ago!" Channah said between sobs. "I've been engaged less than an hour." She yanked the ring off her finger. "When Zeke gave me this, I thought it was the most beautiful thing I had ever seen. Now, it looks ugly and scary, like a symbol of death." Channah rose from the bench. "I gotta talk to Zeke."

"Channah," Mimi pleaded, "don't do anything rash. Think it over. Don't say something you'll regret."

Channah glared at Mimi. "Remember, yesterday, I said how much I appreciated it that you never pressured me to get married?"

"Yes," Mimi said warily.

"Please don't start now." Channah's face was as hard as Mimi had ever seen it. For all her good nature, Channah could be quite stubborn. "I'm headed to the hospital. Thanks for stopping by."

That was a clear signal Mimi shouldn't go with her. Which was fine by Mimi. She didn't want to see Channah break Zeke's heart.

Channah held the ring with her forefinger and thumb. "And please, take this *thing*. I don't want it anymore. It scares me." She dropped it into Mimi's hand.

Mimi closed her fingers around the diamond. It felt sharp and hard.

Channah slung her purse over her shoulder and marched away, tossing the uneaten banana and cereal box in the trash.

Mimi gazed at the black stone sitting in her palm. She wasn't sure she wanted it, either.

CHAPTER EIGHT

MIMI LEFT THE PROMENADE IN A DAZE, with no idea what to do, or where to go. She'd told her dad she wasn't coming to work that day, but decided to go in anyway. As much as the office sometimes drove her crazy, it was home.

She also knew her dad would find out that Channah had broken her engagement eventually; she might as well tell him face-to-face.

After she got off the subway to Forty-Seventh Street, she texted Channah. "I'm so sorry about everything. Are you okay?"

"Not really," came the reply.

"Did you break it off?"

"Yes. For now. You might think it's crazy, but I feel it's the right thing for me and Zeke."

"How did Zeke take it?" Mimi wrote.

"Not well. He said what I did hurt him ten times more than getting beat up last night."

"I'm sorry to hear that."

"I am, too." Channah was being uncharacteristically terse.

Mimi was tempted to try and change Channah's mind, but didn't see much chance of that. She typed, then erased, several responses. Finally, she sent Channah a line of hug emoticons. There was nothing else to say.

MAX REACTED HOW MIMI EXPECTED.

"She's calling off the engagement because of a curse?" he bellowed, bouncing off his seat. "Where does she think she's living? Disney World? Maybe I should call a fairy godmother. She can sing the curse away."

"Dad, Channah's very sensitive and she's been through a lot. She might not be thinking all that rationally right now. She just needs more time."

"But I didn't give her the diamond to hurt her!" Max's scalp was red. "I thought it was beautiful, and she should have it. Is that so wrong?"

"No, it isn't," Mimi said. "And she probably knows that. She just feels the curse, or whatever it is, has cast a shadow over her engagement. It might not make sense, but people aren't always logical."

"But they shouldn't be crazy!" Max took out his phone. "I can't believe she's acting like this. Let me call her. What's her number?" Max had owned a smartphone for a year, but hadn't yet grasped he no longer had to memorize everyone's contact info.

"Don't!" Mimi lunged for the phone. "You two will just end up screaming at each other. The best thing to do is give her time, and hope she'll change her mind."

Max put the phone down. "I can't believe it. Yesterday, I was so happy you were bringing someone into the office. I thought maybe you were starting to take a real interest in the business. And now look. You've made a huge mess, and ruined the tiny bit of *naches* we've had around here."

This infuriated Mimi. "Do not blame me for this! It wouldn't have happened if you hadn't—"

Mimi was ready to tell her father this was all his fault, because of his stupid decision to give Zeke the diamond.

But he probably knew that. And it probably gnawed at him. Why upset him more? They all felt bad enough.

"You know what?" Mimi said. "Never mind. We just have to hope Channah comes to her senses. She's her own woman, who can make her own decisions."

"I know," Max groused. "I hate that." He turned toward his computer, and half-heartedly started typing.

Mimi couldn't bear to see her father so sad. For so long, he'd wanted Channah to be happy. And now he'd helped blow that up.

Mimi went back to her desk and phoned Michael. She told him about the busted engagement, and he also reacted like she expected.

"That's nuts," he said. "Channah seems like someone with a good head on her shoulders. I can't believe she'd cancel an engagement because of a supposed curse. I'm surprised she's acting like this."

"Yeah." Mimi paused for a beat. "You know what's weird? My father said almost exactly the same thing."

"He did?" Michael groaned. "Oh God. Do me a favor. If that happens again, don't mention it." He cleared his throat. "Anyway, a colleague from my precinct wants to talk to you about this Rosalyn Lowery situation. Are you available?"

"I'm at the office now."

"Wait a sec," Michael said. He put Mimi on hold for a few seconds. "Okay. Can Detective Brill come over in about ten minutes?"

Mimi was intimidated to speak to one of the "difficult guys" Michael had snickered about, but she couldn't say no. "We'll be here."

Michael seemed to sense her hesitation. "It will just be a quick chat."

Ten minutes later, Mimi was happy to meet Detective Brill— Detective Rita Brill.

She was a small, thin African-American woman, dressed in a brown paint-suit, with silvering hair and glasses perched on the edge of her nose. She warmly greeted Mimi and Max, saying she'd heard "great" things about them.

From there, she morphed into a strict professional, quizzing Mimi and Max on every interaction they had with Rosalyn, from Mimi's Facebook exchanges through her visit to the office. Mimi was impressed by her thoroughness; she asked every question multiple times, and when Max answered something, she double-checked it with Mimi, and vice versa.

She finished by asking about Mimi's past investigations, causing Max to grumble: "Mimi never should have gotten involved in those. You agree with me, right?"

"It probably wasn't the best idea from a safety standpoint," Brill said. "But it seems to have worked out okay."

Max pouted and folded his arms.

By the time they were done, they'd spent two hours discussing Rosalyn's twenty-minute visit. So much for a "quick chat." Mimi's memory felt squeezed dry.

Detective Brill took pictures of the diamond, brooch, and lawyer's letter. "I think we're done," she said, closing her notebook. "Do you have any questions?"

"I guess my main one is," Mimi said, "was the brooch stolen?"

The detective drummed her fingernails on her notebook. "That's certainly something we're looking at. From what we know, Shepherd Lowery sent his sister-in-law the brooch shortly before he died. So, it's hard to say that Rosalyn Lowery obtained it illegally.

"Of course," she added, "that doesn't mean some lawyer won't make an issue of it. That's what they're paid for. Have you been contacted again, by that private investigator or anyone else?"

"No," Mimi said.

"We haven't heard from anyone either," said Detective Brill. "From the paperwork you showed me, it certainly seems like Rosalyn Lowery had legitimate title to that brooch. And you appear to have followed proper second-hand purchase procedures.

"Though, I will say one thing. Under New York City law, when you purchase a diamond off the street, you have to hold it for five days before you resell it. And while you may not have technically violated the law, I don't know if it was the smartest idea in the world to give that diamond to your receptionist as an engagement gift."

Max lowered his chin, like a chastened child.

"Fortunately," Detective Brill said, "she gave it back to you."

"Yes, it's in our safe now," Mimi said. "Our receptionist didn't want it, because of its quote-unquote 'curse.'"

"I don't blame her." Detective Brill turned to Max. "What were you thinking, Mr. Rosen, giving her a cursed diamond for an engagement ring?"

Max leaned back on his chair, and mumbled something unintelligible.

"Here's my advice," said Detective Brill. "Securely lock away both the diamond and—what did you call the brooch, the tuck-us?"

Max nodded.

"And they're together?" Brill asked.

"Yes," Mimi said. "We've remounted the diamond on the brooch. Everything is like it was and locked away."

"Good," the detective said. "Let me know if you hear from anyone."

Detective Brill left on an upbeat note, telling Mimi and Max it was "lovely" meeting them.

After she left, Mimi became anxious about keeping the diamond in their office for the next few days. Like Channah, she wanted to be rid of "that thing."

Mimi didn't believe it was cursed. At least, she didn't think she did. But she was nagged by that persistent voice, the one that underlies everything from superstitions to lottery tickets, the voice that won't stop asking, "What if?"

CHAPTER NINE

AFTER DETECTIVE BRILL LEFT, MAX RECEIVED A CALL, which he passed on to Mimi. "It's from Zeke," he said. "He's hoping you can help out with Channah."

"No, Dad," Mimi objected. "I can't help him. Tell him I'm not here. I don't want to talk to him."

"I don't want to talk to him either," Max said. "That's why I'm transferring him to you."

Mimi growled at her father, and picked up the phone.

"I really need your help, Mimi," Zeke said. "Please."

He sounded bad; he was stammering more than usual, and when he described Channah calling off their engagement, his voice broke. It was hard for someone so logical to understand something so incomprehensible.

"I've told Channah a million times," he said, "I'm not worried about the curse. I told her, even if, God forbid, I do get killed, I will die happily, as I was married to her."

"That's sweet," Mimi said.

"I thought so," Zeke said. "So did she. But it wasn't enough to change her mind."

"I'm sorry," Mimi said.

"I just wish Channah would think about this logically. Like, what do we know about this cursed diamond? How do we know this curse is real?"

"Of course, it's not real," Mimi said. "Curses don't exist."

"I didn't mean it that way. I agree, curses are fake. But how do we know this diamond was actually cursed? Just because some people say it was, doesn't mean it's true. And let's say, for the sake of argument, somebody did curse it. Did that person have the proper qualifications to curse something? I'm guessing it's a specialized field.

"We need more information on this diamond. I've read as much as I can but every site says the same thing. They say there's a curse but don't provide any evidence for it. The whole thing could have been a publicity stunt. Or an urban legend. It could have been completely made up."

Mimi mulled this over. "That's a good point. I'll look into that."

"Please do," said Zeke. "If we can prove this diamond was never cursed, that might be the only thing that convinces Channah."

After Mimi hung up, she hit Google with a vengeance, hunting for every morsel of info on the Prince Corthoff diamond and its supposed hex. There wasn't much, and, like Zeke said, just about every page said the same thing. Its Wikipedia entry was based on a long out-of-print book, which was only available, used, for two hundred bucks.

She did find an extensive entry on the Heartbrooch on a site about famous jewels, which showed a refreshing skepticism.

"For all the legends and wild tales that surround the Prince Corthoff, very little concrete information exists about the black diamond's origins or history.

"According to a 1920s newspaper article, a British soldier stole the diamond from the eye of a statue in an Indian temple during the Siege of Delhi in 1857. Afterward, the temple priest decreed that anyone who owned it would suffer terrible misfortune.

"The story claims the soldier who stole it didn't feel any immediate bad effects. But within three months, all the men in his regiment had died except for him. Some succumbed to then-prevalent diseases. Others perished in combat. Individually, each death was explainable. Collectively, it was unusual that almost an entire battalion should die in such a short period of time.

"Broken-hearted at the demise of so many of his comrades, the soldier returned to London with the diamond, and sold it for a huge amount to a local jeweler. Afterward, the soldier went on a massive bender to celebrate, and got so drunk, he fell into the Thames River and drowned.

"There are many reasons to be skeptical about this story, which apes the nativist tropes of the pulp tales of the era. The article says the London jeweler eventually sold the diamond to Russian Prince Grigor Corthoff, its purported namesake. But like so many of the legends surrounding this gemstone, the Prince's ownership has never been proven.

"What *is* known is that Corthoff's family was eventually executed. Yet, their demise was almost certainly caused by the Russian Revolution, not the diamond.

"It's possible that G.V. Washbrun, the jeweler that bought the Prince Corthoff in the 1920s, concocted the story of the curse to increase the diamond's marketability. The people there were no doubt aware of how Louis Cartier played up the supposed curse of the Hope Diamond to increase public interest. We may never know for sure, since the Washbrun company no longer exists, having gone bankrupt in 1939. The end of the Washbrun company is often attributed to the curse—although the Great Depression is a far more likely culprit.

"After that, Washbrun's heirs spent the next eleven years in court fighting over the gem, the most valuable object the company owned.

"A few decades later, the Prince Corthoff and its history caught the eye of Wyllis Lowery, the second-generation CEO of high-end jeweler Lowery Inc. Wyllis was every bit the showman as Louis Cartier, and surely couldn't pass up a good promotional opportunity. Lowery put out a monograph on the diamond which mostly parroted existing lore, with a few obvious embellishments thrown in.

"The most authoritative source on the diamond's history is likely the Lowery company archives. The company is known for keeping detailed records on every piece they've created. However, they have a policy of only giving out information about a piece's origins to its owners, and since the Heartbrooch remains in their vaults, they declined to answer our questions.

"In the past, the company had said that, given all the tragedies that befell the family following the creation of the brooch—including the deaths of Wyllis Lowery, and his father, Nicholas—they will never sell it, nor have they displayed it publicly since its introduction. So, unless Lowery ever sells the brooch, the questions surrounding it will remain a mystery."

But, of course, now, the brooch *had* been sold—to Mimi. She could get those answers.

Mimi called Lowery's headquarters, and requested the archive department. When asked what this was in reference to, she said the Heartbrooch. "I'm its current owner, and I want to learn more about it."

After sitting on hold for what felt like an eternity, an official-sounding woman asked her name. A minute later, a high-pitched voice came on the line. "You said your name is Mimi Rosen?"

"Yes."

"Great to hear from you. I'm Archibald Lowery, CEO of Lowery."

The minute he boomed out his name, Mimi felt a tickle in her throat . . . which didn't make sense. Yes, Archibald Lowery was an important jewelry executive, but he was also married to her friend.

"Hi, Mr. Lowery," she said, then wondered why she called him that. "I'm very sorry to hear about Rosalyn. We were once close friends."

"Thank you. I appreciate that." He paused. "Though honestly, I don't believe I ever heard her mention you."

Charming.

"We worked together on the night shift at *The West Jersey Metro*," Mimi said. "Lately, we had drifted apart. Which is a shame, because I really liked her."

"Gotcha," Archibald said. "You told our receptionist you own the Heartbrooch. I assume you work for the diamond company she sold it to."

"Yes."

"Great. You can return the brooch at any time. Just deliver it to our store on Fifty-Seventh Street."

Mimi was taken aback. "That's not why I called. Why would I return it to you? We just bought it."

Archibald's voice turned stern. "Because you have to. Rosalyn sold that piece to you illegally."

"Actually," Mimi said, getting her back up, "we just spoke to a police officer, who said Rosalyn had legitimate title to it."

"I'd like to see you prove that in court," Archibald declared. "I'll give you a hint: you can't.

"Of course—" he softened his tone, "we'd rather not go that route. I'm currently at our store on Fifty-Seventh Street. It would be in our best interest to meet. There's certain things regarding this transaction, and Rosalyn's involvement in it, that you may not know. I'll happily fill you in, on a confidential off-the-record basis."

The words "confidential off-the-record basis" got Mimi's journalistic juices flowing. After Archibald repeatedly cajoled her, she agreed to visit the Lowery castle and meet the King.

CHAPTER TEN

BEFORE HEADING TO THE STORE, Mimi did some quick research on Lowery Incorporated. It was founded by Archibald's grandfather, Nicholas, but it really entered the public consciousness thanks to the tireless showmanship of his son Wyllis.

But Wyllis' high profile came with a price. After he was killed in a robbery, his wife Claudia took the reins. She was considered such a fearsome businesswoman she was nicknamed the "Piranha in Pearls."

Later, her sons, Archibald and Shepherd, joined the business, and became embroiled in an embarrassing public fight over control of the company. Archibald claimed Shepherd did nothing but collect a paycheck; Shepherd accused his brother and mom of cooking the books. Eventually, Archibald bought out his brother's share of the company.

"Archibald Lowery and his mother will face a formidable task making the venerable jeweler relevant to modern consumers," opined one newspaper after the settlement. "Some people find its 57th Street flagship intimidating."

When Mimi arrived at the flagship, she found she agreed with those people.

The store's front door was so lavish, it was almost a jewel itself. Its steely gate was slathered in gold and topped with Lowery's signature cursive "L."

Mimi pulled on the door handle. It was locked. The store "every-one dreams of entering" didn't let everyone cross the drawbridge.

Mimi made eye contact with the poker-faced guard standing in the front window. He pressed something on the wall, and the door buzzed. Mimi had apparently made the cut.

A doorman opened the door and declared, "Welcome to the Kingdom of Love." After Mimi stepped inside, the guard asked her to open her pocketbook, and frisked her with a metal wand.

When Mimi finally made it to the Lowery main floor, all the rigamarole felt worth it. This store was *something*. The carpet was so plush, Mimi felt it might swallow her. In its center hung a glis-tening chandelier, the size of a refrigerator, which almost dared you not to gawk at it. Mimi had read somewhere it was the larg-est chandelier on the East Coast, though she wasn't sure who kept track of such things.

Every window was draped with bright silk curtains. The tables were topped with porcelain vases bursting with bright red roses. An orange fire blazed in the fireplace. The overall effect was a stud-ied hominess, if your home was a mansion dotted with jewelry cases.

The floor was mostly empty, though she did spy some elderly customers, talking with also-elderly salesmen. The salesmen were all lanky Ichabod Crane types, who spoke in hushed tones while bent over the jewelry cases. The youngest person on the floor was a beautiful blonde twenty-something sales assistant in a tight-fit-ting dress who acted as a kind of human mannequin, awkwardly displaying a diamond necklace for an older man, who was clearly checking out more than the jewelry.

When Rosalyn first visited Archibald's world, she said she felt like "Dorothy entering Oz." Mimi now understood what she meant.

Mimi was approached by one of the Ichabods, who bowed and asked if he could help her. When she replied that she had an appointment with Archibald Lowery, he marched to a display case, opened a drawer, and picked up a phone. After talking to whoever he needed to talk to, he summoned Mimi and asked for her ID. He returned it with a smile that disappeared as quickly as it came. A security guard accompanied Mimi on the elevator to the top floor. When Mimi entered the Lowery executive suite, she was struck by how un-striking it was. It was just a generic corporate office, staffed with regular people, nothing like the mini-Versailles downstairs.

Archibald's office was, of course, huge—though, like her dad's, it was lined with wood paneling that probably hadn't been changed since the seventies.

On one wall hung a framed magazine cover, bearing the words, "They Call it Glowery: Inside New York's Rudest Store." *My God,* Mimi thought. *They like that reputation. They thrive on it.*

There were also several shots of Archibald's dad, Wyllis Lowery, posing with royalty, First Ladies, celebrities, and other famous wearers of jewelry. The photos showed a diminutive man with white hair and an open grin, his head perpetually ducked in the "can I help you" pose. He seemed the epitome of the friendly, crinkly-eyed jeweler, eager to show off his garden of delights.

But there was another, more formal portrait of Wyllis, which hung on the wall across from Archibald's desk, and it made him seem a lot more intimidating. His hard eyes glared—one might even say glowered—down at his son, warning him not to screw up what he'd built.

There were no pictures of Archibald. Maybe this was truly for security reasons, but Mimi's first impression was that he was both unimpressive and unattractive—tubby and bespectacled, with a head of thinning black curly hair. His features looked like they had been smushed together to create a permanent scowl. His stubby hands stuck out of his monogrammed sleeves. He didn't look like a CEO of a glamorous jeweler . . . more like its accountant.

Mimi figured Rosalyn wasn't all that upset about his no-photo policy. It's one thing to boast you're Mrs. Archibald Lowery; it's another when people see the guy.

The security guard led Mimi to a chair in front of Archibald's desk. Mimi gave him a quick smile, which he didn't return.

"Again, Mr. Lowery," she said, "I'm very sorry to hear about Rosalyn."

"Thank you. It's been a difficult time." Archibald said this quickly, as if he wanted to get the condolences part of the conversation over with.

"Like I told you before," he said, "I'd prefer to settle this Heartbrooch matter without going to court. I've spent way too much time with attorneys and I don't particularly care for it. They cost a lot of money and never use it to buy jewelry.

"I can prove that the Heartbrooch is the property of this company. My father designed it as a gift of love for my mother, right before he passed away. You have no legal right to it."

Mimi shifted in her seat. "Just so you know, that's not what Rosalyn told me. She said that you and your brother Shepherd had a dispute over the business. And after Shepherd sold his shares, he received the Heartbrooch as part of the settlement."

"That's true as far as it goes," Archibald said. "The family did buy out my brother's share of the business. He received several million dollars, none of which he deserved. Since most of this company's value is tied up in inventory, he also received a large amount of jewelry, including that brooch.

"As my late brother was extremely skilled at spending money, but less so at making it, he sold just about every item we gave him. But, significantly, he did not sell the Heartbrooch. Why was that, you ask?"

Archibald spun the miniature globe on his desk. "Because he wasn't allowed to. The Heartbrooch is one of the most historic pieces in our collection, so Lowery Incorporated had the right of first refusal to any sale. So while he could legally transfer his interest to Rosalyn, she had no legal right to sell it without our approval. And now that she's deceased, any title she held reverts to me."

"Okay," Mimi said. "If all that's true, why did Rosalyn sell it?"

Archibald blew out a gust of air. "My deceased wife, I'm sorry to say, had a spending problem. The more she wrote about clothes, the more she felt compelled to buy them. From what I hear, they're quite competitive about fashion at *The Look*. They apparently spend most of their days judging each other's wardrobes. I'm not sure when they find the time to put the magazine together.

"My family isn't exactly poor, but she was spending so much, I had to put her on a strict budget. She even started shoplifting, which caused a number of unpleasant situations. She's lucky that I know a lot of upscale retailers, put it that way."

He leaned over his desk. "By the way, how much did Rosalyn sell you the brooch for?"

"Twenty-five thousand," Mimi said.

Archibald almost laughed. "That's it? I was thinking she'd sell it for far more. I'll happily match that. My lawyers charge that much a week."

Mimi cleared her throat. "Right now, I can't sell you anything. There's a mandatory five-day waiting period."

Archibald nodded. "Correct. But that policy was put in to help victims of theft, which in this case is us."

Mimi edged forward on her chair. "It doesn't matter. We have to obey the law. And you're not the only person laying claim to the brooch. Right after we bought it, I received a call from a private investigator, who said he's working for the Tomaso estate. He claimed the brooch belongs to them."

"The Tomaso estate?" Archibald shook his head and chuckled. "There's no such thing. If there was, they would have contacted us. Whoever called you was probably some idiot."

"Well, here's another issue," Mimi said, "and it's a big one. We may be able to get millions for that brooch at auction. It's a Josephine Tomaso original, the last piece she ever designed. Why should we sell it to you for far less than it's worth?"

Anger flashed in Archibald's eyes. "Because it's stolen and you had no right to buy it in the first place. Isn't that a good enough reason?"

"You haven't proved that."

"If we must, we can prove it in court. We'd just prefer not to."

Mimi brought her arms to her chest. "Why not, if your case is so strong?"

Archibald exhaled noisily. "I wasn't going to bring this up, but the Heartbrooch was designed by my father for my elderly mother, to commemorate his undying love for her. It's always held a special place in her heart.

"My mother is in her eighties, and she's frail and in failing health. Having to testify about the brooch in court would destroy her emotionally and possibly physically. Do you want the death of a sick old lady on your conscience?"

Mimi heard a loud noise. She turned around with a start. A door at the side of the room had swung open.

A tall older woman in a bright green dress stepped out. "All right, Archibald," she said, her voice suffused with annoyance. "Don't overdo it."

Archibald lowered his head. "Sorry, mom."

CHAPTER ELEVEN

CLAUDIA LOWERY MIGHT BE IN HER EIGHTIES, but the "Piranha in Pearls" was so imposing that Mimi reflexively leaned back when she entered the room. Archibald's mother was tall and thin, with obviously-dyed black hair which hung in a bob. She stood ramrod straight, and sported a vault-full of bling—a gumball-sized diamond on her finger, shiny red rubies on her ears, and, appropriate for her nickname, snow-white pearls around her neck.

"If you don't mind," she said, with more than a touch of ice in her voice, "I've overheard a bit of this conversation and I had to step in. Archibald has been extremely polite to you. I won't be.

"I am quite familiar with our agreement with my son Shepherd. Rosalyn had absolutely no right to sell that brooch. If you don't return it to us, we will let our lawyers handle it. And trust me, you do not want that. They're monsters, those people. Complete animals."

"That's true," Archibald said. "They work for me, and even I'm scared of them."

Mimi turned to Claudia. "Mrs. Lowery, I understand you feel that your company owns the brooch. But I don't appreciate your threats. There's a waiting period we must respect, and if you feel you have a claim to this item, call my lawyer. I didn't come to make a deal."

"Then why are you here?" Claudia asked.

"Because Archibald invited me," Mimi said. "I'd called the store over something completely different. I was trying to reach the archive department to find out information about the brooch."

Archibald and Claudia appeared baffled.

"What kind of information?" Archibald said.

"This is going to sound stupid," Mimi said, sucking in her breath, "but we gave the black diamond to our receptionist for an engagement ring, and when she learned it was cursed, she called off the engagement. So I thought, if we could get information about the diamond's history, and find out if it was actually cursed or not, that might change her mind."

"You are correct," Claudia said. "That does sound stupid."

"We can look in our files," Archibald said. "But obviously any talk of a cursed diamond is claptrap. I can't believe anyone sensible would believe that."

"Rosalyn did," Mimi said.

"To repeat," Claudia jumped in, "I can't believe any sensible person would believe that."

"Once you give us the brooch," Archibald said, "we'll be happy to search our files and provide you the name of the relevant witch doctor. Most likely, my father invented the curse for publicity purposes."

Archibald's desk phone rang. "Give me a second. It's client services." He picked up.

"Ah yes, the Dubai sultan-ette," he told the person on the other line. He put his hand over the phone, and turned to his mother. "Remember, the four-million-dollar necklace we spent three months designing to her exact specifications? She just told the salesperson she's not, quote-unquote, 'vibing with it.'"

"Really?" Claudia said. "We made that piece exactly like she asked. It's completely hideous."

"Apparently, she's quite discerning about her vibes," said Archibald. He spoke again to client services. "I'm guessing she's looking for a little CEO attention. I'll be right down."

"It's amazing," Claudia spat. "Some of these people are so tight with their money, you'd think they'd earned it."

Archibald walked to the large wooden closet on the right wall, and pulled open the door, revealing a row of identical black jackets, with two tuxedos hanging in the corner.

He removed one from its hanger, and slid his arms into it. "I'm sorry, I must depart. Those billionaire butts don't kiss themselves."

Archibald stared at the full-length mirror mounted on the closet door, and tightened his tie and adjusted his jacket. "It was lovely meeting you, Miss Rosen. I hope we meet again, when you're returning our stolen jewel. As I mentioned, we are happy to reimburse your father the twenty-five thousand dollars he paid." He turned toward her. "I assume we have a deal." He held out his hand.

Mimi didn't want to shake. She didn't want to have anything to do with him. "No, we don't."

"Why not?" Archibald said. "Are you looking to make a profit? How about thirty thousand?"

"Honestly, Mr. Lowery," Mimi said, raising her voice, "this isn't about money. I'm a little disturbed by your behavior." She sat up in her chair. "Maybe this is none of my business, but it doesn't seem like either you or your mother are all that broken up about your wife's death. Rosalyn was just killed yesterday, and you've repeatedly disparaged her, and are treating this like it's a normal workday. You seem more upset about losing this brooch than losing your wife."

At this, the cleaning woman, who'd been clearing the teacups, swung her head toward Mimi and offered a telltale smile.

"Again, you're correct," Archibald said. "That is none of your business.

"As you may have surmised, we are not a heart-on-our-sleeve kind of family. We've weathered a lot of rather unpleasant incidents, and we've often been betrayed by those close to us—including, I'm sorry to say, my late wife. We work with very valuable items, and live under constant threat that what happened to Rosalyn, and happened to my father, might happen to us. We've had our family issues dissected in the press. Perhaps that has hardened us a bit. But if you've been through what we have, maybe you'd understand.

"Of course, I'm upset that Rosalyn was killed. I may seem calm, but emotionally I'm a wreck. Rosalyn was my wife and I loved her very much."

The cleaning woman rolled her eyes as she took out the tea tray.

"I'm quite upset, too," Claudia added, though unlike her son, she didn't sound remotely convincing.

"I don't believe that sitting around, moping, solves anything," Archibald said, brushing off his sleeves. "And unfortunately, since my late wife's picture was on the front page of the newspaper today, we've been besieged by sympathy calls and client visits. We don't have the staff to handle this kind of crunch. So, I have no choice. I must do my job, no matter how much I'm grieving." His voice turned sharp. "I hope that's okay with you."

Mimi didn't answer. What he said sounded both reasonable and horrible.

Archibald removed his glasses, and stuffed them in his pocket. That made him look better, but still not great.

"You told me that you worked on the newspaper with Rosalyn," he said. "Were you once a writer?"

"I wouldn't say I was *once* a writer," Mimi said. "I haven't written professionally in a while, but I plan to—"

"Please," Archibald butted in. "I find it quite tedious when writers whine about their careers. I used to hear that all the time from Rosalyn.

"You may not realize how Rosalyn and I met. When she was working at the PR firm, she helped write the company history we produced for our hundredth anniversary. Now that our one-hundred-and-fifteenth is coming up, we're planning an updated edition.

"We want to produce a beautiful coffee-table book, with an incredible layout and gorgeous illustrations. No one will read it, of course, but it will look amazing.

"Assuming we have a deal for the Heartbrooch, would you be interested in working on that? Our history is quite fascinating. Did you know, for example, that Lowery was the first American jeweler to use brass filigree?"

"No," Mimi said. She didn't know what brass filigree was, or whether that was all that fascinating.

"One thing, Archibald," said Claudia. "We agreed that we wouldn't call it the Lowery family history, as that makes it sound like we're stuck in the past. We want to focus on how our brand has built on its legacy. So we're calling it: the Lowery family heritage."

"Ah yes." Archibald gave a dutiful smile. "Would you be interested in writing the Lowery family *heritage*?"

Mimi blinked incredulously. She didn't want anything more to do with this obnoxious family, or to chronicle their history, or heritage, or whatever they're calling it. "I'll be honest, I'm not—"

"It'll pay fifty thousand dollars," Archibald said.

Mimi's mouth dropped. "Let me think about it."

CHAPTER TWELVE

B Y THE TIME MIMI LEFT LOWERY, the sun had set and it was dark. It had been a long day. Between Channah calling off her engagement, the meeting with Detective Brill, and her very strange talk with Archibald and Claudia Lowery, Mimi was ready to head home and decompress.

But then she spotted the cleaning woman from upstairs, the one who emitted the nod and eyeroll. She was standing outside the store smoking, the orange tip of her cigarette glowing in the dark.

Mimi was at first tempted to keep walking. But something about this woman made Mimi want to stop and talk to her. Of course, that would mean Mimi was sort-of investigating Rosalyn's murder. But this was only an attempt. The woman might not speak to her.

"Excuse me," Mimi said. "Weren't you just upstairs cleaning Archibald Lowery's office?"

"Yes," the woman replied, with a slight Southern lilt. She was short, stout, and intense, her eyes alert and assessing under a shock of brown hair.

"My name's Mimi. I noticed upstairs that when I criticized Mr. Lowery for not being more upset about the death of his wife, you smiled at me. And when Archibald Lowery said he loved his wife, you rolled your eyes. Do you mind if I ask why?"

The woman scanned Mimi suspiciously. "Why do you want to know?"

"Rosalyn was a friend of mine. I'm curious."

"Rosalyn was my friend, too," the woman said, amid a stream of smoke. "But curiosity can be dangerous."

"I'm well aware," Mimi said.

The woman flicked her cigarette to the street, then ground it into the pavement with her foot. "You know, in all the years I've worked for those people, you're the first person to notice my eye-rolling? And I roll my eyes constantly."

"So why'd you do it upstairs?"

"Walk to the Columbus Circle subway," the woman said. "I'll meet you there in five minutes."

MIMI DIDN'T WAIT LONG. The woman approached the station, caught her eye, cocked her head, and said, "come with me." They crossed the road to Central Park.

The streets were packed with commuters rushing to the subway. Mimi and the woman—who gave her name as Darlene—walked, slowly and deliberately, the other way.

When they entered the park, Darlene led Mimi down a dimly lit path, their only companions a skateboarder, a homeless man, and a furtive couple making out.

"So how long have you worked for the Lowerys?" Mimi asked.

"About four years. I work at both their store and their estate in Larnsdale."

"What's that like?"

Darlene frowned. "It's not easy. I spend all day bending down and picking things up and it kills my back. Some nights, I come home, and my whole body aches. I just need to earn a little more money so I can live with the rest of my family in Florida. Should take two or three years."

"If it's so bad, why don't you quit?" Mimi asked.

Darlene shrugged half-heartedly. "I never finished high school, so I don't have many other job options. I hated waitressing, because you have to be friendly all day. Here at least, you don't have to talk to anyone.

"It pays pretty well. And I find it entertaining. The Lowerys don't realize, I hear all their craziness. They think I'm an idiot, that I don't understand what they're saying. But I follow it all. It's like watching the *Real Housewives*, but with ugly people.

"It's funny. The Lowerys are always nervous someone will steal their jewelry. If they don't have every last piece accounted for at the end of the day, they'll make the entire store staff stay until they figure out where it is. But I get something from them that's far more valuable: information."

Mimi's stomach tingled. This woman was the perfect source. "So tell me," she said, "why did you smirk and roll your eyes upstairs?"

"I liked Rosalyn. We were friends. It's sad, what happened to her. When Archibald said he loved her, I knew that wasn't true. Archibald didn't love Rosalyn, at least not toward the end. She and him were always fighting."

"What about?"

"He's a jerk," Darlene spat. "He thinks he's so important, because he's CEO of a famous jeweler. Really, it's his mother who has the last say on everything. Rosalyn used to tease him about that, which always made him furious.

"Archibald wanted Rosalyn to have a baby, someone he could pass the store onto. And she couldn't. So, that was a problem. Then, they got her the magazine job and she started spending tons of money on clothes, which drove him crazy. He watches every penny, that guy."

"Here's something I'm curious about," Mimi said. "Rosalyn told me that she and Archibald's brother, Shepherd, had a history. Did she and Shepherd ever—?"

"Oh yeah." Darlene giggled. "You know the good stuff, huh?"

"So they had an affair?"

"No," Darlene frowned. "It was a one-time thing, at a wedding or something. But that was enough. When Shepherd's wife found out about it, she walked out on him. And Archibald went nuts."

Darlene abruptly spun around. She was now walking out of the park. Mimi had no choice but to follow.

"I should return to the store," Darlene said. "I've told you enough."

"You can't say more?"

"Not right now," Darlene said. "But I can always give you more information on the Lowerys."

"That would be great." Mimi couldn't believe her luck. She scribbled down her number and handed it to Darlene.

"No problem. I used to pass information onto Rosalyn all the time. We had kind of an alliance."

"Really?"

"Yeah. It began about a year ago. I saw Rosalyn sitting in one of the fancy gardens they have at the estate, and she didn't look so good. I said, 'are you okay?' At first, she was startled to hear me speak. She looked like the cat was talking.

"But we started to chat. She told me how unhappy she was. This was right after her little hook-up with Shepherd. She'd just had a fight with Archibald, and he threatened to kick her off the estate. And she was scared because she had nowhere to go.

"I told her: don't worry about it. I had just heard Archibald and Claudia talking in the library. They said that since Shepherd's marriage was ending, it wouldn't look good if the Lowery family had two divorces in one year. And they didn't want the media to find out that Shepherd had slept with his sister-in-law.

"And Rosalyn thought that was funny. She said the family once had a public scandal, so they think that the whole world is obsessed with them. But really, only old people care about them now. We had a good laugh about that. After that, we talked a lot."

"About what?" Mimi asked.

"The usual things. Life. Love. Her problems, mostly. Not that my life's so great, but she was the boss, so her problems came first. And if I heard something interesting, I'd tell her. But I only did it under three conditions. And if I talk to you, you must follow them, too."

"Sure," Mimi said.

"First, you gotta keep everything I say confidential. It can't be traced to me. I can't afford to lose my job."

"Of course," Mimi said. "That's a given."

"Second, we gotta be real careful how we talk. So, if you want to get ahold of me, don't call. Write me on Signal. That's the app that keeps everything secret."

"No problem," Mimi said. "I'll add it to my phone."

"And third, like I said, information is valuable. So if I tell you anything, it'll cost you."

Mimi stopped walking. "You're going to charge me?"

"Sure." Darlene stopped, too. "Why would I risk my job for nothing? I gave you a couple of samples to whet your appetite. I know a lot more. You just gotta pay for it."

Mimi gulped. "How much?"

"This is Lowery we're talking about," Darlene said. "Nothing's cheap."

And with that, she strolled away.

MIMI GOT HOME, GOBBLED A MICROWAVED DINNER, and called Michael. She told him about her talk with Detective Brill, but didn't mention her meetings with the Lowerys or Darlene. If she did, Michael would scold her for investigating, and she'd say she wasn't, even though she basically was. Instead, she said the rest of her day was "boring."

"That's good," he said. "You could use a little boring."

"Definitely," she smiled.

After she hung up, she resolved not to think about the brooch for the rest of the night. She stretched out on her recliner and tackled *The New York Times* crossword puzzle. This much-needed downtime was interrupted by a call from an unknown number, which she let go to voicemail. Afterward, she played the message, and instantly regretted it.

"My name is Vanessa Lowery," said the voice, which sounded both firm and distressed. "I was formerly married to the late

Shepherd Lowery. I believe you recently purchased an item called the Heartbrooch. I need to talk to you. That piece belongs to me."

Mimi put her head on the back of her chair, closed her eyes, and tried not to scream.

CHAPTER THIRTEEN

M IMI MET VANESSA LOWERY THE NEXT MORNING at a classic New York diner. They sat in a back booth, at a grey Formica table with a wobbly leg. It was breakfast time, and the place was packed. Clanging dishes and shouted orders provided a nonstop soundtrack.

Shepherd Lowery's widow was a pretty, rail-thin brunette who appeared in her late thirties. She had a long face and a sharp chin, which made her look like a somewhat weathered aristocrat. Her eyes had obvious bags under them, but they were intense enough that Mimi felt they were boring into her. Mimi thought she resembled someone, and finally realized who: Rosalyn, without the dye job.

Vanessa clutched her tea between her long skinny fingers, and launched into her life story. She first met Shepherd Lowery as a nanny for his kids. "I used to say we fell in love. Now I just say we had an affair." Their marriage lasted six years, until Shepherd was again unfaithful—this time with his sister-in-law.

"Why do you think he—" Mimi tried to phrase this delicately. "Ended his life?"

"I blame Rosalyn." Vanessa took a sip of tea. "I know that's a terrible thing to say, given what happened, but when Rosalyn slept with Shepherd, that killed both his marriage and his jewelry business. And that was the beginning of the end for him."

"How did sleeping with Rosalyn affect his jewelry business?"

"Because I was running it," Vanessa said. "Shepherd couldn't manage that company by himself. Even his father didn't try that. I was the one with the organizational skills. I knew my way around a balance sheet. Shepherd knew jewelry. That was it.

"When it first started, the company had a little success, and it went to his head. He basically sank his entire life savings into the company, and it all went down the drain. He died in major debt. Which was ridiculous. He was born rich. He received millions in the settlement with his family. He was a *Lowery*. But he was so desperate to prove himself, he didn't watch his money. And if you're not careful, it can disappear very quickly.

"At the end, he was in real bad financial shape. He owed money to this local loan shark, who was threatening to come after him. And he didn't want to ask his family for help. He was too proud for that.

"I feel bad for him," Vanessa continued. "But he brought his problems on himself. He had a real self-destructive streak. He never did what was best for himself. He only wanted to get even with his family."

"Why was that?" Mimi asked.

Vanessa stared into the distance. "It goes very deep, into the weird family dynamic the Lowerys have. Shepherd never fit in with the rest of his family. He was the black sheep. Later in life, he was diagnosed with ADHD, but growing up, his family just thought he was dumb and lazy. 'Our big disappointment,' they called him. That bothered him to no end. He'd say, 'I'll show them I'm not stupid.' He spent his whole life trying to prove he wasn't a failure.

"Even when they brought him into the company, it was in a junior role, and he didn't mesh with the culture. He would wear jeans, when everyone else was super-formal. He would come to the office on a skateboard. His mother hated that. She wanted another son like Archibald, who just follows the rules and never has an original thought.

"And the thing is, if his mom and brother kept an open mind, they'd have seen Shepherd could have done a lot for that company. He had a vision to modernize it. He'd spent his entire life around jewelry. He knew the business, and he could judge quality. He had a much better sense of current jewelry trends than they did. But he wasn't interested in the boring classic stuff the store specializes in. So when they ignored him, he just checked out. They were willing to keep paying him, but these stupid lawyers convinced him to take legal action against the company. In the end, Shepherd had no choice but to take the paltry deal they offered him—a few million dollars and some jewelry. They made it extra-chintzy just to spite him.

"You have to understand, a family business is not like a normal company. When you've been told your whole life you're too stupid to run the business, like Shepherd was, it's a double blow. You've been rejected by your job *and* your family. After he left the business, he was incredibly depressed. He felt like he was worthless.

"When we got married, he said I gave him a new lease on life. We decided to go into business for ourselves. We would take the ideas he had and use them. He knew if Lowery didn't change, it would die."

"You think so?"

"Of course." Vanessa straightened her spine. "You ever go in there? Look at the customers. They once did a survey. Their core shopper is a white woman, over sixty, with a five-million-dollar net worth. Basically, old rich ladies who are halfway to dead. Does that sound like a growing business to you?

"The only reason that place stays open is because of its name, and the fact that they own the building, so they don't pay rent. They've had several offers to buy the company, but Archibald and his mom refuse to sell. Probably because they're skimming off the top, and don't want people to know. But when they die, that place will die with them."

"That makes sense," Mimi said.

"And you know who else thought so? Your friend Rosalyn. She wanted the store to appeal to a wider clientele. But the Lowerys were scared they'd ruin their image if they offered affordable product—and when I say affordable, I mean a fifteen-thousand-dollar entry price point, which is still ridiculous. So, they got Rosalyn a job at a magazine. Which kept her happy for a while. But eventually she grew tired of Archibald and wanted a way out.

"That's why she wanted the Heartbrooch. She knew if her last name wasn't Lowery, she wouldn't have that big job at *The Look*. She'd accrued a lot of debt from buying so many clothes, and needed a lot of cash if she was going to leave Archibald. She could only do that by getting that brooch."

Mimi tried to get her head around this. "Rosalyn told me that Shepherd gave her the brooch because it was cursed."

"Come on," Vanessa scoffed. "That's not a reason you'd give someone a valuable piece of jewelry. It's certainly not a reason Shepherd would do it. He was basically broke."

"I guess." Mimi rubbed her temples. "But on Facebook, Rosalyn told Shepherd she wanted nothing to do with him."

"She just wrote that so Archibald would see it," Vanessa said. "Shepherd was obsessed with Rosalyn. He thought, 'Archibald had taken so much from me, I'm going to take what's his.'

"After they slept together, Rosalyn played Shepherd like a fiddle. She knew how much he hated his brother. And she convinced him to give her the brooch."

Mimi shuddered. That didn't sound like the Rosalyn she knew. Was she really that devious? Mimi was starting to see her old friend in a new light.

"By the end, Shepherd's life was a mess," Vanessa said. "We had split, he wasn't talking to his family, and he had this loan shark after him. The only thing that kept him going was his bitterness toward his family. But at some point, he realized they'd won. They'd ruined his life. And so he did what he did." Her eyes turned red.

Of all the people Mimi had spoken with—Rosalyn, Archibald, Claudia, Darlene—Vanessa was the only one who showed any distress about Shepherd's death.

"Though honestly," Vanessa added, "part of me believes that Shepherd didn't kill himself. I think he was murdered."

"Why do you think that?" Mimi asked.

Vanessa's manicured nail tapped her tea cup. "Because I knew Shepherd. For all his problems, he wasn't the type to kill himself. He was a fighter. He always said, 'I never give up.' And he never did. That was both the best and worst thing about him."

"But who would kill him?"

"I don't know," Vanessa said. "Maybe the loan shark he owed money to. Or even the Lowerys."

"You think the Lowerys would kill their own family?"

"It's possible. There was a lot of bad blood between Archibald and Shepherd, especially after Shepherd slept with Rosalyn. The Lowerys are not good people. I'd be happy if I never saw them again. Unfortunately, I see them all the time now, since I live on their estate."

"Hold it," Mimi said. "You live on their estate? Why?"

Vanessa's mouth formed a semicircle. "After Shepherd and I separated, they knew I was bad off financially, so they let me stay in one of the three guest houses they have out back. I've lived there six months."

"What's that like?"

"It's okay. The houses used to be the servants' quarters, so they're kind of small. Their cleaning woman, Darlene, stays in the house next door, so every now and then I talk with her.

"And of course, their estate is amazing. Most days I can just walk around and forget about everything. Sometimes Shepherd's children, my step-kids, come over, and I watch them. The family likes that, because they don't have to deal with them. Basically, after all this time, I'm still their nanny."

"But isn't it weird living there?" Mimi asked.

"Sure, it is. Especially when Rosalyn was alive. She'd slept with my husband and broke up my marriage. My place was right underneath her window. I'd look up and see her shadow and it was like a knife in my heart.

"Mind you, the Lowerys aren't putting me up to be nice. The last thing they want is for a newspaper to discover one of their family members living in a trailer somewhere. So, they let me stay in one of the houses out back and give me a small stipend. But that's how they operate. They have a lot of secrets, and they try to keep people in their tent. Trap them, really.

"But that's where they've messed up." She lifted her eyebrow and an off-kilter smile formed on her face. "They think that by keeping me on their estate, they're keeping an eye on me. But actually, it's me watching them."

Mimi was digesting this when Vanessa turned to the Heartbrooch. Like everyone else, she considered it hers.

"Shepherd and I weren't officially divorced when he died. We were only separated. And since Shepherd didn't have a will that anyone can find, I am entitled to his possessions. And the only thing he had of value was that brooch.

"But I don't want it for me," she added quickly. "It's for Shepherd's children. I helped raise them, so I feel like they're my children too. That piece is an important part of their family history. Shepherd would want them to have it. He always told them that they'd get it. Because it's the Heartbrooch, and those children were his heart.

"I've talked to lawyers about contesting his giving Rosalyn the brooch. They think I have a case because he gave it to her right before she died, and he did it under false pretenses.

"But lawyers are expensive. That's why I thought you might just give it to me. I'll pay you back when I'm on my feet again. I'm sure the Lowerys want it for themselves, but please, I beg you, don't give it to them. You'll be helping the people who destroyed my husband. You'll kill him a second time."

Mimi didn't know what to make of this sob story. Vanessa certainly seemed like she was in authentic pain. But Mimi wasn't going to just hand her the brooch. That was nuts.

"I understand what you're saying," Mimi said. "But that piece may be worth several million dollars, and there's several competing claims to it. I can't just give it to you."

"But that brooch is mine." Vanessa's voice grew louder. "I've explained why."

"I agree, you have a compelling claim to it. We just need to determine the right thing to do."

"In other words, you'll see who offers you the most money." Vanessa's face contorted to a scowl. "I thought you might be a decent person, but obviously I was wrong. How stupid of me to think that anyone associated with this family, could be in any way decent."

"Please, Vanessa," Mimi said, "I don't want to fight with you. I don't want to fight with anyone. We didn't ask for this. We just need to go through a process."

Vanessa slapped a ten-dollar bill on the table. "This should take care of my coffee. It's not like I have tons of money, but take it. You have so much else that's mine."

"Oh come on," Mimi said. "In a perfect world, I agree, you would get the brooch. But I can't make any commitments right now. I hope you understand that."

Vanessa stood up and put on her coat. "It's not a matter of understanding. That brooch is mine. And if I have to go to court to get it, I will."

"If that's what you're gonna do," Mimi said, "get in line."

Vanessa stood a full six feet tall, and when she bent over the table, she got so close to Mimi's face, it was chilling. "I'm not like Shepherd. I'm not going to let my bitterness destroy me. I'm going to use it as fuel."

Vanessa strode out of the diner, her head held high.

AFTER MEETING WITH VANESSA LOWERY, Mimi returned to her office, where she was greeted at reception by an uncharacteristically glum Channah.

"How are you doing?" Mimi asked her.

"Fine, I guess," Channah said, tilting her head back and forth. "You probably want to talk about the engagement. I'm not in the mood right now."

"Okay," Mimi said. "Can I ask if it's still off?"

"It is," Channah whispered.

"All right." Mimi sighed. "If you ever want to talk—"

"I know. And I appreciate that. I'm sorry. I'm not trying to be rude. It's been a rough couple of days and I need time to figure things out."

"I understand. I hope my dad didn't say anything."

"He did."

Mimi moaned. "Oh God, Channah. What happened?"

"What do you think happened?" Channah's nostrils flared. "We ended up screaming at each other. Let's just say he's lucky I'm still working here."

INSIDE, MAX WAS ITCHING TO GIVE his side of the story.

"I tried to talk to Channah, very grown-up and calmly," he said. "At first, it was fine. She was listening to me. I explained that I didn't give her the diamond to hurt her. She said she understood that. I told her curses don't exist. She agreed with that, too. I thought things were going well."

"And then what happened?"

"I said, 'so don't be a *meshugana*.' Then, she got very hostile."

"Dad, don't you think calling her 'nuts' may have upset her?"

"I'll admit, it wasn't the best choice of words," Max said.

"And then you started screaming at her?"

"No! She yelled at me first. But yes, I yelled back. What do you expect me to do? She wouldn't listen to reason."

"Maybe because the voice of reason is supposed to be a soft, measured voice, not someone shrieking at you."

"*Eh*," Max said, waving this away.

"Dad, we can't force Channah to do something she doesn't want to do. It's *her* life. Not mine. Not yours. Hers." Mimi took a breath. "Anyway, we've said our piece. There's nothing else we can do."

"Fine," Max grumbled. "Then let's stop talking about it. I'm tired of the whole thing."

"Good, because I have something important to discuss.

Remember, I got a call from a private investigator demanding that brooch back?"

"Yeah." Max's eyebrows came together. "What happened with that?"

"Nothing. But now the Lowerys are laying claim to the brooch. And so's Vanessa Lowery. She was married to their son Shepherd, the one who gave the brooch to Rosalyn."

"All these people want that stupid thing?" Max said. "I don't think I've ever had an item that was so in demand."

"Yes, but unfortunately, some of those people are threatening to take us to court. We need to talk to our attorney."

Max scrunched up his face. "We have to go to Rabinowitz? *Oy.* This thing really is cursed."

CHAPTER FOURTEEN

A FEW HOURS LATER, MIMI AND MAX WERE HEADED to the office of their lawyer, Elliot Rabinowitz. Max complained the whole way there.

"Every time I see the guy, he spends half the time telling me these stupid stories. I pay him three hundred dollars an hour. If he tells me a ten-minute story, that's fifty dollars. Granted, some of his stories are funny. But they're not fifty dollars-funny."

Sure enough, for the first five minutes of their meeting, Rabinowitz held forth on the basics of estate law, relaying what he called an "interesting story" about a case he had thirty years ago. Mimi didn't find the story all that interesting, and the only part she retained was something she'd heard Rabinowitz say before— "we have an expression in my business: the bigger the diamond, the bigger the problem." After which he laughed so hard, his belly jiggled.

"Let's get to *tachlis*," Max said, mindful, as always, that Rabinowitz billed by the hour. "Are we getting sued or not?"

Rabinowitz adjusted his wire-rim glasses. A black *yarmulke* sat on his silver mane. "I spoke with the attorney handling Shepherd Lowery's estate, and he told me the transfer of the brooch was completely legal and above-board. So while Rosalyn Lowery may not have had the right to sell it, you will likely be considered a good-faith purchaser, which means under the law you have a certain immunity."

"So, we're good?" Max's face brightened.

"Not necessarily. The problem is Shepherd Lowery used this brooch as collateral for a bunch of loans. When his jewelry business went bust, all the different creditors tried to recoup their losses. The problem is there's one brooch, and five creditors."

"That can't be legal," Max said.

"It isn't," Rabinowitz said. "In fact, it's a crime. And some of the people who he pledged the diamond to as collateral are not exactly rabbis, if you know what I'm saying. It's possible some of them might take you to court. They're not going to win, but at this point, they may feel they have little to lose, and they'll just try to recoup what they can."

"Great." Max's head sunk into his hands. "It's been two days and I'm already tired of this stupid brooch. Can't I just sell it and make it go away?"

"Possibly," Rabinowitz said. "Except they might come after you for the proceeds."

"At this point, I don't even care about the money," Max said. "I just don't want to spend the rest of my days in court. I was willing to take a major hit on this thing and give it away as a gift. Can't I just give it to charity or something?"

Mimi was amused her father would rather lose twenty-five thousand dollars on a diamond than incur more legal bills. That's how much he hated paying lawyers.

"Unfortunately, no." Rabinowitz raised his hands. "At least not now. You have to respect the waiting period. It will expire in a few days, but it's possible some of these creditors may try to get an emergency injunction against you selling it. So for now, just hang on to it, and make sure you don't discuss this case with anyone."

"Good luck getting Mimi to do that," Max said.

Mimi shot her father a dirty look.

"The other issue," Rabinowitz said, "is the Lowery people might come after you. They're the biggest threat. They have enough resources to keep you tied up in court for years."

"Years!" Max complained. "That's the last thing I want."

"I'm getting the feeling you don't like lawyers, Max," Rabinowitz chuckled.

"I hate being here," Max said. "I'd rather get a root canal."

This made Rabinowitz laugh uproariously. "Come on, Max. We lawyers aren't so bad. It's only ninety-five percent of us." Rabinowitz cracked up again. "Don't worry. Worst case scenario: this goes on two to three years."

Max let out an anguished cry. "And what's the best-case scenario?"

Rabinowitz shrugged. "It might go on a few months. I don't know."

"What do you mean, you don't know?" Max hollered. "I'm paying you to know! How about the scenario where I get to live my life without this nonsense? That's the only scenario I want."

"Max, it's okay," Rabinowitz said.

"That's easy for you to say," Max said. "You're the one making money here. I don't want to pay for your new summer home."

"Max, you must think I have cheap taste in real estate." Rabinowitz laughed again. He was enjoying this. "I'll call the Lowery attorneys, see what they're looking for." He reclined on his chair. "I remember, years ago, I had a case against Lowery. They were threatening to sue this client of mine. It's a funny story."

"If you don't mind," Max stuck up his wrinkled hand, "I don't want to hear it."

"No, Dad." Mimi touched his arm. "Let him tell it. It might be worth hearing. They're threatening to sue us, too."

"So—" Rabinowitz settled into story-telling mode. "Years ago, I represented this *frum* diamond dealer. Nice guy. Unfortunately, he passed away recently. *Nebach*. That reminds me, I have to send his wife a card."

"Could you get on with the story?" Max interrupted.

"So my client told another dealer some gossip about Wyllis Lowery. That's the father of Archibald, the guy who runs the company now. He said that Wyllis was having an affair with this young designer, some Italian lady."

"Was it Josephine Tomaso?" Mimi inched forward. "She designed the brooch we have."

"I think so," Rabinowitz replied. "Anyway, my client said he would never do business with someone with such loose morals. And word of this got back to old man Lowery, Wyllis' father. In those days, he was one of the biggest buyers at the diamond club. He filed a formal complaint against my client with the head of the bourse. Back then, there were strict rules against *lashon hara*.

"So, I called the general counsel at Lowery. I remember it clearly, I told him, 'why make a big deal out of this? Even if Wyllis is seeing this girl, it's not the worst thing in the world. She's a very attractive young lady. The whole thing doesn't make him look bad. Now, people will think of him as this big ladies' man.' And the lawyer laughed and said, 'you know, you got a point there.'" Rabinowitz giggled.

Mimi blanched and muttered under her breath.

Rabinowitz apparently heard this, because he turned to her. "Obviously, those were different times. I just thought that was a funny story. That attorney was very sexist, agreeing with me like that.

"Anyway, they dropped the complaint. Though around the same time, Wyllis Lowery was killed. So that probably would have ended the whole thing anyway." He became pensive. "Come to think of it, that isn't such a funny story."

"So, hold it," Mimi said. "Do you think there's any connection between Wyllis Lowery getting killed and this alleged affair?"

Rabinowitz raised his shoulders. "Who knows? There were rumors to that effect. Apparently the designer's family had ties to the Mob. But this all happened years ago. It doesn't matter anymore."

As MIMI WALKED BACK TO THE OFFICE with her father, she Googled Wyllis Lowery's murder, and found a webpage with some particularly interesting information.

There's always been speculation whether Josephine Tomaso—who had a reputation for being temperamental and hot-headed—was involved in the murder of Wyllis Lowery. Friends have said that the famous designer was in love with Wyllis, the company's then-CEO, though it wasn't clear if the interest was reciprocated. Some friends of Wyllis called her a "stalker."

What's undeniable is that, several months after Tomaso began working with the Lowery company, Wyllis Lowery was killed in a reputed robbery—an event many attributed to the black diamond's fabled curse.

But sources say there's compelling evidence that what happened to Lowery wasn't a robbery at all, but a pre-arranged hit, possibly set up by Tomaso, whose father was reputedly a Mafia kingpin. Witnesses saw Tomaso fleeing the scene right after the shooting. That same night, she returned to her native Italy, and never designed jewelry or spoke in public again. Tomaso's current whereabouts are unknown, and she is believed to have died a long time ago.

"Why are you reading that?" Max asked. "Are you going to investigate a thirty-year-old murder now?"

"No," Mimi said. "It's just information that might help us with our case. Of course, I'm not investigating."

The real answer was: maybe.

THAT NIGHT, WHEN MIMI ARRIVED AT HER APARTMENT in New Jersey, she found an envelope slipped under her door, with "Mimi Rosen" written on the outside. Inside was a typed letter from "George Morton, private investigator."

"Dear Ms. Rosen: As I've indicated, my client, the family of Josephine Tomaso, will not rest until it gets back its stolen brooch.

"I've been watching your movements. I saw you visit the Lowery offices, talk with their cleaning woman, and meet with Vanessa Lowery, in an obvious attempt to sell the Heartbrooch. That brooch belongs to its TRUE OWNERS, the Tomaso family.

"The Tomaso family is not stupid. They do not play games, and do not give up. This is your last warning."

Mimi became gripped by fear. She was being stalked by an investigator who worked for a family said to be associated with the Mafia. This guy knew where she lived, and was apparently following her.

Mimi inspected her driveway and sidewalk. They seemed empty, though she didn't look that hard; she didn't want to see anyone. She rushed into her apartment, locked the door, and called Michael.

"Jesus," Michael told her. "Make sure you save that note, and call Detective Brill tomorrow and tell her about it. Nine times out of ten, these guys are full of hot air. Unfortunately, you don't want to be in the small percentage where they're not. If you want, you can come to my place."

Mimi said no; it was ten p.m., and it would take an hour to get to Brooklyn.

"I can drive over to you," Michael said.

Mimi considered this; Michael was still at work, and didn't sound all that enthusiastic about making the trip. She decided not to push it. "No, it's fine." She looked around nervously. "I'll probably stay at your place tomorrow, though, and after that—until we figure out who this guy is."

"That's fine," Michael said. "Stay calm. There's no point in panicking. Chances are this is nothing. Before you go to sleep tonight, inspect all your doors and windows, make sure they're locked, and check that your alarm works. Keep your phone next to you in bed, and if you hear anything—even if it's something that may be nothing—call 911 immediately. Don't worry that you're bothering them. Err on the side of caution."

"Okay." She took a breath. "You're not really relaxing me right now."

"You'll be fine," said Michael. "Be calm but cautious."

Mimi had planned to spend her night doing research. Instead, she triple-checked her locks and jumped into bed, terrified.

CHAPTER FIFTEEN

"THAT NOTE *IS* CREEPY," DETECTIVE BRILL TOLD MIMI on the phone the next morning. "I am not seeing any listing for a private investigator named George Morton. And from what I can tell, he appears to be using a burner phone.

"You could try for a restraining order," she continued. "But that might be difficult since we're not sure who this guy is. You'll need a lawyer. Do you have one?"

"My father does but—" Mimi paused. "Let's hold off on that for now."

"Mr. Morton is definitely someone we will keep an eye on. If he contacts you again, hang up and block the number. Stay aware of your surroundings. If you see him, or if you detect anything suspicious, call for help."

Mimi also told Detective Brill what she'd learned, about Rosalyn sleeping with Shepherd, and the possible long-ago affair between Wyllis Lowery and Josephine Tomaso.

"Very interesting," Brill said. "There's quite a bit of intrigue surrounding that brooch of yours. Thanks for the info. Keep in touch and stay safe."

FOR MIMI, "STAYING SAFE" MEANT STAYING AT MICHAEL'S place in Brooklyn for the foreseeable future.

That night, Michael whipped up fettuccini alfredo for dinner; he was a surprisingly good cook. For most of the meal, Michael—napkin tucked into his shirt—raved about how well dinner turned out, while his dog Louie whined and begged for scraps.

Halfway through the meal, Michael cleared his throat and put down his fork. "So, I just spoke with my colleague, Detective Brill."

"Yes, we talked this morning," Mimi said, as she twisted noodles on her fork. She wasn't sure where this was going, but judging from his tone, it wasn't anyplace good.

"She said you've learned all sorts of information about this case. She was impressed. She thinks you're a good detective."

"That's nice of her to say."

"You don't realize how nice," Michael said. "I've known her for fifteen years, and I'm still waiting for her to say that about me."

"I told her, yes, you're a sharp cookie. But I was also a little disappointed to hear that you're investigating again, because I know how dangerous that is, and I've told you a million times not to do it."

"Oh, come on, Michael," Mimi said. "I'm not investigating! Just doing a little research."

"Really? If it was just a little research, why didn't you tell me about it last night?"

"Because I thought you'd react—" Mimi paused. "Like you're reacting." She sipped water to soothe her suddenly dry mouth. "I was only finding information about the curse. To help Channah."

"Oh yeah?" Michael aimed his eyes at her. "Detective Brill said that you found out juicy information about these people's personal lives. Not sure what that has to do with a curse."

"That stuff came up! It's background." Mimi was trying—she sensed in vain—to prevent this discussion from spiraling into an argument. "And by the way, those people contacted me."

"They *all* contacted you?" Michael's face turned stony. "How about the Lowery cleaning woman? Did she call you too? Because I heard you talked to her. I assume you weren't seeking her expertise on a one-hundred-year-old curse."

Mimi threw her arms in the air. "Okay, you're right. I did ask one person a few questions." It wasn't easy dating a detective; he was skilled at parsing words. "I saw her on the street, and we got to talking."

"So you were walking down the street and started chatting with a random cleaning woman?"

Mimi tossed her fork on the table. He'd broken her again. "All right! I admit it! I was curious. My father's business might get sued so I wanted to find out more about the Lowerys. But that doesn't mean that I'm doing a formal investigation."

"Correct. Because you can't do a formal investigation. You're not a formal investigator!" Michael inhaled a large amount of air through his nose, trying to calm himself. "I'm not trying to start a fight here."

"You could have fooled me!" Mimi felt a headache coming on, above the bridge of her nose.

"I understand that you're curious," Michael said. "I'm well acquainted with that part of your personality. And it goes without saying that you've uncovered an impressive amount of information in a short period of time. But Detective Brill said that sick-o P.I. saw you talk to those people and that's why he left you that note.

"I'd be extremely cautious about speaking with people involved in this case. If I can just plead with you, one more time: do not investigate. You could get hurt or even killed. It's a seriously stupid thing to do."

"Fine," Mimi declared. "I won't." She hoped that would settle things, but was surprised how detached and distant that sounded. "Let's finish dinner."

They sat and ate, not saying a word, with the only sound the scraping of their forks on their plates. The silence only widened the gulf between them.

Mimi knew there was truth to what Michael was saying. Investigations *were* dangerous.

On the other hand, they got her juices flowing. They made life

interesting. They made her feel like more than just someone working for her father's company.

Mimi felt a jumble of emotions: guilt, anxiety, and anger over the
phrase "seriously stupid." After letting it simmer, anger won the day.

"Let me just say, Detective," Mimi said, breaking the silence.
"You may call me 'seriously stupid,' but I solved several murders."

"I didn't call you that," Michael said through gritted teeth. "I
just—"

"Let me finish," Mimi said.

Michael flinched.

"I am well aware that investigations are dangerous," Mimi said.
"But you don't need to go crazy every time I do a little research. It
feels like you're Ricky, and I'm Lucy, and you keep telling me not to
be in your show. I'm a grown woman, capable of making my own
decisions."

"Right," Michael said, raising his voice. "You're a grown woman
who's nearly gotten herself killed on several occasions. You need to
let professionals do their jobs."

"Don't yell at me," Mimi said, though she was yelling, too. "I
put up with a lot. You barely talk to me about your work, because
you're so nervous I'll start my own investigation. Did you treat
your ex-wife that way?"

"No."

"And why am I different?"

"She was a cop."

Mimi swallowed. "Fair point."

"And honestly," Michael's finger sliced the air, "when she was
dealing with difficult cases, sometimes I'd get so worried I wouldn't
sleep for days on end. I can't begin to describe how awful that was."
Michael shook his head and gulped a half-glass of wine.

"I'm asking you to respect my choices," Mimi said, surprising
herself with her firmness. "Even if you think they're stupid or dangerous, they're *my* choices, and you need to understand that. And
if you can't do that, then—" Mimi knew what she wanted to say,
and felt she had no choice but to say it. "We're through."

Mimi sat, panting heavily. The minute those words flew out of her mouth, there was no taking them back. But this argument was inevitable. This issue had loomed in the background of their relationship for too long. If they couldn't resolve it, they probably *were* through.

"That's a nice thing to say!" Michael sputtered. "I'm trying to prevent you from getting hurt, and this is how you treat me! Maybe you should leave!" Beneath the rage, Mimi could hear the hurt in his voice.

This argument was building, escalating, spinning out of control. They were both so dug in, they were powerless to stop it.

"I will!" Mimi threw her napkin down. She no longer wanted to eat Michael's fettuccini. It didn't taste that good anymore.

She walked to the closet, and put on her coat, angrily tugging each sleeve, while Michael sat and shoveled food in his mouth. When she reached the door, she stopped and turned around.

"Actually, Michael, I don't know how to say this but—"

"What?" he growled.

"Can I sleep on your couch? I'm nervous about that note."

Michael wearily shook his head. "Sure."

FOR THE REST OF THE NIGHT, Michael stayed in his room and watched TV. Mimi heard its muffled sounds through the wall as she lay on his couch, reading her phone and worrying she'd screwed up another relationship.

At around ten, Michael came out, a pillow clutched in one hand, a white sheet and blanket drooping from the other.

"Here you go," he said, handing them to her.

Mimi said a clipped "thanks," and decided to treat this as a peace offering. "Listen, before we do something we both regret, can we talk calmly and rationally?"

"Sure," he said. He pulled up a chair next to the couch. He wanted to work this out. That was a good sign.

She sat up and took his hand. "You know I care about you."

"Of course I do. And I care about you, too." His voice was an odd mix of gruff and tender. "But that's why this matters to me. I don't think you're stupid. Not at all. You're the smartest person I've ever met. But I don't want you putting your life in danger. I hope you understand that.

"I come from a police family. And when you're part of that world, you understand there's a certain amount of danger involved. There's always the possibility that one day that person you love might not come home. It's not something you dwell on, but it's always there. It's part of the deal.

"And now I have a girlfriend who isn't part of that world, but she keeps getting involved in these horrible situations. And it's a million times worse. Because I know, if Detective Brill got in a bad spot, she'd be able to handle herself. Because she's had years of training. And you haven't."

Mimi had spent the last two hours mentally rehearsing arguments why Michael was completely wrong about this. Now that he was sitting in front of her, the words wouldn't come.

"I understand that," she said, her voice breaking. "I get nervous about you, too. It's not easy being a cop's girlfriend. So yes, I get it."

She had nearly gotten to the "but," when he broke in.

"Good. I'm glad. I've been a detective for twenty years. It's serious work. I'm willing to bend on lots of things. We can even go to foreign movies. But I won't change my mind about you investigating. Can you just stop, please?"

Mimi felt for Michael. He looked sad. He looked sweet. His agreeing to watch foreign films was a major concession. Two days ago, she'd be thrilled with that.

But he didn't understand how recent events had affected her. Her friend had been murdered, Channah had broken her engagement, and her father's business was under threat. She couldn't just sit back and let all that happen. She needed to try to make things right. And she didn't want her boyfriend freaking out every time she asked someone a question.

"I can tell you I won't investigate, if it will make you feel better." Mimi paused, and hunted for the right words. "But, as you know, I've said that before. I am going to do what I feel is right. I don't know what that is right now. I'm not planning on investigating. But if I think it will help, then yes, I'll do it, whether you approve or not."

"Got it." Michael threw the pillow and blanket on the couch. "Have a nice life." He trod back to his bedroom, shut the door, and turned on the TV.

THAT NIGHT WAS ANOTHER SLEEPLESS ONE for Mimi. At around six a.m., Mimi changed into the work-appropriate clothes she'd brought to Michael's place. Before she left, she spent a few minutes petting Louie, and gave him a goodbye kiss on the head.

"Maybe I'll see you again, big fella." She scratched under his chin. "But probably not."

On her way to the subway, Mimi felt glad that she and Michael had talked. They were handling this like mature adults. Yet, as she sat on the platform—waiting for the train they usually took together—she burst into tears.

She would miss Michael—and his damn dog.

CHAPTER SIXTEEN

I F COPING WITH HER OWN RELATIONSHIP DRAMA wasn't enough, Mimi found herself again dealing with Channah and Zeke's.

"Did you hear anything from the Lowery people?" Zeke texted her. "I'd love to tell Channah there's no curse on the diamond. That could ease her mind a lot."

It took Mimi a while to formulate an answer. She couldn't begin to describe her meeting with Archibald and Claudia Lowery.

"I did," she wrote back. "But it's complicated. We have to give them back the brooch before they tell us anything."

"Hope you can work something out," Zeke responded. "I'd really like to have something to tell Channah. Can you ask them again? Please."

"I'll try," Mimi wrote, "but they're very difficult to deal with."

Zeke didn't write back, and his silence drove her nuts. She didn't need yet another fight in her life. "All right," she wrote. "I'll call them."

BEFORE MIMI TALKED TO ARCHIBALD LOWERY, she phoned Elliot Rabinowitz.

"I need something from the Lowery people," she said. "Can I try to strike a deal with them one-on-one?"

"Look, kid, it's a free country," Rabinowitz said. "I can't stop you. But I wouldn't recommend it. There's a lot that can go wrong. It's better you let an attorney handle it."

"I know," Mimi said. "But I have some specific things I want."

"What can I say? Just don't do anything crazy. I want your father to be able to pay me."

Mimi agreed to not sign any document without him reviewing it, and he gave her a few points to insist on.

Mimi made sure she hung up quickly so her father wouldn't gripe about the legal bill. Then she took a breath, and called Archibald.

"I want to make a deal," Mimi told him. She spoke fast, so he wouldn't interrupt. "I'm sick of this brooch. It's making everyone miserable, including me and my father. I'm willing to let you have it. But I have a couple of conditions. They are all non-negotiable.

"First, we don't want to get sued. My father doesn't want to spend any time in court. I spoke to our attorney. He said we can transfer liability. That means if the sale is challenged, all the expenses will fall on you, including legal fees. I don't want to bear any responsibility for this going forward. And I don't want to hear about this brooch again."

"I'll check with our attorneys," Archibald said. "But that should be fine, given that any legal challenge is unlikely, as we have clear title to the brooch—"

"Yeah, yeah." Mimi cut him off. "That's one of the things I don't want to hear again. By the way, that means you'll pick up any legal fees we've already incurred."

"How much are those?" Archibald asked.

"Three hundred dollars. But my father is sensitive about that kind of thing."

"We can swing that," Archibald said, sounding amused.

"Third, as we agreed, my father must recoup the twenty-five thousand dollars he paid for the brooch. He isn't looking to profit off this, but he shouldn't lose any money, either."

"Done."

"Fourth, I need information about the origins of the Prince

Corthoff diamond. In particular, I need to know whether it's cursed or not."

Archibald emitted a low chuckle. "Good Lord. What kind of information could there be about whether a diamond is cursed? Isn't common sense enough?"

"I don't care if it sounds crazy," Mimi said. "That point is non-negotiable. I want as much information on that diamond as possible."

"If you insist," Archibald said with a sigh. "I'll check our archives. We have pretty extensive files on our items. Is that it?"

"One more thing. I'll agree to write the company history for seventy-five thousand dollars."

"I offered fifty," he said. "I thought you weren't looking to profit off this."

"I said my *father* wasn't," Mimi said. "I need the money."

Mimi held her breath. She'd never received such a large sum for her writing—or for anything, really. Seventy-five thousand dollars would get her out of debt and then some.

"That shouldn't be a problem," Archibald said. "We're glad to have you on our team."

Mimi found that phrasing interesting. Vanessa had warned her, "The Lowerys like to keep people in their tent. Trap them, really."

"Do we have a deal?" Archibald asked.

"Yes, in principle. Our attorney has to review anything I sign."

"Certainly. I'll have a contract written up in the next hour, and assuming he approves it, I'll send a messenger to collect the brooch this afternoon."

"I can't give it to you this afternoon. Under the law, we can't sell the brooch for five days. We have to wait 'till Saturday."

"That's tomorrow," Archibald said with a laugh.

"Right," Mimi said. "We can't sell it before then."

"How about this? Come to our estate in Larnsdale tomorrow. We'll get the deal done, and begin work on the company history."

"Your estate?" Mimi was intrigued. Rosalyn once described the Lowery compound as "a house out of a PBS drama, like something from a dream."

"I guarantee," Archibald said, "you've never seen anything like it."

Mimi didn't relish spending time with the Lowerys, but she'd probably need to for the book anyway, so she might as well do it at their fancy estate. She could use a change of pace, something different and exciting. Spending the day at a PBS-level house certainly sounded better than being stuck in her drab apartment, ruminating over her break-up with Michael, and worrying about the private detective. Of course, if Michael knew she was going, he'd be furious, but one good thing about breaking up with him was she no longer had to worry about that.

"How about you come over around one p.m. Saturday?" Archibald said. "We'll have a nice lunch. And make sure you have the Heartbrooch."

"You want me to bring the brooch?" Mimi eyed the company vault.

"Absolutely. Delivery of the item is, as you put it, non-negotiable."

Mimi checked Google Maps; Larnsdale was located in upstate New York, just outside the Hudson Valley, about an hour by car. "Honestly, I'm not comfortable driving all that way with such an expensive piece. That feels like a security risk."

"Don't worry," Archibald said. "You'll be perfectly safe. You won't have to drive. We'll arrange a helicopter."

A helicopter? This was shaping up as quite the adventure. Screw you, Michael.

CHAPTER SEVENTEEN

ON SATURDAY, MIMI LEARNED A NEW FACT: she lived near a helipad.

She had never been there before or knew it existed. Given it was hidden behind a parking lot, she apparently wasn't supposed to. After showing her ID, Mimi waited a few minutes in the ultra-comfy departure lounge, the brooch lying in her purse. She was repeatedly offered mimosas, but she turned them down.

Mimi had a lifelong fear of heights, which made the thirty-minute helicopter ride, and its attendant bumps, both exhilarating and terrifying; at a few points, she wished she'd accepted a mimosa. Mimi had always imagined a helicopter ride would be cramped and uncomfortable, but this was flying rich person-style, and the helicopter had refreshments, onboard Wi-Fi, and a plush white seat that she melted into.

The Lowery family home—Farrington Manor—was one of a number of fairy-tale estates the helicopter passed over, huge tracts of land featuring gingerbread mansions amid acres of green. The Lowery estate wasn't the nicest one she saw, but it was quite impressive, especially to someone who'd woken up in a cramped one-bedroom where she felt lucky the toilet flushed.

The helicopter landed on the Lowery lawn, and Archibald greeted her with an extended hand and practiced smile; he was dressed in a blue blazer, a button-down shirt, brown slacks, but no tie. Mimi had spent an hour stressing over what to wear, before picking out a nice blouse and pants, and everyday shoes that weren't quite heels. And just like when Rosalyn came to the office, she felt underdressed.

"Welcome to my not-so-humble abode," Archibald said, then let loose a bark of a laugh that was five times deeper than his normal voice, and came from the back of his throat. The bark-laugh was so goofy, it was almost endearing—and so startling, Mimi couldn't help but chuckle along, even though she'd forgotten what the joke was.

"How was your flight?" he said.

"Amazing," Mimi beamed.

Archibald then went into a long explanation about how they'd just switched helicopter providers, because the last one was providing "substandard" service. Mimi tuned him out and surveyed the grounds.

Farrington Manor was an imposing red brick Gothic house, which was too large to take in with one glance. It was beautiful, if somewhat generic. Some parts had a real grandeur; others resembled a gussied-up local library.

The stadium-sized lawn surrounding it was dotted with trees, flower gardens, and well-placed brooks, and was bracketed on either side by woods. Brown and orange leaves littered the grass; they made lovely crunching sounds when Mimi stepped on them. A man stood nearby, vacuuming them up.

"Let me take you on a tour," Archibald declared, before delivering what seemed like a well-practiced history of the estate.

"My grandfather, Nicholas Lowery, built Farrington Manor at the height of the Gilded Age. He was catering to an ultra-affluent clientele, and they all had places like this, so he wanted to prove he was one of them.

"It took my grandfather three years to construct this white elephant, which he financed with smoke and mirrors. He took out multiple loans against his diamond inventory, but fortunately, none of his bankers found out. They tend to frown upon that kind of thing. But then the best entrepreneurs aren't big on rules." He grinned at the old man's moxie.

"You may be wondering about the name."

Mimi wasn't, but nodded politely.

"My grandfather met a rich Englishman named Farrington and wanted an English-sounding name for the manor. That was all the rage back then. He nearly gave it one of those English double names, like Farrington-Longsberry, to really Brit it up. Fortunately, my grandmother talked him out of it."

As with Lowery, home of ninety-nine-carat diamonds, the Lowery estate was all about the numbers, which Archibald happily rattled off. It comprised some eighteen acres of land, including four acres of forest, three lakes, and fifty-nine species of plants. The main house was fifty feet tall, and its roof deck, which Archibald's grandfather built specially, offered "spectacular" views ten miles in every direction. Mimi didn't know if Archibald was giving a tour or trying to sell it.

"Let's walk to the mansion." He took her elbow, and they trekked toward the house. The elbow grab was a bit presumptuous, but she excused it as old-fashioned manners.

Inside the mansion, there were more marvels to gape at—and more numbers for Archibald to recite. The manor had eleven bedrooms, two libraries, fifteen fireplaces, and ten bathrooms. Mimi almost asked why there were more fireplaces than bathrooms, but figured there was no point questioning such things.

The entry hall was light and airy, but the rest of the house reflected its turn-of-the-century roots, with everything draped in different shades of brown—from dark maple to light tan, and almost every variety in between. And while the place was well-maintained, even the dim lighting couldn't hide the fact this was an old house, not free of the occasional crack and hole.

Archibald marched Mimi through the mansion, his pot belly leading the way, as his footsteps echoed throughout the vast house. Aside from the occasional servant, the place was empty, eerily so.

Archibald proudly pointed out the features of each room: the marble hallway was made from real African marble; the library molding came from a Peruvian forest's "very best wood"; and the sitting room's Persian rugs were actually from Persia. Mimi felt like she did when visiting a museum—she was initially excited, then enchanted, then overwhelmed, then jaded, then ready for lunch.

Fortunately, by that point, they'd arrived at the second-floor terrace, where a table was set for two.

The servants pulled out their chairs, and they sat down. Mimi marveled at the view. The terrace was positioned just over the estate's rolling hills, which stretched down to the Mamaroneck River. The morning had been mostly gray, but the sun was starting to peek through the clouds, and when it hit the water just right, it gleamed blue, like a Lowery sapphire.

The servants put Caesar salads in front of them, and offered glasses of white wine. Mimi wasn't planning to drink that day, but figured, what the hell.

"Everything here is lovely," she told Archibald.

"Thank you. I chose my parents very carefully," he said. "That was a joke your friend Rosalyn used to tell. Of course, her choice of family didn't work out so well.

"Sorry." Archibald set his napkin on his lap. "I shouldn't disparage Rosalyn. You might call my behavior 'disturbing' again." He was still smarting from Mimi's comment at his office.

"I'm sorry I said that," Mimi said. "It was a knee-jerk reaction. I know everyone grieves in their own way."

"Yes." Archibald swirled his wine glass. "Rosalyn's death was a huge shock. I haven't truly come to terms with it. It's hard to believe she's gone."

"Do you have any idea who killed her?" she asked.

"None whatsoever," he said. "And the police haven't either. From what I hear, in situations like this, the authorities suspect the husband first. Fortunately, that isn't the case here. My family has long had excellent relations with the local police department.

"It was probably some idiot. Or person she was involved with. I wasn't exactly sure what she was up to in the last months of her life."

He took a sip of wine. "As you may have discerned, Rosalyn and I didn't exactly have a perfect marriage. It was not a pleasant moment when I learned Shepherd sent her the Heartbrooch. I'd rather not discuss why."

That sounded like a license to pry. "I can guess," Mimi said. "When Rosalyn came to our office, she mentioned that she and Shepherd had a history."

"Ah yes. My late wife did enjoy displaying our dirty laundry in public." Archibald's mouth became a straight line. "She said that they had 'a history.' Interesting way to put it. I'm not sure the word 'history' is accurate, as it signifies something in the past. Shepherd wouldn't have given Rosalyn the Heartbrooch unless they were involved until the very end."

This puzzled Mimi. "But Rosalyn told us that Shepherd gave it to her—"

"Yes, because of the curse. She told me that, too. That explanation is as nonsensical as the curse itself. I don't believe a word of it. Shepherd would never have given her such a valuable item for such an absurd reason." Archibald finished his wine. A waiter quickly refilled his glass.

"In a way, Rosalyn and Shepherd were well-matched." He gazed at the horizon. "They were both impulsive, immature, prone to attention-getting stunts. I tried not to let their antics bother me."

He toyed with his fork. "I'm not saying I was a perfect husband. I can be impatient. I get very caught up in my work. But I carry the weight of this company on my shoulders. It's a one-hundred-year legacy. Which is mostly on me.

"In a way, my brother was lucky. He didn't have that burden. He was able to do what he wanted. Which, in his case, was skateboarding and video games."

"Did you always plan to join the family business?" Mimi asked.

"No, that was planned for me," Archibald said. "When it was obvious that my brother was not the sharpest tool in the shed, my father picked me to run the company. Mind you, this was when I was fourteen years old." He bark-laughed again, though it sounded hollow.

"In college," he continued, "believe it or not, my major was English. I studied classic romantic fiction. I dreamed of being an author. I wrote quite a bit in those days."

"Really? Were you good?"

Archibald's shoulders bounced up and down. "I thought so. I'm not sure the rest of the world agreed. That dream lasted maybe a month. I quickly grew up. Struggling writers can't enjoy this kind of lifestyle."

He thrust his stubby hands out at the river. "Look at this view. A lot of people pretend they wouldn't want to live like this. But I don't believe them. Who *wouldn't* want to look at this every day? It's beautiful. Almost paradise." He beamed, gazing down on it all. "Don't you want this?"

"I guess," Mimi said. "Though, honestly, this isn't something I ever aimed for. When you work in journalism, you don't expect to make a lot of money."

Archibald raised an eyebrow. "And yet you did it."

"Sure. The work was great and we all had fun. Rosalyn probably told you stories from our newspaper days."

"Not really."

"Oh." That stung. "Well, it *was* fun. I was also interested in, you know—" Mimi always felt silly saying this next part. "Changing the world."

"And did you?" Archibald asked.

"What?"

"Change the world?"

That felt like a jab, but Mimi decided not to treat it as one. "I guess not. The world's still a mess. So's journalism, for that matter." She took a sip of wine. "I was out of work for a long time. Which is why I now work for my father's diamond company. I guess I grew up, too."

"Funny," said Archibald. "For both of us, growing up meant working for our parents."

God, what a depressing thought. Mimi drank more wine—this time, a big gulp.

The servants whisked away their salads and delivered the main course—lamb, in truffle and artichoke sauce.

"Rosalyn had a nice career," Mimi said. "I always envied her position at *The Look*."

"Really?" Archibald said, wolfing down a forkful of food. "She would have loved to hear you say that."

"Come on," Mimi said. "She wasn't that kind of person."

Archibald grinned wryly. "Ah, but she was. Rosalyn was one of the most envious people I've ever met.

"But there's nothing wrong with that. Envy is a wonderful emotion. It's the backbone of my business. It's the basis of all luxury brands. Luxury isn't about what we put on our bodies. It's about what happens in our brains. Including envy. *Especially* envy. Sometimes I think the best luxury marketer would be a well-trained psychologist.

"That's what many people in this industry don't understand," Archibald continued, as food crunched in his mouth. "Your average diamond dealer gets excited whether a stone's a G color, or V-whatever clarity. But that's not where you make money. You make money on the intangibles. The story. The experience. And the most important thing: mystique."

He lifted his chin. "Do you know that wine you're drinking is three hundred dollars a bottle?"

Mimi tried to look impressed. "It's nice."

"Have a sip."

He was staring at her so intently, she had no choice but to drink.

"Now that I've told you how much it costs," he said, "does it taste better?"

Mimi didn't know how to answer that question. The wine tasted somewhat better. But it was fine before. "I guess so," she hedged.

"Of course, it does," Archibald said confidently. "Because now you know it's special.

"Take this so-called cursed diamond. Why don't people talk about cursed napkins, or cursed toothpicks? Because gemstones are special. They have a mystique. On one level they're just rocks. On another, they can stir profound emotions.

"When people wear a diamond, they feel different. Maybe they feel wealthy, or loved, or important. But they feel *something*. And if gemstones affect people positively, it's easy to believe they can affect them negatively as well. You don't have that with other objects. That's the power of mystique.

"The same is true, by the way, of the Heartbrooch. What makes it so valuable? It was Josephine Tomaso's final design. It has an air of mystery.

"Personally, I consider Tomaso's designs florid and over-the-top. But the reason her pieces are so sought-after is because there's so few of them. She stopped designing, and became a recluse. She's like the J.D. Salinger of jewelry. That makes her work more valuable than if she spent five decades creating endless variations of the same nonsense.

"You take her legend, and put it together with the curse, and it's a fascinating tale for some rich lady to tell her friends. Because what else are those people going to talk about? Their tennis game? Those women are bored. We give them fantasies to fill their days.

"My father always said, 'a good jeweler is a good storyteller.' Because there's nothing more powerful than a good story. Stories are how we make sense of life."

"I never thought of it that way," Mimi said.

"I do. I have to. It's what puts this food on my table."

The waiters brought out dessert—a rainbow-colored fruit sorbet so sumptuous, Mimi could feel the different flavors dance on her tongue.

"Speaking of the Heartbrooch"—Archibald snapped his fingers at an attendant, who handed him a folder—"here's the paperwork for our transaction." He pulled out a stack of papers the size of a phone book. "It includes everything we discussed on the phone. Just sign it, hand over the brooch, and we can start our project."

Mimi rifled through the papers. They were packed with legal jargon, climaxing in a non-disclosure agreement.

"Can someone email this to my attorney?" Mimi asked. "He told me not to sign anything before he examined it."

"No problem. I'll email him now. Hopefully, he can turn this around quickly."

Then it dawned on Mimi. "He can't right now. It's *Shabbat*. He won't be available until after sundown."

Archibald's nose twitched. "Oh, really? I hoped to have this done today. Why didn't you tell me that before?"

"Sorry." Mimi squirmed. "When you told me to come this afternoon, I didn't think about it. Just email the contract to him. Once the sun sets, I'm sure he won't take long getting back to you." Mimi paged through the documents again. There was no historical information. "Did you get any background on the diamond?"

"Ah yes," Archibald laughed uneasily. "We couldn't find our file on that particular piece. It has gone missing, somehow. But I assure you, we searched for it very extensively. It's quite an important piece for my family so perhaps it was loaned out for research.

"So, unfortunately, we have nothing new to offer you there. But as I've explained, the so-called curse is almost certainly a fiction. And between us taking on your legal liability, and the price we're paying you to write the family history, we feel our offer is more than generous."

"I understand that," Mimi said. "But when we spoke, I told you I needed that information. I said that was non-negotiable. I can't give you this brooch without it."

Archibald's face curdled. The sky grew dark behind him.

"If it's really that important to you," he said, "I can contact our company archivist. Maybe there's something in our files that he missed. He can probably get you something by tomorrow."

"I don't want to disturb his weekend."

"Please," Archibald scoffed. "He always works weekends. It's no bother at all. How about this? Can your lawyer get back to us on Sunday?"

"I'm sure he can."

Archibald sat up on his chair. "Then, why don't you stay at the estate tonight and we'll sign the deal in the morning?"

This offer caught Mimi by surprise. She fiddled with her dessert spoon. "I don't know if I can stay over. I don't have a change of clothes."

"That's no problem. Rosalyn had a big enough wardrobe to clothe a Third World country." He looked her up and down. "You're about her size. You should be able to find something in there that fits you. There's more than enough items to choose from. I wouldn't even call what she had a closet. More like a warehouse."

"I don't know," Mimi said. "I would feel weird wearing clothes that—"

"Belonged to a dead woman?" Archibald said. "You think they're cursed, too?"

Mimi's cheeks flushed. "No, it's just that—"

"I guarantee half the clothes in her closet, she didn't even wear. But if you don't want to stay tonight, you're welcome to return to New Jersey. Though I'm not sure why anyone would want to do that."

Mimi's brain was too foggy from all the wine and food to offer a coherent response.

Archibald put his hand above his eyes and gazed at the sky. "I wouldn't recommend taking a helicopter right now anyway. It's about to drizzle, and from what I hear, it might pour later, and that would not be a particularly safe time to travel. It'll be far better if you leave tomorrow, when the weather will be clearer. You don't have any big Sunday plans, do you?"

"No," Mimi admitted. With her fear of heights, there was no way she would ride in a helicopter during a downpour. And spending the night at that estate would certainly be an experience.

"Then, stay!" Archibald said, suddenly exuberant. "As you may have noticed, we have plenty of space here. You can sleep in our main guest bedroom." He pulled the napkin from his lap, dabbed his mouth, and stood up. As far as he was concerned, the issue was settled.

"If you pardon me, I have to get our archivist moving on his curse-debunking. And I'll make sure we send the contract to your attorney. We'll settle everything tomorrow and then get to work on the company history." He touched his forehead. "I'm sorry, my mother would kill me if she heard me say that. The company *heritage*.

"Anyway, go upstairs and rest up. Dinner's in the main dining room at seven. My mother will join us. She'll be a good source of information for this project."

Mimi glanced at her watch. It was three-forty-five. She felt so bloated—like she'd swallowed a bowling ball—that she couldn't imagine another big meal in three hours. And she didn't relish breaking bread with scary Claudia.

"Darlene," Archibald barked. "Take Miss Rosen to the guest bedroom on the third floor."

Darlene came out on the porch and nodded at Mimi. They put on a passable show of not knowing each other.

"Come this way," Darlene said.

Mimi followed Darlene down a long winding corridor, then up a tall staircase. At the top of the steps, Darlene looked around to make sure they were alone, then grabbed Mimi's arm and whispered in her ear.

"Good to see you here," she said. "You know where Archibald's having you stay—the third-floor guest bedroom. That's where Rosalyn used to sleep when they didn't get along."

"How often did that happen?" Mimi asked.

"The last two years."

"And I'll be sleeping there?"

"Yes." Darlene nodded knowingly. "Archibald has plans for you."

CHAPTER EIGHTEEN

DARLENE LED MIMI INTO THE SPARE BEDROOM. Like the rest of Farrington Manor, it was big, brown, and beautiful, though parts showed as much age as elegance.

It was dominated by a massive four-poster bed, walnut desk, and oversized mirror, which self-conscious Mimi tried not to look at. A television screen was mounted on the wall—one of the house's few concessions to the twenty-first century.

Two windows—framed with red velvet curtains—faced the back of the property, and offered a glimpse of what appeared to be a guest house. Could that be where Vanessa stayed? And if it was, what must it have been like for Rosalyn to see that house every day, knowing she'd ruined Vanessa's marriage? Were they deliberately placed in each other's line of sight, to hurt them both?

Darlene opened the curtains, straightened the flowers on the dresser, and readied the bed, singing to herself throughout.

"How are you?" Mimi asked.

"Not great," Darlene said, as she fluffed the pillows. "I miss Rosalyn. It's strange. Sometimes, when I come here, I feel her presence. Not in a spooky way. I just sense that she's around here somewhere."

"You were close to her, weren't you?"

"I guess," Darlene said wistfully. "We were friends. I admired her. I certainly admired her closet." She walked to the edge of the room, and opened the door. Rosalyn's closet was indeed massive—almost a room in itself—and crammed with clothes. Mimi felt she could rummage through it all day.

"It's something huh?" Darlene said, before returning to the bed and pillow-fluffing.

"It is," Mimi said. "Darlene, you don't have to keep making the bed. It's fine how it is."

Darlene dropped the pillow. "Have a nice afternoon."

Mimi tapped her arm. "Before you go, do you think any of Rosalyn's old things are still here? I'm not talking about her clothes, I mean, other stuff." She hesitated. "Things that might be worth looking at. That might give me an insight into her."

Mimi instantly regretted saying that; Darlene might find wanting to comb through a dead woman's possessions creepy. Luckily, Darlene not only understood, she was right on board.

"Rosalyn kept a journal. She once told me, 'if something bad ever happens to me, find my diary.'"

"And did you?"

"I tried. But she never told me where it was. She was worried I'd read all her secrets and sell them to someone. I told her that was crazy. But by the end, she was pretty paranoid. The only thing she said was, 'it's hidden in a book with my name on the cover.'

"I looked through that whole bookcase." Darlene pointed to the wooden structure, crammed with books, in the corner of the room. "I couldn't find anything with her name on it. Maybe you'll have better luck." She patted Mimi on the shoulder and left.

Mimi began examining the books, but couldn't find anything with Rosalyn's name on it, either. Combing through all those books would be a huge job, and she lacked the energy to rifle through each one. All the food and wine at lunch had left her woozy. She kicked off her shoes and dove into the bed. It was the largest bed she had ever laid on. It was raining outside, and she could hear the wind whip against the walls.

Mimi wondered if she could feel Rosalyn's presence, like

Darlene did. "Rosalyn," she found herself saying. "If you're here, give me a sign." She added, with a smile, "and tell me where your damn diary is."

Mimi lay on the bed as still as a statue, waiting for a signal from her old friend, though she had no idea what that would be. Maybe an alarm would go off, or a bird would fly in the window, and point its beak at the diary. But there was no alarm, no bird, and no signal. Mimi couldn't feel Rosalyn's presence. She just felt alone, in a big, strange room, in a big, strange house.

For the last few years, Mimi and Rosalyn had been more Facebook friends than real ones. But now, Mimi longed to talk with her again, and tell her how sorry she was that they'd drifted apart, and how sad she felt that she'd died.

Mimi yawned and lifted her knees to her chest. The bed was quite comfortable. The sheets were silky smooth and felt cool against her cheek. Her head sunk into the pillow. It wasn't long before she drifted off.

Mimi slept soundly, until she saw Rosalyn's face in a dream—and it jarred her awake. She opened her eyes, and caught her breath. She sprang from the bed and vowed to stay awake. She had work to do.

She walked into the adjacent bathroom, and splashed cold water on her face, to clear the fuzz from her brain. She scanned the room. Maybe the book wasn't in the bookcase. That might be too obvious.

She rummaged through the corner desk. She opened and shut all its drawers, but they held mostly credit card bills and old editions of *The Look*, as well as one lone copy of their old newspaper, *The West Jersey Metro*. Mimi started paging through it, and got so lost in nostalgia she had to remind herself to resume her search.

She returned to the bookcase. She found an anthology of photography from *The Look*. If Rosalyn compiled it, her name would be on the cover. She didn't. Mimi paged through it, anyway. She didn't find a diary. She didn't even like the photos.

The bookcase held a wealth of fashion books, but the only one Rosalyn appeared to have read was *High Fashion for*

Dummies—probably to cram for her job at *The Look*. It was stashed behind other books, along with a cluster of self-help titles, including tomes on dealing with depression, conquering compulsions, and leaving a loveless marriage. Some appeared well-thumbed. Mimi examined them all. They provided painful insights about Rosalyn's mental state. None held her diary.

The bottom shelf held a long row of classic books, including *Jane Eyre, Turn of the Screw, Rebecca, The Moonstone, We Have Always Lived In the Castle, The Maltese Falcon,* and *The Wizard of Oz.* Something made her linger on *The Wizard of Oz.* It was the only children's book, and Rosalyn had once compared herself to Dorothy. Then it hit her. *The Wizard of Oz.* That contained her name: Roz.

Mimi opened it and found its middle had been hollowed out, and another book stuffed inside. The second book had a red cover and a padlock. Bingo!

But Mimi couldn't celebrate just yet. She may have found Rosalyn's diary, but she had to circumvent its padlock. Mimi wasn't exactly an experienced lock-picker.

One late night at the newspaper, Roz had given Mimi a tutorial on that very subject. Mimi couldn't remember what she said, except that it required a small, sharp object.

Mimi hunted through her pocketbook, but the only pin she had was connected to the Heartbrooch. She removed the pin from its latch, and considered using it, but didn't want to damage such an expensive piece. She scoured Rosalyn's medicine chest, and found a Swiss Army knife—the type Rosalyn used to carry in her Jersey girl days. Perfect.

Mimi searched online and discovered a video detailing how to break into a diary on a site called Lockpicking 101. Mimi carefully followed its instructions, and before she could think, *hold it, there's a site called Lockpicking 101?*, she heard the fateful click that signaled success. Mimi had aced her first try at "light B and E."

She opened the diary, and suddenly, her old friend was talking to her again.

CHAPTER NINETEEN

T HE FIRST ENTRY IN ROSALYN'S DIARY was dated about three months before she died:

> Hello! I'm journaling again. My therapist thinks it will be helpful, and give me a forum to vent, because God knows I need to. She also said it might be good to keep a record of all the crazy goings on here, just in case—well, you know. Just in case.
>
> My latest problem, and the reason I started seeing a therapist, is I started shoplifting again. It's been two weeks since I got caught at Saks and I'm still mortified. After Archibald bailed me out, I had to listen to him lecture me for hours. He talked to me like I was a child. He pretended he was upset but I could tell he was loving it.
>
> My therapist said all the dumb things I've done lately—sleeping with Shepherd, the shoplifting, the out-of-control spending—are "cries for help." No kidding. I'm stuck in a miserable marriage, and I have no way out.
>
> I am dying to leave Archibald but I can't. My credit card bills are astronomical, and there's a clause in my prenup that lowers my payout if I've committed adultery—as Archibald happily reminds me every time we argue.
>
> At least he's helping with my credit card bills, though not out of the goodness of his heart, because I'm not sure he has one. He and

*his mom don't want to see a bankrupt Lowery family member end
up in the papers.*

*So, that's my first diary entry. Not my best writing, but it's better
than prattling on about fabrics or hemlines or whatever I do at work
all day. Did it make me feel better? Not really. I have a lot more vent-
ing to do.*

From there, came page after page of complaints, about
Archibald, Claudia, and Eloise, her boss at *The Look*.

But one entry struck Mimi as especially interesting:

*The weirdest thing happened today. I got a package from Shepherd
Lowery with the Heartbrooch, the most famous piece the company
produced. It came with a note. "This is yours, forever." Weird!*

*I'm petrified that Shepherd's going to start stalking me again. Last
year the family stopped me from getting a restraining order against
him. They told me not to worry, since he hadn't been to the estate in
years. They just didn't want word of it getting out. They're in denial
about how far off the deep end Shepherd is. And of course, Archibald
said that it was my fault Shepherd was stalking me since I slept with
him.*

*I'm just going to hope this was a one-time thing and I never hear
from Shepherd again.*

Mimi ripped out a blank page from the diary, grabbed a pen,
and started taking notes. "This contradicts Vanessa's theory that
Rosalyn manipulated Shepherd into giving her the brooch," she
wrote. "Rosalyn seemed genuinely surprised that Shepherd sent it
to her. At least, that's what she wrote. She wouldn't lie in a diary.
Would she?"

The next entry was even more interesting. Rosalyn had swiped
the file on the Heartbrooch from the Lowery archives—which
explained why Archibald couldn't find it.

Rosalyn was especially intrigued by the mock-up of the original design:

The original Heartbrooch didn't just say 'JT' and 'WL.' It said, 'JT LOVES WL.' And on top of the original sketch, Wyllis wrote, "It's beautiful. Just like you. Love you forever." Gag.

On my brooch, the word 'loves' has been polished off. There's zero trace of it. It's obvious why.

The Lowerys have always said that Tomaso "stalked" Wyllis, and he never did anything with her. That was, not surprisingly, a lie. Every time you think you've learned all this family's dirty laundry, a few new loads come tumbling out.

"So, Wyllis Lowery and Josephine Tomaso *were* having an affair," Mimi wrote. "Perhaps more!"

But Rosalyn wasn't done.

The file also has lots of information about the Prince Corthoff diamond's curse. I should probably say "curse" in quotation marks, because I don't believe in that kind of thing. But now that I've read all this info, I can't say for sure.

Apparently, neither can anyone else. The file includes a long memo from the archivist who worked for Lowery in the 1980s. He examined every document connected with the Corthoff, and still has no idea if it was actually stolen from an Indian statue. He said information about it is sparse, and its actual origin is "one of those great gemstone mysteries that may never be solved." He noted there was a theory that the curse was invented for publicity purposes, but said that couldn't be proved or disproved either.

He does list all the tragic incidents, including the deaths of the Corthoff family, connected to people who owned the diamond. One man went insane and was institutionalized. Another killed his lover. A delivery guy carrying the diamond was supposedly killed in a car crash.

Which doesn't mean the diamond's cursed. The archivist said you could probably take any gem that's been around 100 years, and chances are you'd find a long list of tragedies associated with it. He said you'd have to calculate the "normal" number of tragedies connected to a diamond, and see if the number here was higher. Yet, it's hard to look at a list like that, with one horrible episode after another, and not get spooked.

Unless you're Wyllis Lowery. With typical Lowery compassion, he seemed thrilled about the tragedies and wrote a memo calling the curse a great marketing hook. He said the company should buy the Corthoff and promote the hell out of it. "Things that are bad luck for other people are always good luck for me," he said.

He recommended the diamond be cut into three pieces, to make it more salable, but that Lowery should announce that they did it to defeat the curse. Wyllis even ordered his team to add a few fake names to the list of dead.

A little later, Wyllis was himself added to the list, when he was shot in the middle of the street. If that isn't karma, I don't know what is.

MIMI HAD FINALLY RECEIVED AN ANSWER to the curse question, though it wasn't a particularly satisfying one. Even the Lowery archivist didn't know if the diamond was actually cursed. Mimi wanted to examine the complete Lowery file, but Rosalyn had squirreled it away in a safe deposit box.

Mimi read on:

Last night was hell. Archibald found out Shepherd sent me the Heartbrooch and made all sorts of threats. He said Shepherd would never have given me that brooch if we weren't still sleeping together. I told him that's ridiculous. Archibald knows that I wanted to get a restraining order against Shepherd. But he didn't care. He said he can never believe what I say, because I'm not trustworthy. I hate him.

He said that while one instance of adultery would lower my pay-out, having a full-fledged affair would wipe it out completely. He said if we got divorced, The Look would probably fire me and I'd be penniless, though if I was lucky, the Lowerys might allow me to live in their third guest house, next to Darlene and Vanessa. The prospect made him almost giddy.

Mimi chewed her pen as she read the next entry:

I just heard my brother-in-law Shepherd died. He drove his car off a cliff near his house.

With his usual tact, Archibald told me this over dinner, and then complained to the chef that his chicken was underdone. He said his mother is devastated, but she sure isn't showing it. She acted like the same old cold fish as usual.

Shepherd and I had a strange relationship. Even when I was dating Archibald, we would flirt. He was cooler and cuter than his brother. Which isn't saying much.

But we never really talked until their cousin's wedding. Shepherd and I ended up hanging out in back of the country club while everyone else was in the reception hall. We'd each had a bit to drink, and shared some stuff we probably shouldn't have.

We both said we felt out of place in the family. I told him about my shoplifting. He talked about his skateboarding. He asked if the family was scandalized when he married his nanny. I said, "you have no idea."

I was surprised how much he knew about jewelry. I'd never checked out his line before, because Archibald said it was garbage. When Shepherd showed me a piece, it was nice! Very wearable and pretty. Definitely something I'd wear, more than that creepy out-of-date Lowery stuff. I told Shepherd that his brand could be even bigger than his family's. I kind of exaggerated that part, but he said he appreciated it.

We talked about his family issues, because of course every Lowery has HUGE family issues. Wyllis was murdered when he was young. And right after that, someone told him his dad has been targeted by the Mafia, which totally traumatized him. For months afterward, he put chairs in front of his bedroom door at night, because he was petrified the Mafia was coming to get him.

His mother never had time for him because she was busy running the company. And Archibald was the "golden child," who teased him and called him dumb.

I told Shepherd he had a lot going for him. He was smart and talented. I may have even said cute.

Then, we started kissing, and twenty minutes later, we hooked up in the back seat of his car. Which was incredibly stupid. I can't believe I did it. But here's the thing—it was fun! Just like shoplifting is fun. A girl needs to have a good time now and then. And the fact that it was in his back seat, definitely added a little spice. I felt like a teenager again.

It may have been TOO good, because afterward, Shepherd told me he loved me and we should run away together.

That totally freaked me out. I said, look, Shepherd, what we did was nice, but you gotta be realistic, all we did was have sex in the back of a car. He got so mad when I said that. It was the first time I realized he had a screw loose.

I begged him to keep what we did quiet. But of course, he told everyone. He was proud of it.

When Vanessa and Archibald found out, they went nuts. Archibald ended my clothing allowance, which is why I'm now drowning in debt. And Vanessa filed for divorce, leading Shepherd to go full-on stalker. He popped up everywhere. He left me creepy notes, saying he'd been tracking my movements. He told me he was the type of person who never gave up, and he wouldn't leave me alone until I gave in. It was scary. He was so envious of Archibald, he desperately wanted to take something that belonged to him. Even if that "thing" was me.

Eventually, I got my lawyer to threaten him with a restraining order, and he backed off. I hadn't heard from him in months, until last week, when he sent me the brooch, then wrote to me on Facebook.

Shepherd was clearly starting to lose his mind again, but, honestly, I wouldn't be shocked if he didn't really kill himself. Shepherd was way too stubborn for that. He also knew a lot of dirt on the family. Claudia and Archibald clearly considered him a nuisance and an embarrassment. Did they hire somebody to kill him? I'd like to think that they wouldn't, but with this family, you never know. Maybe I'm just getting paranoid.

Even so, I feel a lot safer knowing Shepherd's dead. But here's the weird thing: him sending me that brooch was one of his last acts. It could be his attempt to stick it to me from beyond the grave, by saddling me with the diamond's curse. Or supposed curse. Whatever.

It creeps me out beyond belief. Shepherd is the latest death associated with that diamond. I don't think the diamond's cursed, because I don't believe in that kind of thing. But it's not a diamond I'd necessarily want to own. Yet I do.

Mimi found those words chilling, since the person who wrote them was now also dead.

The next day, Rosalyn wrote:

Last night, Archibald and I had another nasty argument. He'll never forgive me for sleeping with Shepherd. I doubt he cares that I was with someone else; he's just mad that it was his "idiot brother." At one point I said Shepherd wasn't as stupid as he thought. That really made him nuts.

He called me all sorts of names, like "born crook" and "Jersey trash." Let's just say he was lucky I didn't have my knife on me, because I might have been tempted to use it. I gotta get out of here, before I do something crazy.

"Wow," Mimi wrote. "After this, I'll never complain about my family again. I mean, I will, of course. But jeez."

Rosalyn's next entry began:

All day, I've been planning my exit. That brooch is worth a lot of money. I just got in touch with this big jewelry collector, who's apparently one of the world's biggest experts on Josephine Tomaso. When I told him I wanted to sell the Heartbrooch, he almost fainted. We're having a teleconference Monday morning. If he offers me a decent amount of money, I'll start packing my bags. Shepherd may have given me that brooch because of its "curse." But it could be my lifeline.

Leaving here won't be easy. I've gotten used to this lifestyle. But

I no longer enjoy it. The only thing I'll miss is talking with Darlene. She's become my closest friend. I'd like to stay in touch with her, but it's not easy having a friend you can only reach through Signal.

There could be difficult days ahead. The Lowery lawyers will put me through hell. I may lose my job. I have huge debts. Basically, I'll be starting over.

But I'm not some pampered rich girl who can't survive on her own. I'll wait tables if I have to. I've taken care of myself before. I can do it again.

I will get out of here. I know it. I can feel it. It's time to escape this nightmare, and have a good life.

Mimi checked the date on that entry. Rosalyn wrote that the night before she died. The remaining pages were blank.

Once Mimi closed the book, she realized something. For the past week, she'd been telling herself—and Michael, and her dad—that she wasn't investigating Rosalyn's murder. Yet, if that was true, why was she taking notes on her diary?

It was terrible learning how unhappy Rosalyn was, but Mimi found reading those determined words on the final page the hardest part of all. That was the Rosalyn she remembered—the brave, brash Jersey girl.

Someone had extinguished that flame. That person would have to pay.

CHAPTER TWENTY

Mimi's thoughts were interrupted by a knock on the door.

"It's Archibald."

"Hold on," Mimi called out, as she hurriedly picked the diary and knife off the floor and stuffed them in her purse. "Come in."

Mimi ran to the door, but Archibald had already cracked it open. "I want to remind you that dinner is in fifteen minutes." He opened the door further, and peered inside. "I trust you have found the accommodations acceptable."

"Lovely," Mimi said.

Archibald walked in, eyes darting around the room. He stopped in front of the books on the floor. "I see you've made yourself at home."

"I was reading some of Rosalyn's books," Mimi said, blushing.

"O.K.," he said, pronouncing each letter separately. He strode to the far wall. "This is the nicest spare bedroom we have." He gestured at the window. "I just wish the view was better. This only shows the back of the estate."

"The view is fine," Mimi said. "Mine is just piled-up garbage cans." She pointed to the outside cottage. "Is that the guest house?"

"Yes. It's one of three." Archibald loved his numbers.

"Is that where Vanessa Lowery is staying?"

"Correct." Archibald scrunched his eyes. "If you don't mind me asking, how did you know that Vanessa was staying there?"

Mimi tensed up. "She once reached out to me, about the Heartbrooch."

"Oh God, don't tell me that Vanessa believes it's hers?" A smirk crawled up his face.

"She thought because she's Shepherd's widow—"

"She's Shepherd's *estranged* widow. They were legally separated when Shepherd went to that great skateboard park in the sky. Her claiming that brooch certainly takes nerve, considering we're providing her free room and board. But it certainly wouldn't be out of character—or should I say, lack of character."

"You'll have to speak to her," Mimi said in a small voice.

"I will." Archibald strolled to the door. "Dinner is at seven, sharp, in the second-floor dining room. Just go to the bottom of the stairs, turn left. You can't miss it. It's absurdly large. And if you want to wear any of Rosalyn's clothes, there are plenty to choose from."

Mimi glanced down at her outfit, which, Archibald had just implied, wasn't nice enough. Mimi turned to Rosalyn's closet and made a show of sifting through it.

After Archibald left, Mimi couldn't stop thinking about Vanessa Lowery. Mimi had long considered Vanessa the most sympathetic player in this drama. Now Mimi might have gotten her in trouble.

Mimi peered out the window at the little guest house out back. One of its windows glowed with a yellow light. A figure moved behind the shade. That must be Vanessa. Mimi decided to call, and relay her chat with Archibald.

"Hi Vanessa. It's Mimi Rosen. I'm at the Lowery estate."

"Oh hello, Mimi," Vanessa replied frostily. "May I ask what brought you here? I assume you came to sell the Heartbrooch."

Mimi exhaled wearily. "I did. I know you might be disappointed to hear that, but I needed something from the Lowerys."

"Yes," Vanessa snickered. "Money."

"No, not that. I wanted information on the diamond. And

actually, I don't need it anymore. I found what I was after in some of Rosalyn's old writings."

"So you won't sell them the brooch?" Vanessa sounded skeptical.

Mimi took a breath. "I don't know. I haven't made up my mind about that. We'll see what they offer."

"Mimi, I am warning you, do not sell them that brooch. That will be the biggest mistake of your life. They will offer you a huge pile of money, but the Lowerys know how to trap people. Look at how they've trapped me. No matter how much they give you, you will live to regret it."

"Got it," Mimi said.

"I'm serious," Vanessa said, her words gaining speed and force. "These people are dangerous. Remember, I told you I believed that Shepherd didn't actually kill himself, that he was murdered. Yesterday, I was contacted by a local detective. He told me certain things about Shepherd's suicide were suspicious. For instance, the night he died, people broke into his house, and stole his computer.

"Now that I think about it, you should probably leave the estate now. The Lowerys know you have that brooch. And if you don't sell it to them, they'll find a way to get it. I'm not saying they will hurt you. But I wouldn't put it past them."

Mimi was unnerved by Vanessa's warnings, but also by her intensity, which was palpable even through the phone.

Mimi assured Vanessa she'd be careful. Then, she hung up; it was nearly time to eat. Mimi grabbed one of Rosalyn's dresses that looked like it would fit. She quickly changed into it, and headed down for dinner.

CHAPTER TWENTY-ONE

W**HILE** M**IMI'S** **AFTERNOON** **AT** F**ARRINGTON** M**ANOR** had begun to jade her to large displays of wealth, she still gasped when she saw the Lowery's dining room. It was indeed "absurdly large," about the size of a high school gym. A long candle-lit wooden table stood in its center. It could probably hold dozens, though tonight, it only sat three.

Archibald was stationed at the head of the table, and his mother Claudia sat to his right, about a foot away. Mimi was placed across from Claudia, bringing her face-to-face with the "Piranha in Pearls."

Claudia was wearing a dress the color of a tomato, and a set of milky-white pearls around her neck. (*Maybe she likes that nickname*, Mimi mused. *Because she sure wears pearls a lot*.) Archibald wore a different blue blazer, button-down shirt, and tan slacks than he did at lunch, though he again wore a blue blazer, button-down shirt, and tan slacks. Both Archibald and his mother were quite dolled up for a family dinner. Mimi wore a pink dress from Rosalyn's closet but again felt underdressed.

Claudia told Mimi it was nice to meet her, though they'd met before. Mimi didn't bother to correct her.

A server announced the main course was scallops and shrimp, preceded by salad, risotto, bread, and—by that point, Mimi was no longer listening. She had zero appetite. Her stomach was still stuffed from lunch.

When the meal came out, every plate was piled high with food, which was arranged so beautifully, Mimi didn't feel right eating it. She nibbled her dinner, while Archibald and his mother heartily bit into theirs.

Halfway through the salad, Archibald started delivering a capsule history of Lowery Inc.—"for the book," he said.

"Lowery, the company I am proud to lead, was built by two legends in the industry. I live every day in their shadow."

Archibald's grandfather, Nicholas Lowery, was a short, scrappy diamond merchant who recruited the "most distinguished looking man he could find" to impersonate him when he applied for bank credit. He loved jewelry so much, he had the store's entire inventory committed to memory. "Every time he parted with a piece, it was like saying goodbye to a child," Archibald said.

On the other hand, his son Wyllis' "first love was promotion. My father believed Lowery didn't sell jewelry. It sold mystique. More than that, it sold magic.

"My father once had a one-hundred-and-fifty-carat diamond cleaved on live television. One false move, and millions of dollars would be gone. The entire audience held its breath. The cleaving was executed flawlessly. But afterward, the cutter fainted dead away." Archibald's eyes sparkled and dimples formed in his cheeks. "The press spent the next few weeks debating if the cutter really fainted or if it was just a publicity stunt."

Mimi had read about that. "So what happened? Did he really faint?"

Archibald smiled knowingly. "Let's just say he got up afterward, and leave it at that. The point is, we got a huge amount of press out of it. That was my father's genius. He was a master at understanding what people want, and feeding it to them."

Claudia didn't pay much attention to Archibald's recitation, except when he credited her with keeping the business going after her husband died, which earned a polite nod.

"Lowery Inc. has been approached many times by big luxury houses wanting to purchase our business," Archibald said. "We have consistently, but firmly, said, 'no, thank you.'

"Those conglomerates kill the character of the brands they buy. They turn everything into a high-end Apple store. My father and grandfather worked hard to build this company. We don't want our reputation sullied. We want it celebrated.

"That's why we're writing this book. It will be called—" He spelled out the title with his hands. "*The Lowery History: 115 Years of the Kingdom of Love.*"

"Archibald." His mother threw him a look.

"Oh, sorry, Mother. I did it again. I should have said 'The Lowery Heritage.'" He shook his finger. "And, Mimi, now that you're overseeing this project, you need to take ownership of it. You should have corrected me when I said 'history.' Remember. It's 'The Lowery Heritage.'"

Mimi was beginning to wonder if even seventy-five thousand dollars would be worth this crap.

"I'm quite excited about this project," Archibald said. "We'll start it right after we settle matters with the Heartbrooch."

Another mention of the Heartbrooch. They really wanted that thing.

"Speaking of which," he continued, "just before we sat down to eat, I had a long talk with our company archivist. He found the file with all the background on the Heartbrooch. It includes a letter from my father stating that he invented the curse as a publicity stunt. So, you can rest assured that the hex, or curse, or whatever you want to call it, was total claptrap, as I figured. That diamond didn't date back to the 1800s. It was discovered in Africa in the 1970s, like most diamonds from that era. My father, being a master showman, wanted to spice up its backstory.

"The archivist will email me those documents tomorrow. And assuming your lawyer signs off on everything, we'll be set."

Mimi took another nibble of her food and stared at Archibald, knowing what he'd just said was an outright lie. Rosalyn had taken the file the archivist had just miraculously discovered, and whatever "document" this guy was spending the night preparing would almost certainly be, in Archibald's words, "utter claptrap."

Perhaps Archibald was like his father. He'd figured out what Mimi was after, and was feeding it to her. He just didn't know she'd already found it.

Mimi was tempted to call Archibald on his lie, but she couldn't think of any way to do that without admitting she'd read Rosalyn's diary. Plus, she figured, it wouldn't be the worst thing in the world if Archibald whipped up some document saying the diamond was never cursed. That was what Zeke wanted. Curses weren't real, anyway. She might as well get a fake document about a fake curse.

Mimi plastered a grin on her face and said, "great," but couldn't resist adding, "I thought you said the information on the brooch was missing."

"It was," Archibald said, without missing a beat or changing his expression. "But after lunch, I called the archivist and lit a fire under him. He knew if I was calling on a Saturday, it had to be important. He did a much more thorough search, and lo and behold, he found the file."

"I'd love to see it," Mimi said.

"Why?" Archibald asked. "You're not going to own the Heartbrooch after tomorrow."

"It might be useful for the book. It's one of the most famous pieces produced by the company. It was the last item Josephine Tomaso ever designed."

"Oh, no one cares about Tomaso," Claudia said, speaking up after a long period of silence. "She's old news."

"I don't know about that," Mimi said. "She has a devoted online fanbase."

"Big deal," Claudia said, with a wave of her hand, as if Tomaso was a bug she could swat away. "What doesn't have a devoted online fanbase? You can probably find one for a heat rash.

"The truth is, Josephine Tomaso was never that famous, or renowned, or respected. The only reason people talk about her is because of all the pictures of her looking glamorous and beautiful, like she was this brilliant young innocent. In reality, she was flighty, immature, and a nightmare to work with. Her designs were absurdly sentimental. Wyllis' greatest mistake was getting involved with her."

"You mean involved in a business sense?" Mimi said.

"Of course," Claudia said. "What do you think I meant?"

Mimi wriggled in her chair and took a breath. "I know that she and your husband did business together. But, there were also rumors that he—" She grasped for an easy way to finish that sentence, but couldn't come up with one.

It didn't matter. They knew what she meant.

"You are correct, there was talk that Miss Tomaso was attracted to my father," Archibald jumped in, keeping his mother in view. "That is not surprising. My father was a very charming man. But he stayed devoted to my mother. They had a remarkable love story, which that brooch commemorates." He must not have rehearsed that lie, because he was far less believable delivering it than his last one.

"Okay," Mimi said. "So Josephine Tomaso and your father were never involved?"

"Of course, they weren't." Archibald let out a small unconvincing laugh. It didn't sound like his standard bark, more like a bleat. "That's just gossip."

"It's trash, is what it is," Claudia said, with a voice that lowered the room temperature twenty degrees. "Tell me, Miss Rosen. Where did you hear that?"

"It's a long story," Mimi said.

"I'm a woman of leisure," Claudia said. "I have plenty of time."

"I can't tell you," Mimi stammered. "I'm a journalist. I can't disclose my sources."

"Sources?" Claudia's eyes hardened into dark rocks. "Oh, how lovely, Archibald. You've invited *Us Weekly* for dinner."

"Let's change the subject," Archibald declared with a tight smile.

"Sure, why not?" Claudia said, straightening her back. "That's what they always tell women, let it go, move on, don't pay attention to what people say, just forget all the catty gossip and humiliating comments. I ran Lowery Incorporated for fifteen years, at a time when virtually no women ran jewelry companies. What did I get for all my hard work? A bunch of ugly rumors and a sexist nickname. Even today, little Miss Josephine is the main woman associated with the brand. Apparently, I'm not young and beautiful enough for anyone to care about."

"Please, Mother—"

Claudia shot him a glare.

Archibald nervously wet his lips. "Miss Rosen, you are witnessing the directness that made my mother such a successful businesswoman. Obviously, the topic you have raised is a quite emotional one. Once again, I suggest we discuss something else."

"I don't know if I care to," Claudia pronounced, dropping her napkin on the table. "I'm not sure I want this woman at my house. You told me before you thought she was snooping in Rosalyn's room. She's clearly spying on our family."

"I wasn't snooping," Mimi said, though that comment made her join the legion of liars. "Those rumors about your husband have been around for decades. You're a famous family. Of course, people are going to gossip about you."

"Right," Claudia said. "Our family is famous. Therefore, all our trials and tragedies should be fodder to entertain the masses. I know that's how journalists think. Pardon me if I find that appalling.

"I shouldn't have to remind you that we are human beings, with real feelings. Yes, we've had issues, and horrible things happen to us, and they may be fun for you to gossip about, but I can assure you, they were no fun to live through. It's true, there were issues in my marriage, quite unfortunate ones, and some of the parties involved were not particularly subtle about it. It was quite humiliating. It's not something I like to talk about and certainly not something I consider suitable dinnertime conversation."

Almost every vein in Claudia's neck popped. "I had a son who died recently. Did you plan to discuss that over dessert?"

Mimi felt like she'd just been mauled by the Piranha in Pearls. She was about to defend herself, but noticed that Claudia's eyes were no longer lit with fury. They were pink.

"I'm sorry, Mrs. Lowery," Mimi said in a soft voice. "It was just something I was curious about. I didn't know bringing it up would upset you so much. We discussed Rosalyn's cheating at lunch."

Archibald sank his head in his hands. That wasn't a convincing argument. The ensuing silence felt endless.

Mimi moved her chair away from the table. "I no longer want to stay here tonight. I'd like to go back to New Jersey."

"Let's not be overdramatic," Archibald said. "We've already decided you're sleeping over tonight. It's too late to order a helicopter."

"I could call an Uber," Mimi said.

"You don't need to do that," Archibald said. "It's fine if she stays, isn't it, Mother?"

"I suppose," Claudia said, her fork playing with her food.

But Mimi had made up her mind. Between Claudia's scolding, Rosalyn's writings, and Vanessa's warnings, Mimi had no desire to spend another minute at the Lowery estate. Archibald urging her to stay only made her more anxious to leave.

Mimi took out her phone. Uber promised a car would be there in ten minutes, which, in her experience, meant fifteen. She bristled when she saw a ride to New Jersey would cost two hundred dollars. She couldn't afford that. She was ready to admit defeat.

Before she could, Archibald, who'd been eyeing her intently, raised a warning finger and declared, "Be careful, Miss Rosen. If you leave this house without giving us that brooch, we will sic our lawyers on you. And I assure you, that will not be pleasant."

That settled it; Mimi didn't care how much the ride cost. She pulled the trigger on the Uber.

"See you in court." Mimi rose from the table. "And by the way, Archibald, Rosalyn was too good for you."

Archibald responded with a fusillade of threats. Mimi ignored them as she stormed out the door.

MIMI HURRIED ACROSS THE LOWERYS' PROPERTY to the front gate. Security lights illuminated the first part of the lawn, but the rest was as dark as the Corthoff diamond, except for a few strips of moonlight that streamed through the trees. The frigid wind lashed her body, and the cold air seeped through her skin to her bones. The rain had turned the grass wet and chilly. Icy droplets splashed against her ankles.

She heard stirring, apparently coming from behind a bush. Out of the corner of her eye, she spotted a dark shape. It was a man, approaching her with a swift, menacing gait. The grass crinkled under his feet.

The man flashed a light in her eyes. "Excuse me, Miss. I'm Lowery estate security. Can I ask who you are and what you're doing here?"

Mimi felt a wave of relief. "I'm Mimi Rosen. I was a guest of the Lowerys. I'm just going to the front gate to catch an Uber."

"Okay," the man said. "I'll need to see some form of identification." He put away the light and began walking toward her. He walked with a slight limp.

"Sure. Just a second." She took out her phone, to illuminate her purse, and for a second it shone on him. He was tall, brawny, clad in jeans—and had a black mask over his face.

Her heart began to pound against her ribcage. Whoever this was, he was no security guard.

"Who are you?" Mimi called out, before deciding she didn't want to know. "Don't come near me!"

"You stay there!" he yelled. "Don't try to get away!"

She reached into her pocketbook and fished out the switchblade she'd found in Rosalyn's room. She brandished it in her trembling hand.

"I have a knife," she yelled. She shone her phone on it, so he could see she wasn't bluffing.

He kept walking toward her, faster now.

Mimi's heart leapt to her throat. If this guy wouldn't be stopped by a knife, it was time for plan B: run.

CHAPTER TWENTY-TWO

MIMI SPRINTED BACK TO THE MANOR she'd just dashed out of, the man speed-limping behind her. It sounded like he was getting closer, but she didn't dare look over her shoulder.

Mimi ran up the porch stairs to the entrance to the manor. Trembling, she banged on its giant front door, as loud and hard as she could. She spied a doorbell and began pushing it frantically. She could hear it echo in the great hall on the other side of the door.

She turned her head. The man was still coming after her, but when he'd reached the illuminated part of the lawn, he moved slower and more carefully than before.

She continued to bang and scream, until the door finally swung open.

There stood Archibald, his face as red as his dragon-patterned silk robe. "Dear God. Are you back *already*?"

He had only opened the door a crack, but that was enough for Mimi to wedge herself in the house. "There's someone outside," she said in a strangled sob. "He's coming after me."

Archibald gazed at her skeptically. He opened the door further and poked his head outside. "I don't see anyone."

Mimi summoned the courage to peek out the door. The man *had* disappeared—or at least retreated to the area beyond the security lights.

"There was someone out there," Mimi protested between heavy breaths. "He had a black mask over his head. And he was chasing me."

Archibald's perma-smirk was working overtime. "Nonsense. This estate is extremely well-guarded. It's almost impossible to penetrate. If what you're saying is true, that would represent a major security breach. Perhaps you've watched too many horror films. Or maybe you're using this as a pretext to apologize."

Mimi's brain swam. "What are you talking about? Why would I apologize?"

"Because I was just on the phone with our lawyers," Archibald said. "And if you don't return our property, I assure you, they plan extremely aggressive action."

"Why are you so obsessed with that stupid brooch?" Mimi screamed. "I don't appreciate threats, especially after what I just experienced. But that seems to be how you operate. I know how you threatened Rosalyn."

"I did nothing of the sort," Archibald declared.

"Yes, you did," Mimi said. "Rosalyn told me how you threatened her after she got the brooch from Shepherd." This was half-true; Rosalyn had written that in her diary, so that was how Mimi was "told." "You told Rosalyn that if she left, she'd be penniless."

Archibald spun his eyes skyward. "That wasn't a threat. That was the cold reality. Our prenup was extremely well-drafted, at least from my point of view. It certainly didn't allow for repeated instances of adultery."

"You also threatened her that, if she left you, she'd lose her job at *The Look*."

"I merely mentioned that as a possibility," Archibald said, smiling with half his mouth. "She never would have gotten that position if my mother wasn't friends with the editor. Rosalyn had very little knowledge about fashion, except for how to spend large amounts of money on it."

"So, basically," Mimi said, her hand on her hip, "you threatened her."

"If that's how you want to label it, fine," Archibald said. "I'm not sure how you expect a man to act when his wife cheats on him with his own brother."

"At lunch, you said that you didn't let that bother you."

"I said I *tried* not to let it bother me," Archibald said, his voice growing louder. "I'm a busy man. I run a multi-million-dollar company. I don't have time to get distracted with my family's idiotic theatrics. But of course, it bothered me. It was devastating!" He winced; that admission seemed to startle even him.

"Then why didn't you get a divorce?" Mimi asked.

"Because my mother had just had one of her two sons separate, thanks to your friend Rosalyn. I wanted to spare her the pain of having two sons divorce in one year. My mother is in her eighties and has been through a lot. She's a lot more fragile than she comes across.

"You think you know the truth about me and Rosalyn, but you don't. I loved Rosalyn, very much." His voice grew softer. "I thought she loved me, but it turned out she only loved this." He gestured around the mansion.

"Obviously," Archibald continued, "this isn't something I like to talk about. But she did hurt me, very badly, just like her death hurt, as did Shepherd's, as did my father's." His face grew pink and his voice rose to a scream. "It's all been quite painful!"

He breathed in and regained his composure. "I hope I've cleared the air on subjects that are none of your business. Any other wounds you wish to pick at?"

Claudia appeared atop the double staircase that dominated the front hall, wearing a robe that shimmered even more than Archibald's. "What is going on here?" she asked, her voice booming across the foyer. She gazed down at both of them. "Archibald, I thought that woman was gone."

"She did, but she came back," Archibald said. "She claimed there was a man outside chasing her."

"A man?" Claudia said. "Who?"

"Nobody," Archibald said. "I just checked. There's no one out there."

"There was someone!" Mimi stamped her foot. "Why would I make that up? I don't see why you don't believe me." It hit her. "Unless that man was working for you, and that was your attempt to get the brooch back."

"Archibald, make this woman leave," Claudia demanded. "I don't want her in my house one more moment. She's dishonest and a snoop. Her presence makes me feel unsafe."

Mimi's phone beeped with a text: "Hello. Your car is at the front gate."

"Don't worry, Mrs. Lowery," Mimi said. "My Uber just came. He's at the entrance outside." She turned to Archibald. "Can you let him drive up here? I don't want to go back out on the lawn."

Archibald theatrically groaned and pulled his phone from his robe pocket. "If that's what it takes to be rid of you, I'll let the car approach the house." He typed a bit, then put the phone away.

"What a mistake it was having you here," he growled. "It's obvious you never planned to give us that brooch. I bet you didn't even bring it."

"Of course I brought it." Mimi absently patted her purse.

Claudia noticed. "Archibald," she called from the top of the stairs. "The brooch is in her pocketbook. Grab it!"

Archibald awkwardly heaved toward her, as Mimi clutched her purse to her chest.

"Don't you dare steal the brooch!" Mimi said.

"Why not?" Claudia declared. "He has every right to. It was stolen from us. Get it, Archibald."

Mimi's adrenaline was still pumping from her outdoor encounter. When Archibald again fumbled toward her pocketbook, she screamed, "I will not let you take it!" She reached into her purse and pulled out the switchblade. "I have a knife."

Fear flashed on Archibald's face. "What do you plan to do with that?"

"I don't know." Mimi stared at her hand; she couldn't believe she was brandishing a knife for the second time in five minutes. This time, she held it firm and steady. She felt the power of it, which terrified her.

"Are you going to stab me?" Archibald asked.

The question shocked Mimi. "I wasn't planning on it."

"Archibald, get the brooch!" Claudia screamed.

"I will not, Mother," Archibald said. "She has a knife."

"She just said she wouldn't use it," Claudia said.

"I did not say that," Mimi said. "I said I wasn't *planning* on using it. I might, hypothetically."

"She's bluffing," Claudia said. "Take it from her, Archibald."

"Mother, do not dare this woman to stab me!"

A car horn honked outside. "That's my Uber." Mimi dropped the knife into her purse and opened the door. "Later, guys. It's been fun."

She sprinted out of the house, then raced across the porch and down the stairs. The car was waiting at the front entrance, just like she'd asked. Mimi jumped in the back seat.

"Get me out of here, quick," she shouted as she fastened her seatbelt.

The car sped toward the front gate, to Mimi's great relief.

"I know this is a long trip," Mimi said. "I appreciate you making it."

"Yeah, sure," said the driver, as he zipped past the entrance to the estate. "So where we going?"

"Somerset, New Jersey," Mimi said. "The app should give you the address."

"Right," the driver said. "Just wanted to make sure."

Mimi checked his dashboard; he didn't have his phone mounted, like most Uber drivers. His voice sounded vaguely familiar, but she couldn't quite place it.

The car raced down the tree-lined road outside the estate. It was going way too fast, and Mimi had no idea if it was headed in the right direction.

"Maybe you should slow down," she said.

The driver didn't respond.

Mimi's phone rang, with a call from an unknown number. She picked up. "Is this Mimi?" said a voice.

"Yes."

"This is Tony, your Uber driver. I'm waiting for you."

"But—" Her breath got caught in her throat. "I'm in an Uber now."

"I don't know about that. You ordered a ride with me ten minutes ago, and I've been waiting outside this estate for the last five minutes. This guy at the front gate told me he'd come and get you, but I think he just drove past. Was that you in the back seat?"

She didn't have to check the app to understand that, yes, the man on the phone was her actual Uber driver, and the guy in the front seat was . . . she didn't know. She hung up.

"Who are you?" she shouted at the man behind the steering wheel.

"I'm your Uber driver. Can't you tell? I'm driving!" He was now flying down the road.

"You are going way too fast. You need to slow down. I demand you stop this car."

"Actually," he said, "I think I'll go faster." Which he did.

Mimi's stomach flipped. "Stop this car, or I'm jumping out."

"I wouldn't do that if I were you," the man said. "At this speed, if you hop out, you'll break your neck. Trust me. I know what I'm talking about."

Mimi frantically scanned her surroundings. The driver was right. She had no escape. Her seatbelt was a trap.

Mimi flashed her phone around the back seat. Right next to her was a black hood. Her blood ran cold.

She was stuck in a car with this guy, and she had no idea where he was going, or who he was.

CHAPTER TWENTY-THREE

MIMI SCREAMED AT THE DRIVER TO STOP and kicked the back of his seat. But instead of slowing down, he sped up.

He gazed in the rearview mirror. He was wearing sunglasses and a hat, and most of his face was covered with a bushy black beard.

"I believe we spoke a while ago," he said. "My name's George Morton. I'm a private investigator, working for the Tomaso family."

"That's a lie," Mimi shouted over the sound of the speeding car. "I checked on Google. There's no private investigator by that name."

"Well, look at Miss-Handy-With-A-Search-Engine. You're right, that's not my real name. That's why they call us private investigators. We like to keep things private.

"The point is, I warned you not to sell that brooch. It belongs to the Tomaso family. I can only think of one reason why you'd go and talk with the Lowerys, and it's not to see their new tennis court."

"I didn't make a deal with the Lowerys, and I'm not going to," Mimi said. "And I'm not making a deal with you, either, creep. Now, stop this car!"

"Yeah, that's not happening," he said.

"I am not talking to you until you stop this car."

"You don't get to negotiate terms here," the driver chuckled. "I'm in control and this is the only deal I'm offering: take me to wherever you have that brooch, hand it over, and I'll leave you alone. I'm through playing games."

"What happens if I don't agree to that?"

"You don't want to know."

He said that so matter-of-fact and coldly, she didn't doubt he was serious.

"All right," Mimi said, close to tears. She needed to end this craziness. "If you really want the brooch, I can give it to you. I have it on me."

"You expect me to believe that?" the driver sneered. "I'm not stupid, lady."

Mimi rummaged through her purse until she finally found the brooch. She pricked her finger on the back pin, which had become unmoored from its latch when she considered it as a lock pick. She pulled it out and flashed her phone on it. "See?"

The driver gazed in the rear-view window. He slammed on the brakes, sending the car skidding to the middle of the road with an ear-piercing screech. Mimi was propelled into the air, but the seatbelt pulled her back with a violent painful snap. Afterward, her back felt like it had been smacked by a piece of plywood.

Neither said anything, as they both sat, gulping down air, absorbing the shock of what just happened. Mimi's heart hammered in her chest.

"Jesus!" Mimi screamed. "What are you, insane?"

"I prefer the term, 'determined,'" the driver responded. "I don't give up. Now hand me that brooch."

Mimi unlocked her seatbelt.

Morton apparently heard that. "Don't think you're going to escape without giving me the brooch." He reached into the back-seat and grabbed her arm, squeezing his nails into her flesh.

Mimi almost screamed in pain, but she clenched her teeth and didn't make a sound; she didn't want to give this guy the satisfaction of knowing he was hurting her. "How do I know you won't kill me if I hand it over?"

"Let's put it this way," the driver said. "If you don't hand it over, your chance of getting killed is one-hundred percent."

"And what if I hand it over?

"We'll see."

That wasn't particularly comforting, but it wasn't like she trusted this guy anyway. He squeezed her arm even tighter, and Mimi couldn't help but scream.

"Give it to me." He held out his hand.

She gripped the brooch, and with her finger, moved the back pin away from the latch. "Here you go," she said—then stuck the pin in the center of his open palm. She kept pressing until she heard the sound she wanted—a shrill, anguished cry. He snatched his hand away, a trickle of blood running down his wrist.

She opened the door to escape. But before she could flee, the man's arm grabbed her throat. He clutched it tight, his face purple with rage. She kicked and trashed and tried to wriggle away but he was a big man, who had her pinned to the seat. He tightened his grip on her neck. Her eyes bulged and her breath grew short.

"I was going to let you go," the man seethed, as his body rose over the front seat. "That's not in the cards now."

She couldn't even beg for her life; his grip was so tight, she couldn't talk.

She stuck her hand in her purse and felt for the pocket knife, which, fortunately, was already open. She lifted it from her pocketbook and plunged it into his arm. He howled in pain. As she drove it into his flesh, he let go of her neck and his arm flailed as he tried to pull the knife out. This gave Mimi enough space to kick open the back door and leap out of the car.

She raced across the deserted street to the forest on the side of the road. She clutched her purse, but it was open, and some things fell out, including lipstick, cosmetics, a mirror, and Rosalyn's diary. She decided not to pick them up; she still had the brooch, her phone, and a madman chasing her.

Mimi barreled deep into the forest, running through plants and bushes, nicking her legs on the occasional thorn. The trees appeared to stretch on forever under the night sky. She heard her pursuer behind her, cursing and yelling.

Until suddenly, he stopped. She didn't know if she'd outran him, or if he was faking her out. But she kept going.

After a few minutes, she decided she'd had enough. Her legs and back were aching and she was gasping for breath. It had begun to drizzle, and her hair and clothes were damp with rain and sweat. She found a huge tree and crouched behind it.

She took out her phone. It was at one percent power and its battery was running out.

She thought about calling Michael, but worried noise might attract the man's attention. So she sent him a text: "Michael, please come and get me. I'm in Larnsdale, New York, in a forest outside the Lowery estate. This guy's chasing me." She sent a Google Map of where she was, though a dialog box oh-so-hopefully warned her that, without WiFi, it would be less accurate.

She attempted to call an Uber, but opening that app was the last straw that killed her phone battery. She didn't know if Michael had received her message, or if he'd be able to find her. She wasn't even sure he'd try.

All she knew was she was exhausted, and had a very good chance of dying that night. She thought about running again, but that would mean making noise, and the guy might hear her. She lacked the mental energy to determine her best move, and decided to keep hiding behind the tree.

She sat on the ground, and placed her purse on her head for respite from the rain. She was cold and shivering and her head was filled with fresh new nightmares. Yet she was so tired none of that mattered. She leaned her sore back against the tree. The world melted away and she went to sleep.

CHAPTER TWENTY-FOUR

MIMI AWOKE A FEW HOURS LATER, groggy and confused. It took a few seconds to grasp where she was—in a forest, soaking wet, resting against a tree—and to remember, with a shudder, how she got there.

It was early morning. Birds were chirping, and the sun supplied scattered shards of light. Mimi stood up and brushed the dirt off herself. Her clothes were damp from the night before and her back wasn't letting her forget she was nearly in a car crash. She had no idea how she'd get home, and whether the Uber driver was anywhere nearby.

She heard a man calling her name. Her anxiety level spiked, until she realized who it was.

"Mimi!" Michael called. "Where are you? Are you here?"

"Yes!" she hollered. "I'm here."

Michael ran through the bushes, crackling every twig in his path. It took a few rounds of them yelling back and forth, but eventually they found each other. When Mimi finally saw him, she felt a surge of emotion and gratitude. She wasn't clear on the correct protocol, given they were officially broken up, but couldn't restrain herself. She ran into his arms, sobbing. He clutched her tight.

"I'm so happy you're here," Mimi said, holding him close, a giant lump in her throat. "How'd you find me?"

"It wasn't easy," Michael said. "I've been driving around all night looking for you. The map you sent gave me a general idea where you were, but I spent about an hour going back and forth on this highway, until I spotted some skid marks. I got out of the car, and saw your stuff by the side of the road. I've probably been wandering in these woods for a half hour. I can't believe I finally found you."

"I can't believe it either." Mimi couldn't stop crying.

"I don't get what happened," Michael said. "What are you doing here? Where have you been?"

Mimi nuzzled her head in his chest. "On the moon."

AFTER THEY GOT INTO MICHAEL'S CAR, Mimi told him about her time at the Lowerys, and her Uber ride from hell with "George Morton," supposed private investigator. Michael listened more like a detective than a boyfriend; he said "uh-huh" a lot, and constantly followed up with "then what?"

They stopped for breakfast at the first diner they could find. When Mimi finished her story, she braced herself for a tirade about how stupid she was to visit the estate. But instead Michael said, "Thank God you're okay. The whole thing sounds terrible. I'll call the local police, make sure they find this maniac."

It was only after the food arrived—pancakes for her, steak and eggs for him—that Michael brought up what was clearly on his mind.

"I'm sure," he said, cutting into his steak, "you don't want another lecture."

"No, I don't," Mimi said.

Michael half-shrugged. "Okay." The table fell silent.

"You know what?" Mimi said. "I'm sure you're dying to point out I got in trouble again. So have at it. You came all the way here. You've earned the right to rub it in. Go ahead. Let it rip."

Michael released a weary sigh. "There's no point. You never learn, even when things like this happen. Why should I waste my breath?"

Mimi threw her utensils on her plate.

"Do you think I want this?" she said. "Do you think I want people to try and kill me? I don't ask for this."

"Oh please," Michael said. "You don't end up in these situations by accident. You make an active choice to get involved. And you keep thinking it won't end up like this, and it always does.

"I've given up trying to stop you. I just want to know: why? You're still recovering from your other two investigations. Why on Earth would you do this to yourself?"

Mimi tried to answer, but couldn't.

"Maybe you're some kind of adrenaline junkie," Michael continued. "Or maybe you still want to be a reporter. Or you think you're gonna save the world. But you can't help yourself. You say you don't like these little adventures, but I don't believe that. I think that you do. I don't know why, but you do."

Finally, Mimi had enough. "Maybe I don't want to see someone get away with murder. Or my father's business ruined."

"You have a lawyer and the police for that. Come on. There must be another reason."

"It's because—" Mimi hesitated. She was about to say something she'd long believed but had never said out loud. "I'm good at this."

"What?" Michael barked.

"I'm a good investigator. My whole life, I've never really excelled at anything. I was an okay reporter, but I never got the chance to truly prove myself. I do a decent job for my father. I am okay at most things.

"But this, I'm good at. I notice stuff other people miss. I can put the puzzle pieces together. And yes, I make mistakes. But I've solved two murders. How many people do you know who've done that?"

Michael stared at her, deadpan. "Plenty."

"All right. Non-police."

Michael frowned. "I'll admit, it's unusual."

"And I'll admit, you're a better detective than me. But you can be intimidating. Even the way you just ordered breakfast. It was like you were cross-examining the waiter to make sure the steak was really medium rare."

"I wanted to make sure it was done right!"

"That's fine," Mimi said. "That's how you are. I wouldn't change you. But I'm different. I try to relate to people. I try to understand their motivations, and see the world as they do. And I think because of that, they tell me things."

Michael shut his eyes. This conversation appeared to physically pain him.

"Do you think I'm a good investigator?" Mimi asked.

"No comment."

"You didn't say no," Mimi said. "That's a start. Detective Brill said she was impressed by me."

Michael just grunted.

"And by the way," Mimi said, "let's say, for the sake of argument, I do like these little adventures, as you put it. What does that say about you?"

Michael scowled. "What do you mean?"

"I think you like that I like them. If I were just a regular person, who minded her own business, we never would have gotten together. Did you ever think of that?"

"Oh, that's—" He threw down his fork. "I don't have the patience to analyze all the psychological layers there."

"I don't either," Mimi took a breath. "But I'm really happy you came. I know it was a long trip."

"Of course, I'd come get you," Michael said. "What do you expect? You were in trouble."

"You could have just called the local police," Mimi said.

"Yeah, well, I didn't," Michael said, keeping his eyes on his food.

"I sometimes worry I'm imposing on you."

"You don't impose," Michael said.

Mimi noticed he wasn't speaking about their relationship in the past tense. A good sign.

"We haven't talked in a while," she said. "It's been about—" She counted on her fingers.

"Three days," Michael said.

Mimi smiled. "You've kept track."

Michael cast his eyes down. "I have a good memory."

"Did you miss me?" Mimi asked.

"Well, it's only been three days," Michael mumbled. "But yes, I did. A little."

"A little?"

"I can't quantify it. But I did miss you." He sipped his coffee. "Did you miss me?"

"Of course I did!" She paused. "Would you be open to, maybe, getting back together? I swear, I want nothing more to do with the Lowerys. I'm happy to let Detective Brill figure the rest of this out."

"I'll believe that when I see it. You're not the type to stand on the sidelines. It's admirable, in a way. It just drives me nuts. I know I can't stop you. I don't know what to do—just live with it, I guess."

Michael's phone buzzed. He glanced at it. "It's Detective Brill."

As Mimi polished off her pancakes, Michael gave Detective Brill a quick rundown of Mimi's night in Larnsdale. After which, he grew quiet. Mimi heard him say, "yeah," "okay," "uh-huh," "jeez," and "really, Rita? That can't be right." Whatever she was telling him, it didn't sound good.

"All right," he finished up. "Let's talk later." He ended the call.

"What is it?" Mimi asked.

Michael balled a napkin in his fist. "This morning, while you were taking a nap behind a tree, the Lowerys went to the local police to press criminal charges against you for stealing that brooch."

"We didn't steal the brooch!" Mimi banged her fist. "We bought it legally. Detective Brill knows that."

"They also say you stole a dress."

Mimi glanced down at her outfit. It was Rosalyn's. In the heat of the moment, she'd forgotten to change out of it.

"That's ridiculous!" she said. "Archibald suggested I pick something from Rosalyn's closet. So, I forgot to return it. Big deal. How much is it worth?"

"Two thousand dollars," Michael said. "Apparently, it's some stupid designer thing."

"My God. What's it made out of—gold? If it's such a big deal to them, I'll give it back."

"Let me explain how this works," Michael said. "They don't drop theft charges just because you give something back.

"They also claimed to have security footage that shows you threatening Archibald Lowery with a knife. I told Detective Brill that didn't sound right. You wouldn't pull a knife on someone."

Mimi gulped. "Actually—"

"Oh jeez," Michael moaned.

"I did. Sort of."

"*Sort of?* How do you sort-of pull a knife on someone?"

"It was self-defense," Mimi said. "Archibald was trying to take the brooch from me. And I was still hyper after running from that man. So I took the knife out of my pocketbook."

"And then what?" Michael asked, his eyes big. "Did you threaten him with it?"

"No."

"Are you sure? You never said anything threatening?"

Mimi thought for a second. "Well, actually—"

"Oh God," Michael whimpered. "Not another 'actually.'"

"I said I *might* use it. Hypothetically."

"You said you might stab him?"

"*Hypothetically,*" Mimi stressed.

"You do realize most threats are hypothetical? That's why they're threats." Michael cupped his head in his hands. "I have to say, you're not bowling me over with your great interpersonal skills."

"Very funny." Mimi crossed her arms.

"There's nothing funny about this," Michael said sternly. "You could be facing criminal charges. The Lowerys have a big law firm behind them. You can't ignore this. Luckily, Detective Brill told me they're probably not going to arrest you."

"Probably?" Just the thought that she might get arrested made Mimi want to throw up her breakfast.

"At this point, I wouldn't take anything for granted. Even though you may not have intended to do anything wrong, that video footage could be enough to convince a cop to take you in. My guess is you won't serve any jail time."

That made Mimi feel better—until she thought how far she'd sunk, that she was relieved at not going to jail.

"The Lowerys just want to make your life as unpleasant as possible, so they can get what they want, which is that brooch," Michael said. "But if they're feeling especially vindictive, who knows?

"And there's another problem. I'm a cop, and you're now the subject of a criminal complaint that's being investigated by one of my colleagues. It wouldn't look good for us to associate. I know we just sort of got back together, but we shouldn't talk until this is through. I shouldn't even drive you home."

Mimi tossed up her hands. "Fine. I'll order an Uber." She picked up her phone, then stopped herself. "Actually, can you—?"

"I'll take you home," he said with a deep sigh. "Also—" He reached into his pockets. "Here's your stuff I found by the roadside."

He took out her lipstick, makeup, and mirror. That was everything that fell from her purse, except for Rosalyn's diary. "Did you notice anything else?" Mimi asked. "Like a red book?"

"No," Michael said blankly. "What kind of book?"

"Just a notebook I use to jot things down. It was about the size of a magazine."

"Nope. And I inspected the area pretty thoroughly. If it was there, I would have seen it."

Mimi figured this was probably not a good time to bring up that she'd—accidentally—left the Lowerys with Rosalyn's diary in her purse. But why wasn't it at the side of the road with everything else? The wind could have blown it away, but it didn't move her other things. Maybe George Morton, fake Uber driver, took it. But why would he? What would he want with it?

THEY PAID THE DINER BILL, AND TRUDGED to Michael's car. Michael silently drove out of the parking lot, his lips locked and face grim.

Out of the blue, he leaned toward Mimi and said, "If they do arrest you, and I'm not saying they will—"

"Do you really think they'll arrest me?" That was not how Mimi wanted to begin this trip.

"Of course, they might," Michael said. "The Lowerys are a well-known family. They probably have a lot of pull with the local police. Rita said the only thing stopping them from issuing an arrest warrant is they want to figure out what happened with you and that Uber driver. Apparently, the Lowerys haven't been too forthcoming on that front. But the police will probably want to talk to you soon. It's also possible they'll do more than that."

"Okay." Mimi tried to digest this. The idea that she could be arrested felt crazy, impossible. Michael made it suddenly seem real. "If I have to go to jail, I will. I've solved two murders. I can handle it."

"Oh please," Michael said. "You can't handle jail."

"What are you trying to do, scare me?"

"No!" Michael shot back. "Of course not. I'm just letting you know it won't be fun in there."

"I wasn't expecting it to be a party!"

"It's not worth talking about, because for the moment you're not there, and hopefully you never will be." Michael's hands gripped the steering wheel. "But here's a few tips just in case, you know, they do go after you." He tried to stay matter-of-fact, but at the last part, his voice cracked. "It's against my nature as a cop to offer this advice, but if they do arrest you, keep quiet until you've spoken to your lawyer. I know that will be a challenge."

"Very funny."

"I'm not joking. You have a tendency to talk yourself into trouble."

Mimi brought her arms to her chest. "When have I ever done that?"

"A million times," Michael said. "And whatever they ask you, just give them your name, address, and birthday, and say you won't talk without counsel present. Be polite and cooperative, but stay firm on that point. That's well within your rights, and they'll know that.

"Along those lines, until this is resolved, you shouldn't talk about this case to anyone, including your father, Channah, and me. Only discuss this with your lawyer. Otherwise, you risk undermining your case."

"Really?"

"Yes!" Michael was growing agitated. "Anything you say from now on could be used against you. You have to be extremely careful." His body flinched. "Let's talk about something else."

"Like what?"

"I don't know!" Michael erupted. "Obviously, we can't discuss what's on both our minds. It's strange for me, being on the other side of something like this. Not that I'm the target here, but it feels like—" He groaned. "How about we not talk? Let's listen to the news."

His hand shook as he switched on the radio. For a few minutes, they listened to commercials for fixing bad credit, a public service announcement on the dangers of getting "catfished," and—finally—a travel website.

"Michael," Mimi said tentatively.

"What?" he snapped.

"Maybe after this is over, we can take a trip together. We could both use a vacation. Maybe get away from the city for a while. I haven't gone anywhere in years."

"Didn't you hear what I just said?" he huffed. "This may not be over for a long time. And even when it is over, I'll have a lot of thinking to do."

"Okay." Mimi crumpled her face to keep from crying.

Michael started tapping the steering wheel. His head rolled back and forth. He mumbled, "Ambergris Caye."

"What?"

He turned off the radio. "Ambergris Caye. It's an island in Belize. I'm not saying we'll go there for sure. I'm saying it's a possibility. It's a place I've always wanted to go."

"Why there?"

"It has great scuba diving."

"I've never scuba-dived."

"Really?" Michael said. "Never? It's amazing. You get an incredible view of the ocean."

For the rest of the ride, Michael discussed his love for scuba diving—which he'd only done three times, but acted like an expert on, in a way that Mimi had grown quite familiar with. Mimi mentioned that she'd gone snorkeling once, but had to stop when she became seasick. Michael found that amusing. It was a nice, fun, relaxing conversation. It made Mimi feel a million times better.

WHEN THE CAR ARRIVED AT MIMI'S APARTMENT, Michael asked, "Do you want me to stick around?"

"Of course I do." Mimi touched his leg. "But I assume you want to get back to your daughter."

"Yeah," he said. "I gotta relieve my mom. I woke the poor woman up at ten-thirty last night, to ask her to come over and watch Catherine while I searched for you."

"Tell her I appreciate it," Mimi said. "I've never told you this, but I'd like to meet them someday."

"Yeah, I'm sure. Though, honestly, they're annoyed with you right now. They think you're crazy for always getting involved in these things."

"Okay." Mimi took this in. "Please tell them that I'm nice crazy. And well-meaning crazy. And sometimes even fun crazy."

Michael laughed. "I'll pass that on. I'll admit, if there's a good kind of crazy, you're it."

That prompted a smile. "Thanks. I think."

There was a long pause. It was time for Mimi to leave the car. This would ordinarily be when they'd kiss goodbye. Their heads bobbed and moved toward each other. But it didn't feel right, so Mimi just gave Michael a peck on the cheek. For the moment, that would have to do.

ONCE MIMI GOT INSIDE HER APARTMENT, and double-locked the doors, she felt happy to be home—surprisingly so. She'd always been ashamed of her small rundown apartment. But after her weekend in the lap of luxury, she appreciated the place, in a way she never had before. It might not be much, but it was hers.

She stripped off her tattered clothes—including the ridiculously expensive dress she was accused of stealing—and contemplated a shower. Even that felt like too much. She climbed into bed, wrapped herself in a blanket, and crashed.

She was woken from her sleep by a call on her newly-charged phone. It was her dad.

"How are you?" Mimi asked him groggily.

"Not so good," he answered. "You see, I have this daughter, who told me Friday she was going to fix everything with this brooch that's given me nothing but *tsuris* for the past week.

"And this morning, I was all set to have a nice relaxing Sunday. I figured I'd read the paper, maybe go for a walk. But instead, I get a call from my lawyer, a Mr. Rabinowitz, who, I should mention, charges three hundred dollars an hour. And this Mr. Rabinowitz tells me that actually, my daughter didn't fix everything with the Lowerys, and that, in fact, she now faces criminal charges for pulling a knife on the CEO of one of the world's most prestigious jewelers. Did I dream that, or do I now have to worry about my middle daughter going to jail?"

Mimi groaned. "That's a little reductive."

"I can't wait to hear the whole story. I'm sure it's ten times worse."

"It isn't! It's fine. I didn't do anything wrong. I just can't discuss it right now. Michael said I should only talk about it with our lawyer."

"You know what? That's probably for the best. I've gobbled enough Tums already. Speaking of our lawyer, he also told me that the Lowerys plan to sue my business for five million dollars. They apparently have me confused with someone who has five million dollars."

Mimi's throat tightened, like she was drowning in a sea of bad news. "Dad, I'm sorry. I was just trying to help. There were all these threats against your company and I wanted to settle things."

"Great job you did there," Max said. "Did I mention I'm being sued for five million dollars? You know if they win this suit against me, I might have to declare bankruptcy? I might even have to give up my house."

Mimi couldn't believe how much trouble she was in, and how much she'd caused. "Yes, Dad, I know that. I'm sorry if this is stressing you out. I didn't mean to cause you any problems." Her voice quavered. "I love you and I'll work something out. It'll be okay. I promise."

She started sobbing, and covered the phone so her dad wouldn't hear.

"It's all right, *bubelah*," Max said, suddenly conciliatory. "You don't have to apologize. I love you, too. I know you're trying to do the right thing, which with you isn't always the sane thing. Just call Rabinowitz. He's been trying to reach you all day."

Mimi glanced at her phone. There were three missed calls from Rabinowitz.

"We'll get this straightened out," Max said. "And if the police try anything with you, let them know they'll have an angry old Jew on their hands."

Mimi laughed. "I'm sure that'll petrify them."

MIMI GAVE RABINOWITZ A QUICK RUNDOWN OF HER DAY with the Lowerys, from her arrival to her fight with the scary Uber man.

"Okay," he said, in professional-lawyer voice. "That roughly comports with what the police told me. From everything I hear, the Lowerys have a weak case. I haven't seen the video, but if it shows that Archibald Lowery went at you first, you'll have a credible case of self-defense. We can establish you were a good-faith purchaser of the brooch. And the thing about the dress is just nonsense. They gave that to you to wear, and you left with it. Big deal. That they even brought that up, shows they're just being desperate and vindictive, throwing charges at the wall to see what sticks. I'll use that to discredit their whole complaint."

"That makes me feel so much better," Mimi said.

"Don't feel too good, kiddo," Rabinowitz said. "You're not home free yet. But you're obviously not a thief. If you were going to steal stuff from their big fancy house, you would have snatched more than a dress. I mean, you didn't take anything else from their house, right? Not a tissue, not a tube of toothpaste."

It dawned on Mimi. Her jaw slackened. "Actually," she said meekly. "There might be one more thing."

"One more thing? What is this, *Columbo*? What was it?"

"Rosalyn Lowery's diary," Mimi mumbled.

"Rosalyn Lowery? You mean, the murder victim?"

"Yeah, I found her diary and left with it in my purse." Mimi paused. "I didn't mean to! It just happened."

"Okay," Rabinowitz said. "You should probably hand that over to the police. It could be considered evidence."

"I can't. I dropped it when I was running from the car. Later, Michael found some stuff that I dropped, but not that."

"This diary you took, it's missing?"

"I think so," Mimi said, suddenly in a panic. "Maybe we can send someone to look for it."

"Maybe," Rabinowitz said. "But let me get this straight. You're telling me that you removed a possible piece of evidence in a murder case from the Lowery's residence and you have no idea where it is. Is that correct?"

"Yes." Mimi could almost see him shaking his head in pity and astonishment. "That's bad, isn't it?"

Rabinowitz took a second before answering. "It ain't good."

CHAPTER TWENTY-FIVE

MIMI BARELY SLEPT THAT NIGHT. She just lay in bed, staring at the ceiling, anxious and angry. The Lowerys *did* have a weak case. There was only one reason they'd bring criminal charges against her: to stop her from investigating. Which was why she couldn't quit.

By five a.m., she gave up on getting a full night's rest. She turned on the lights, and took another look at the Heartbrooch—the multi-million-dollar piece she'd placed in a shoebox under her bed, where it lay innocently all night. For the last week, that brooch had dominated her life. It might even ruin it, as it had supposedly ruined others'.

She held it to the light. Was it really cursed? It didn't appear particularly scary, or for that matter, all that valuable. Yes, it had an interesting design, and it was attractive enough, but it wasn't *that* nice. She had no idea why so many people wanted it.

Mimi noticed the back pin was bent—probably from being wielded as a weapon, the only time Mimi had any real use for it.

Mimi wanted to talk to the Lowery expert that Rosalyn consulted the day she died. That person might be key to this. But when she searched online for buyers of vintage Lowery jewelry, every listing was for either a big auction house or small second-hand dealer. No one really stood out as a Lowery specialist. Rosalyn's exclusive buyer was apparently too exclusive for Google.

Mimi did spot a listing for Joey Goulding, a jewelry repairman whose bare-bones website said he'd "spent years as one of Lowery's top craftsmen." His specialty was rehabbing "high-value" Lowery pieces. "I'm also an occasional buyer of Lowery items," it added. His office—in a Forty-Seventh Street basement—didn't look like the kind of place Rosalyn would frequent, but it was the only thing Mimi found that even resembled a lead. She left a message for Goulding at about six a.m. Two hours later, he called back.

"Wow." Mimi glanced at the clock. It was eight a.m. "You get in early."

"I've been busy," said a voice with a New York accent as sharp as a brooch pin. "What can I help you with?"

"I have an original Lowery piece and was wondering if you'd be willing to buy it."

"I don't buy many pieces. Sometimes I take them on consignment. But that's it. What are you looking to sell?"

"It's a famous piece," Mimi said. "The Heartbrooch."

There was a pause, and for a moment, Mimi thought the line went dead. "Did you say the Heartbrooch?" he asked, his voice leaping an octave.

"Yes."

"Wow. I helped craft that piece, many years ago. And you have it?"

"I do."

"Huh," Goulding said. "I read somewhere it was owned by that Lowery woman who died."

That was a clear sign that Goulding wasn't Rosalyn's "exclusive buyer."

"Yes," Mimi said. "Rosalyn Lowery. I was a friend of hers."

"So you have the Heartbrooch? Really? I can't afford to buy that. And honestly, I don't know many people who could. You should try the auction houses."

Rosalyn had specifically said she wanted to avoid that channel, because it would bring too much publicity.

"Yeah, I'm not interested in selling to them," Mimi said. "If you can recommend anyone else, I'd appreciate it."

"No one's coming to mind. That's a real collector's item." He sounded wary, like Mimi was some nut claiming to have a famous piece.

Mimi wanted to keep this conversation going. If Goulding helped craft the Heartbrooch, he might be able to shed some light on it.

"Can I bring it to your shop for repairs?" Mimi asked. "It's a little damaged."

"Really? That kind of piece would be hard to mess up. What's the problem?"

"The back pin's bent."

"How'd that happen?"

Mimi decided not to say that she stabbed a fake Uber driver with it. "Normal wear and tear."

"You can bring it by and I'll take a look at it," Goulding said. "I'll be here all day."

She made an appointment with him for later that morning.

BEFORE THAT, SHE HAD A TEN o'clock meeting with Rabinowitz. When she entered his office, he wasn't the sober lawyer she'd talked to the night before, but his usual genial self. He sank into his brown leather chair and leaned all the way back, a smile spread across his face.

"I have great news," Rabinowitz said. "You'll never guess what happened. I just talked to the Lowery people. They are willing to drop all charges. I've become a great lawyer in my old age."

A sense of calm washed over Mimi. "Did they give any reason?"

"When they heard you were attacked after you left their premises, they offered to drop the charges on humanitarian grounds."

After spending the last day anxious and crazed, Mimi couldn't believe her problems had vanished so easily.

"That doesn't make sense," Mimi said. "The Lowerys don't do anything for humanitarian reasons. That guy who attacked me, probably worked for them. He was on their estate. It's highly unlikely he was there without them knowing it. This sounds suspicious to me."

"It does to me, too, kiddo," said Rabinowitz. "That's not our problem, though. Let the police worry about that."

"But the Lowerys are a big deal in that town. The police may be afraid of them."

"I'm no *maven* on the Larnsdale police department. I don't want to be, either. And I haven't told you the whole story. The Lowerys will only drop the charges under one condition."

"Let me guess. They want the Heartbrooch."

Rabinowitz giggled. "You got it, kiddo. They're willing to recoup what your father paid, and shoulder any costs associated with future litigation. It's essentially the same deal you had with them. They mentioned you were supposed to write something for them for seventy-five thousand dollars. That's out."

"Fine," Mimi said. "I don't want to write that stupid book anyway. But something about this doesn't feel right. I don't like it."

"Unfortunately," Rabinowitz leaned over his desk, his cufflinks gleaming, "in a lot of cases, one party doesn't like how a legal action ends. Sometimes both parties don't. Usually, it's just for the best that they end."

That sounded like a well-rehearsed line.

"This is a good deal," he continued. "The local police might be filing an arrest warrant for you any second, so I strongly suggest you take it. If you're ever arrested, and that Rosalyn diary stuff comes out, you could be in big trouble.

"Let's get this over with." He slapped the desk. "Do you have the brooch with you?"

"Yes." The Heartbrooch was nestled in a plastic bag in Mimi's purse. She took it out and stared at it—wondering, again, what the fuss was about.

"When do they want it by?" Mimi asked.

"Their counsel just emailed me the agreement. You need to sign it now, and after that they'll send a messenger over."

"When would that be?"

Rabinowitz checked his watch. "It's ten o'clock. The guy probably will come over in about an hour. With any luck, this will be settled by lunch."

Mimi flashed back to another time she regularly consulted a lawyer—when she worked at the newspaper. The paper's counsel would make her remove damaging info from articles, so they wouldn't get sued. She would sputter that everything she wrote was one hundred percent accurate, but he'd insist she take out anything that might pose a problem. And in the end, she'd listen.

In retrospect, she should have pushed back more, or convinced her editor to print some of the things the lawyer objected to. But she didn't want to get sued, either. And because of that, she missed a few good stories, and let some bad people get away with some bad stuff.

Now, she was facing something ten times worse than a lawsuit. She didn't want to get arrested. But she also knew—as she had with her past investigations—she was in too deep to stop now.

"We shouldn't agree to this," she declared. "I don't trust the Lowerys. I won't sign it."

The good cheer drained from Rabinowitz's face. "You have to! I spent all morning negotiating this deal. It gets you completely off the hook."

"Yes," Mimi said, "but it also lets the Lowerys off the hook. And that's what they're counting on. Every time they've threatened something, they've backed down, just like they're backing down now. That's despite having all the money, and all the leverage. That's how they operate, through threats and intimidation. It's how they've always operated. It's how they've kept so much secret. We can't let them keep getting away with that."

"Why not? Who cares? That's not our business!" Rabinowitz almost levitated from his chair. "You getting arrested, that's our business. I'm strongly advising you to take this offer. Years ago, I had a client—"

"I don't want to hear a story!" Mimi declared, then cringed.

She was sounding like her dad. She took a calming breath. "I need more time."

"For what?"

"Research."

"Research? What do you think this is? A term paper!" Rabinowitz flung out his arms. "Your neck is on the line. Their offer expires at three p.m. today. It's contingent upon you returning this brooch ASAP. Now, come on. Hand it over."

"How about this?" Mimi said. "I'll give you the brooch tomorrow afternoon. Let me have twenty-four hours."

"I don't think you understand the trouble you're facing."

Mimi dropped the brooch in her purse.

"My God," Rabinowitz cried. "It's like I'm talking to a wall. In fact, I think a wall might actually listen to me. 'Hello, wall. You don't want to get arrested, do you?' 'No, of course not. I'm not stupid. I might be just a wall, but I don't want to go to jail.'"

"Give me twenty-four hours," Mimi said.

"That's fine with me. It's them you have to worry about."

"Call their bluff. They'll back down. I guarantee it."

"What if they don't?"

"Find a way to stall."

His brow wrinkled. "How do I do that?"

"Make something up. You're a lawyer. You're good at that."

Rabinowitz usually chuckled good-naturedly at lawyer jokes, but he didn't laugh then. "I need a reason. They're expecting you to go along with this."

"Tell them you're indisposed. Say you have a medical condition."

"That's true. You're giving me a heart attack."

Mimi smacked the side of the chair. "I got it. This morning, I talked to this repair guy, and said I'd bring him the Heartbrooch to get fixed." She plucked it from her purse. "Look. Its back pin is bent. Tell them we're having it repaired before we return it. You can even send them a picture, showing that it's damaged. They wouldn't want a broken piece."

"You don't think Lowery has repair people?"

"Of course they do," Mimi said. "But if I drop it off at a repair shop, they'll have to wait until it's fixed. We can even show them the slip."

"What are you talking about?" Rabinowitz said. "That piece isn't damaged. The back pin is bent. Big deal. Any repair guy can fix that in five minutes. That doesn't give you a day."

Mimi thought for a moment. "Okay."

She clutched the piece in her hand, and smashed it against the edge of Rabinowitz's desk. When that didn't work, she perched it on the edge of her chair, and banged his stapler against the back pin until it finally broke off. Afterward, she proudly held up the broken brooch in one hand, the pin in the other. "Is it damaged enough now?"

Rabinowitz appeared ready to faint.

CHAPTER TWENTY-SIX

AFTER MIMI LEFT RABINOWITZ'S OFFICE, she walked to Forty-Seventh Street to pay a call on Joey Goulding, former Lowery craftsman turned jewelry repair-guy. His office was located below street level in one of the older buildings on Forty-Seventh Street. The elevator was so rickety Mimi decided to take the stairs.

Goulding's office wasn't actually an office, more a glorified cubby. It was about the size of a bathroom stall, and about as attractive. It was in the rear of a windowless basement, which housed a sea of men all working in similar confined spaces. The air was filled with the faint smell of chemicals.

Goulding had thin tousled white hair, yellow teeth, and a long craggy face. He sported an off-white shirt with an open collar, which revealed an undershirt and red surgical scar. He had a pack of cigarettes in his shirt pocket—Camel, unfiltered.

He sat at a gray wooden desk, with half its paint peeled off. It was covered with tools, stray pieces of gold, and baggies full of jewelry. A photo of Wyllis Lowery was tacked on the side wall.

Goulding removed papers from a chair so Mimi could sit down. When she pulled out the Heartbrooch, his eyebrows rose to his forehead.

"That looks like the real deal." He snatched a pair of glasses from his desk, putting them on after cleaning them with his shirt.

She handed him the brooch. He brought it to his eyes, dumbstruck.

"There's stories the diamond's cursed," Mimi said. "Do you believe that?"

He stopped staring at the brooch and rolled his eyes. "Of course not. That's just silliness. Wyllis Lowery was a master of hype. He knew talking about a curse would bring tons of publicity. Though given what happened afterward, who knows, right?"

He studied the brooch with a jeweler's loupe. "Yep, that's a genuine Lowery hallmark."

He turned it over, and saw the broken pin on the back. "And, you're right, it's damaged. You're telling me this happened with normal wear and tear?"

Mimi shrugged. "Pretty much."

He turned it over again. "This doesn't seem like a normal thing to happen." He peered at her over his glasses. "Classic Lowery jewelry was built to last."

"Aren't all pieces vulnerable to breakage?"

"Sure, but not like—" He took a cigarette out of his shirt pocket, and twirled it in his fingers. "In the days we made this, we prided ourselves on being master craftsmen. We wanted to produce pieces that would last forever. We would spend all night trying to perfect one little detail no consumer would notice. But we would. And so would the guys at the other houses. That kind of thing mattered in those days."

"It doesn't anymore?"

"It does, sometimes. But everything's different now. A lot of the big brands design everything by computer, and they make it in China, because that's where it's cheapest to produce. There's still plenty of good craftsmen, and some of them make excellent stuff. But it's not like the old days, when we'd sweat over every last detail. Back then, there was a human being behind every item.

"Jewelry making is a two-thousand-year-old art, and I feel like my generation will be the last to truly practice it. And working for Wyllis Lowery, may he rest in peace, you had to be on your toes, or you'd be out the door."

Mimi pointed to the picture of Wyllis. "It seems like you admire Mr. Lowery. What was he like?"

"He was not an easy person," Goulding conceded. "He was demanding. Not always nice. He didn't just want everything perfect. He wanted it perfect-plus.

"But at the end of the day, he was honest. Which I can't say for the rest of the family. After Wyllis was killed, I decided I couldn't work there anymore. Especially given the circumstances."

"What do you mean by the circumstances?" Mimi asked. "The robbery?"

"Yeah, that's right." He laughed mirthlessly. "They called it a 'robbery.'"

"Are you saying it wasn't?"

"Hey, hey." He stuck up a bony finger. "I didn't say that. Don't put words in my mouth. I gotta be careful."

"I know some background about the robbery," Mimi offered. "I know that Wyllis Lowery and Josephine Tomaso were romantically involved."

"Well, if you own this brooch, of course you know that. The inscription makes that clear."

"Actually, the inscription has been changed," Mimi said.

"What do you mean?"

"It used to say, 'JT loves WL' on it," Mimi continued. "But now there's just the initials. No 'loves.'"

"Really?" said Goulding. "But how can that—" He inspected it with his loupe. He was flummoxed. "You're right. It's gone. You didn't remove it, did you?"

"No," Mimi replied. "I got it that way."

"Someone's erased any trace of the word 'loves' from the piece. I don't see how—"

"Can I ask a question?" Mimi said. "You said that Wyllis Lowery's murder wasn't an accident. Is that a reference to Tomaso having relatives in the Mafia? Did the Mob kill Mr. Lowery?"

Goulding scowled. "No, that's a bunch of baloney. Who told you that?"

"I don't know. It was talk I heard."

His mouth curved down. "I know where you heard it." He put the brooch down on his desk, as the cigarette danced in his fingers. "The Lowerys. That was the spin they put out. There was a brief moment when people in the trade questioned the robbery story. Everyone knew that Wyllis never traveled with goods. So, they told people it was the Mafia. Which was completely unfair to Josephine. It put this cloud over her when she was unable to defend herself."

"So, what really happened?"

He waved away the question. "I can't say."

"Are you sure?"

"It's an ugly story. You don't want to hear it."

"I understand," Mimi said. "It's old news and not worth talking about."

"Exactly."

"Although, I have to admit you've piqued my curiosity. I'll ask the Lowerys about it."

Goulding's body grew stiff. "You know the Lowerys?"

"Not well. But I've met them a few times. I told you, I was a friend of Rosalyn's. That's how I got the—"

"Yeah, yeah," Goulding interrupted. "Listen, do me a favor. Don't ask them about this. They'll get their lawyers after me. They are really sensitive about their image."

"I understand," Mimi said. "I won't mention your name. I'll just tell them I heard it from one of their old craftsmen."

"Don't say that!" Goulding nearly screamed. "They'll know it was me."

"But what else do you expect me to do?" Mimi said, in her best faux-innocent voice. "You've made me very curious."

Goulding grew jumpy. "Don't say anything. Forget I mentioned it."

"But you told me that, given what happened, this piece might be cursed. Shouldn't I know the truth about what happened? Otherwise, I won't know if my piece was cursed."

"But that's—" His face drooped. "Come on, lady. Give me a break here. I don't want trouble from those people."

"Just tell me what happened," Mimi said firmly. "Then, I promise, I won't mention it to the Lowerys."

Goulding's eyes flicked around his cube, in search of an escape. There was none. She had him cornered.

"All right," he said. "I'll tell you, but don't spread it around. Seriously, I don't want anyone to know I told you this. This is real secret inside stuff. I haven't told anybody this in years."

"I swear," Mimi said. "I'll keep you out of it. My word is my bond."

He drew a deep breath. "I'll tell you what I can. The old man, Nicholas Lowery, who founded the company, was what we used to call a complicated person. That's a nice way of saying he was a prick.

"He was all business, all the time. He used to say that diamonds were like his children. Which was true. His actual kid, Wyllis, he treated like crap.

"He wanted Wyllis to marry someone who would advance the company. So he hooked him up with this woman Claudia. She was kind of difficult, but her father was this big financier, who was basically bankrolling the whole operation. Nicholas needed to keep that guy in the tent."

Wow. Mimi thought. *The Lowerys sure like their tents.*

"But when Josephine Tomaso came into the picture, Wyllis fell head over heels in love with her. You gotta understand, Wyllis was a guy who talked a lot about love and romance in his marketing, but it was no B.S. with him. He believed it. He was a true romantic. And in those days, Josephine Tomaso was a very attractive girl.

"Then Tomaso designs that brooch, and Claudia sees the inscription which says 'loves' on it, and flips out. She reaches out to her father and says, 'you tell Nicholas that if his son doesn't stop playing around, our marriage is over.' This got Nicholas very concerned, since that would have killed the company piggy bank. So the old man sat Wyllis down, and forbid him to see Tomaso again.

But Wyllis was as stubborn as his old man. He said, 'don't worry, the business will be fine.' They got into a huge argument."

Goulding became silent. He appeared deep in thought.

"Go on," Mimi said.

"So now, we're getting to the ugly part. Nicholas, the old man, developed a cockamamie plan he thought would fix everything. He approached this kid in his factory—some moron who wanted to buddy up to the boss—and flashed a wad of bills at him. Nicholas told him the whole story and said, 'I need you to threaten Josephine, tell her to break things off with my son.'

"So, the guy approaches Josephine as she was walking home one night, and makes all sorts of threats. What he didn't know was Wyllis was waiting for her just down the street. And like a lot of jewelers in those days, Wyllis carried a gun. So Wyllis runs up to the guy, starts scrapping with him, and pulls out his weapon. And the guy tries to get the gun away from Wyllis, and they have this scuffle, and the gun goes off, and Wyllis ends up dead.

"Of course, the old man knew who shot his son, but he couldn't say anything. He'd set it up. So, he put out word that his son was killed in a robbery. And the local police bought it, because in those days, lots of jewelers were being robbed.

"But the old man was so horrified about what he'd done, he lost his mind. And one day, he walked up to that beautiful roof deck he'd built on top of that manor of his, and jumped off it."

"That's terrible," Mimi said. "Didn't Josephine Tomaso say anything?"

"No. She was too traumatized. She'd just seen the man she loved, gunned down right in front of her face. She was young, twenty-seven years old, and scared to death. She just wanted to get the hell out of New York. So she went back to Italy, and completely quit the business."

"She didn't report this to the police?" Mimi asked.

"She was too scared of the Lowerys. And once the old man died, she figured, he was the main problem, so what's the point? She just wanted to get on with her life. I don't blame her."

A thought occurred to Mimi. "How do you know all this?"

"Let's just say I heard it from a first-hand source," Goulding said. "The Lowerys are extremely lucky this never came out. It's a real ugly story. It's enough to make you think the brooch truly is cursed.

"Remember, you didn't hear any of this from me. The last thing I want is the Lowerys coming after me."

"I won't say anything." Mimi held up her hand.

"Anyway, that's why I left Lowery. It's a shame, because I loved my job, and I respected Wyllis. But I no longer wanted to be part of that organization.

"If you don't mind, I'd like to inspect this piece a little longer. How about you leave it with me, and I'll call you in a bit?"

Mimi was uneasy leaving the brooch with Goulding; it was now her get-out-of-jail-free card. "Okay, but make sure you give me a repair slip. And don't try to run away with it. My boyfriend's a cop."

"Yeah, yeah, yeah," Goulding said, as he filled out the slip. "Don't worry. I'm not going anywhere, certainly not with that thing."

As Mimi left Joey Goulding's office-slash-cube, she checked her phone. Rabinowitz had sent her five texts—all insisting she call him immediately.

"I don't think the Lowerys are bluffing this time," one said. "You're in serious danger of getting arrested." He'd also left two voicemails, which said the same thing.

"Hi Elliot," Mimi responded, smiling to herself. "Tell the Lowerys I am once again interested in writing their family history. Except this time, it will be the REAL history."

"What does that mean?" Rabinowitz wrote back.

Mimi didn't reply. She was on a mission.

CHAPTER TWENTY-SEVEN

Mimi settled on a bench in Bryant Park to plot her next move. She'd just learned something important about the Lowerys. She needed to find out if all the crazy events in the past had any connection to the crazy events in the present.

She sent Darlene a quick message on Signal. "Can we talk?"

Darlene didn't answer.

She also messaged Vanessa. She didn't write back, either.

Okay, Mimi told herself. *Be patient. They'll get back to you eventually.*

She did hear from Rabinowitz, who kept sending her texts, warning she was about to get arrested. She tried to ignore them, but couldn't help but feel unnerved at his increasingly frantic tone.

She spotted a police officer walking in her direction. Her body froze. Was he coming to arrest her? And if he was, what should she do? Run? Wouldn't that get her charged with evading arrest? Maybe she should call Rabinowitz.

Her heart thumped as the cop drew closer. She turned her face away. He got to her bench, then kept walking. She glanced up at him. He nodded, and strolled by.

Mimi took a breath. The pressure was getting to her. She needed someone to talk to. She considered going to her father's office. But there was one problem: her father. He'd also left her a constant stream of messages, none of which she listened to.

Finally, she called Channah.

"Hi there," Channah said brightly. "I was worried about you. Your father says you're in trouble and no one can find you."

"He's exaggerating. I'm fine. There's just some things I have to figure out."

"Did you hear the good news?" Channah asked.

"No." For a moment, Mimi thought Channah had changed her mind and was going to marry Zeke.

Instead, Channah said, "They caught the three guys who attacked Zeke."

Mimi slapped her forehead. "Really? Wow."

"Yes. Detective Brill called me a little while ago. We're going to the police station to identify them a little later. We might have to pick them out of a line-up. Just like on TV!"

Her voice dropped. "Though, honestly, I don't know if I want to see those guys again, even standing behind glass. They were scary and nasty. Detective Brill said she might call you, since you saw them, too."

"She hasn't called yet," Mimi said. "And for the moment, I am not supposed to talk to her."

"Why not?" Channah said. "She's been super-helpful."

"It's a long story. Did Detective Brill tell you who those men were?"

"Not really," Channah said. "She said they worked for a local player upstate."

"A local player?"

"Like a bad guy. Someone who does illegal things. I think he was a loan shark or something."

"He was probably one of the people Shepherd Lowery owed money to. I know he pledged the Heartbrooch to some shady characters as collateral."

"Hold it," Channah said. "Which one is Shepherd Lowery?"

Mimi forgot how far down the rabbit hole she'd gone. "It doesn't matter." Mimi bit her lip. "Did the police tell you anything else about those guys? I know they followed Rosalyn, too. Could they have killed her?"

"Detective Brill said probably not. Those guys were on the subway, following us, when Rosalyn was, you know—"

"Yeah, that makes sense," Mimi said. "But how did they know Shepherd gave the brooch to Rosalyn? Maybe they were the same guys who broke into Shepherd Lowery's house and stole his computer the night he killed himself."

"Mimi, you've lost me again."

"That's right. I'm sorry. You don't need to hear about all this. I'm just happy those men were caught."

"Me too. Zeke and I are going out to a celebratory dinner tonight."

"So are you and Zeke—?"

Channah's voice turned flat. "No. It doesn't change anything, if that's what you're asking. The engagement's still off. And actually, Mimi, that's something I want to talk to you about. Your father told me how you went to the Lowerys to learn about the curse."

"Yes, I did," Mimi said. "But understand, I didn't do it to pressure you into marrying Zeke. I just wanted to find out—"

"It's fine!" Channah interrupted. "I'm not mad. I appreciate it."

"Okay." Mimi's mind snapped into action. "Because I learned some things. Remember, you asked me, if the diamond wasn't cursed, why did all those terrible things happen to the Lowerys? I know now. Wyllis Lowery was having an affair with the brooch's designer—"

"Mimi, stop!" Channah said.

This so startled Mimi, she actually stopped.

"Of course, there's a reason those things happened," Channah continued. "There's a reason for everything, even if only *Hashem* truly understands it. But that's not what I'm worried about. Don't you get that?"

This confused Mimi. "No."

"Everyone is being so logical about this," Channah said. "Zeke even wrote an algorithm to show me all those events could have been a coincidence. Which was sweet. No one's ever designed an algorithm for me before.

"But what you all don't get is, I know what I'm saying isn't logical. It doesn't matter. When those men attacked Zeke, it reminded me of what happened to Yosef.

"I know the curse is probably fake. But if there's even a one percent chance of something bad happening to Zeke, that's terrifying. Because I've had that happen once. I would never forgive myself if it happened again.

"So that's where I'm stuck. Do you get that?"

"I do," Mimi said. "I wished I didn't, but I do."

"Zeke has been super patient with me," Channah said. "But he wants to get married so badly, I can't keep stringing him along. That's not right. So tonight, I'm going to tell him to find someone else."

"My God, Channah. Do you think that's a good idea?"

"No, I don't. It's a horrible thing to do. I'm dreading it. I want to marry Zeke. But I can't right now. And it's not fair to make him wait and wait and wait. Honestly, I don't know if I'll ever be ready."

Mimi's pulse quickened. "Channah, I know this is not my business, but can you not tell him tonight? Please, wait just a little while longer. Maybe twenty-four hours?"

"Why twenty-four hours?"

"I don't know, but I asked someone else for twenty-four hours to do something, so I figured I might as well do the same with you. I know it doesn't make sense, but hey, neither of us is making sense here, right?"

"Sure," Channah said, stretching out the word. "Oh, hey. Your father's here. He wants to talk to you."

"No, Channah. Do not put him on the phone. I don't want to—"

It was too late. Max had been given—or more likely had snatched—the phone.

"Hello!" he boomed. "Is this my daughter, the fugitive?"

"Dad, I'm not a fugitive! There's no arrest warrant." Her anxiety rose. "Is there?"

"Not that I've heard."

"See? Everything's fine."

"Oh yeah, it's terrific. The police haven't issued an arrest warrant. They'll probably do it five minutes from now but they haven't done it yet. Let's throw a party."

"We can talk later," Mimi said.

"Don't hang up. I have things I want to say to you. You know what really aggravates me?"

"No, and please don't tell me."

Max didn't miss a beat. "I just talked to Rabinowitz. You know, the lawyer I'm paying three hundred dollars an hour to? And you know what he said?"

"No, and please don't tell me."

"All you have to do is give that stupid brooch back and everything will be settled. But he says you won't. What possible reason could you have for not returning it?"

Mimi massaged her scalp. "I can't go into it right now. Can you at least trust I know what I'm doing?"

Max waited a few seconds before responding. "No."

Mimi tightened her grip on the phone. "We can talk later."

"Please. Call Rabinowitz. He's going crazy trying to find you. The poor guy's actually having to work for his money. I'm afraid he'll drop dead from exhaustion."

"I'll think about it. Goodbye."

Mimi hung up, before Max could object to her doing so.

A FEW SECONDS AFTER MIMI ENDED THE CALL, the doubts began. Maybe her father was right.

Yes, she'd discovered the long-hidden story of Wyllis Lowery's death. But that occurred decades ago. She had no idea if that had anything to do with what happened to Rosalyn.

Her only hope was hearing from Darlene or Vanessa, but neither had texted back.

At this point, she might as well give the brooch to the Lowerys. She didn't want to do that, but it was probably her best move. Her investigation wasn't going anywhere.

She called Goulding. "I've decided I don't need the brooch fixed. I'll pick it up now."

"Fine," Goulding said, sounding chipper. "I was going to call you. The brooch is fixed. Told you I wouldn't steal it. I know you didn't trust me."

"I didn't say I didn't trust you, I—"

"Whatever," Goulding said. "I wouldn't want this thing, for any amount of money."

"Why not?" Mimi asked.

"Come over and see."

MIMI RUSHED TO GOULDING'S OFFICE. He proudly brandished the fixed brooch, then dropped it in a plastic baggie and handed it to Mimi.

"I now understand how the brooch broke so easily," he said. "It was what I figured, when I saw that the word 'loves' had been removed without a trace. I even checked with an old friend of mine, and she confirmed it. But if you don't mind, I'll let her tell you about that. She has some questions for you."

"Okay." Mimi inclined her head. "What friend?"

Goulding picked up his phone and dialed. "Josephine Tomaso."

"The famous designer?"

"The one and only," said Goulding. "Except she's not a famous designer anymore. She lives in Europe and goes by a different name, and stays under the radar. But she wants to talk to you. I'm calling her now."

"That is so weird. I thought Josephine Tomaso was dead."

Goulding leaned his phone against a book, as the number rang. "Then say hello to a ghost."

CHAPTER TWENTY-EIGHT

MIMI HAS SEEN PICTURES OF JOSEPHINE TOMASO, marveled at her talent, and read about her wild and crazy seventies days. But now Mimi was about to meet the real deal, if only through a screen.

When Tomaso first appeared, Mimi rubbed her eyes. She thought the former model would be a well-coiffed woman like Claudia Lowery. Instead, Tomaso looked like what she was—a middle-aged Italian woman, wearing glasses, her gray hair wrapped up in a bun. She was sitting in a plain living room on a tattered couch.

In raspy, heavily accented English, Tomaso told Mimi that she lived in the "countryside," but didn't say more than that. Which was fine. Mimi wasn't out to stalk her.

"Miss Tomaso, it's an honor to speak with you," Mimi said.

"Oh please," Tomaso said. "I appreciate you talking to me. You told Joey you own the Heartbrooch and he showed me what you gave him. I have a few questions."

Mimi's heart raced. She remembered that George Morton—the supposed private investigator—said he was representing the Tomaso estate. And while Goulding denied Tomaso was connected to the Mob, it might still be true.

"I purchased it from Rosalyn Lowery," Mimi said, choosing her words with care. "She was an old friend of mine. Unfortunately, she was just killed."

"Okay." Tomaso nodded slightly and leaned forward, intertwining her arms and legs. "And this Rosalyn. She told you it was the Heartbrooch?"

"She didn't call it that specifically."

"How did she get it?" Tomaso asked.

"From her brother-in-law, Shepherd."

Tomaso nibbled on her nail. "I remember Shepherd. He was a little boy when I left America. How did he get it?"

"Shepherd and his brother had a dispute about the family business. He got some jewelry pieces in the settlement. That was one of them."

"Interesting. This is all very strange for me." She picked up a cigarette from the table, and stuck it in her mouth. "It's such a crazy business. That's why I quit. That—and Wyllis."

Mimi's face moved closer to the screen. "I just heard how Wyllis Lowery was killed. Sounds terrible."

"It was." Tomaso struck a match and lit her cigarette. "Wyllis was an amazing man. He had the magic touch with diamonds, with women, with everything. He took his company to a very high level. But his family never appreciated it."

"Why not?" Mimi asked.

Tomaso lifted her shoulders. "That's just how they were. They were cold people. When the father told him not to see me, Wyllis suddenly decided he was madly in love with me and we should run away that minute. Because you could not tell Wyllis Lowery what to do. And if you did, he'd do the opposite."

She took a long drag of her cigarette. "In retrospect, I was quite naive. Wyllis was twenty years older than me. It never would have worked. But I was very young, very unsure of myself. And he painted such romantic pictures. I let myself get swept away." She expelled a cloud of smoke.

"And then to see him, lying on the street, covered in blood—" She paused. She was getting emotional.

A lanky teenage boy entered the room. Tomaso yelled at him in Italian. He skulked away.

"Sorry," Tomaso said, brushing hair away from her face. "I don't want him to hear this."

She took another drag. "It's weird today, thinking about my life back then. I can still remember lying in bed one night, thinking about Wyllis. That's when I came up with the idea for the Heartbrooch. I designed it as a present for Wyllis. We fell in love in twisted circumstances. So I designed a twisted heart. It was a joke, in a way."

She grinned at the memory. While Tomaso no longer resembled her old glamour shots, there was an appealing naturalness to her, especially when she smiled. Mimi could see why so many people—including, apparently, Wyllis Lowery—were so taken with her.

"Unfortunately," Tomaso took a drag, "his wife saw it and that was a problem. But I don't blame her for getting upset. She wasn't supposed to know what I carved on that brooch. I'm sure it was devastating for her."

"So how did she see it?"

"Wyllis liked the brooch so much, he wanted to show it to the world. He could never shut off his business mind. He figured he'd make a splash by unveiling the brooch with that black diamond in it. He knew putting it in a brooch designed by me would generate huge publicity.

"But, I thought, who would put a cursed black stone in a brooch shaped like a heart? It makes you look like you have a black heart. But Wyllis wanted people to scratch their heads about it. Now I think it fit, in a way. The entire family had black hearts.

"That brooch meant a lot to me," Tomaso said. "When I returned to Italy, I didn't take any of my jewelry, except for that brooch. At the time, I was still very much in love with Wyllis, and wanted something to remember him by.

"But I didn't take the black diamond. After Wyllis was killed, I became scared the diamond really was cursed. So I left it in a place where the Lowerys could find it. I figured they deserved whatever bad luck it brought."

Mimi was trying to keep all of this straight. "So hold it. You said you took the brooch with you to Italy. When did you give it back to the Lowerys?"

Tomaso shrugged. "I never did. I never wanted to. When I arrived in Italy, I had no job, no home, nothing. My family had cut me off, because my father didn't approve of a young woman going to New York to become a model and designer. I went through my savings quickly. It was very difficult.

"That brooch was the only valuable thing I owned. I probably could have gotten a hundred *lire* if I melted it down. But I couldn't bear to let it go, because that would mean letting Wyllis go.

"For years, I kept it, because it meant something to me. But one day I was sitting in the backyard, and decided I didn't want it anymore.

"I thought about throwing it in our fireplace, but it's very hard to melt gold with just a fire. I found a blowtorch in our shed out back, and destroyed it that way. I was once so proud of that piece, yet I turned it into a big gold puddle on the floor. I cried, but afterward, I felt better. I didn't even keep the melted gold. I threw it in the garbage. Can you imagine? Throwing gold in the garbage? That's how much I wanted to rid myself of those memories."

"So hold it," Mimi asked. "If you burned the Heartbrooch, then what's this?" Mimi held up the brooch.

"I don't know. It is an imitation of my work. It is a decent imitation; they probably used the same wax model. It has the same design, the same look. That's probably the original black diamond. But it is not my work. You don't see any care in it. I put my soul into every piece. But that piece isn't subtle. It looks like—" She made circles with her hands. "Well, I do not like to say things like this. But it looks like a pair of buttocks."

My God, Mimi thought. *My father was right. It's a* tuchus.

Mimi sat back in her chair, completely shocked. "Did you know this imitation existed?"

"No," Tomaso said. "That's why I wanted to talk to you, to find out how you got it. Because the Lowerys have produced a fake version of my work." She took another drag of her cigarette and reclined on her couch. "But you know what? Now that we're talking about it, I realize I don't care anymore. That's my old life.

"Sometimes I read things on the Internet, and they make me laugh. They said I stalked Wyllis, which was nonsense. They said my father was big in the Mafia. You know what my father did? He was a podiatrist.

"I used to get upset about those stories. Now I think: they are just talking about a dead person, someone who no longer exists.

"I'm happy with my life now. Me and my partner live okay. Not super-fancy, like the old days. But okay.

"It's flattering people are still interested in my work. But that is another world for me. I no longer talk to the friends I had back then. Many of them were great artists, but not so great as people. When I arrived back in Italy, I told myself: 'I know how to be a good designer. Now, I want to become a good person.'"

"And did you?" Mimi asked.

Tomaso shrugged. "I've tried. For the last thirty years, I've taught arts and crafts at a local school. I tell the children to create for the sheer pleasure of it, so they know the thrill of making something beautiful.

"And many of them are quite talented. Some could probably become famous artists, like I was. But I worry about them. They are so sweet and honest and their work is so pure. When you bring fame and money into the picture, it can crush a person."

Tomaso yawned and covered her mouth with her non-cigarette hand. "I am tired. It is late here. This has been an interesting trip down memory lane, but it's reminded me why I left that life behind. I should go. Nice talking with you."

"Thank you for speaking with me," Mimi said. "It was an honor. You're a legend."

Tomaso snuffed out her cigarette and smiled. "I am no longer a legend. I am now just a person. That's much better." With a faint smile, she signed off, and her image vanished from the screen.

Mimi turned to Goulding. "Thanks for that. I enjoyed speaking with her. She seems like a good person."

"She is. A very good person. She's been through a lot. Things we're all still getting over."

Something clicked for Mimi. "You're an old friend of hers?"

"Yes."

"Didn't she say she never talks to any of her old friends?"

"Well, you know." Goulding began to fidget. "Her and me, we have a bond."

"And you said you heard the story of Wyllis Lowery's murder from a first-hand source. That was her, right?"

He wet his lips. "Yeah."

"But you mentioned some things she wouldn't know. Like how Nicholas Lowery got that guy to threaten her."

He bounced around on his chair. "I may have heard that from someone else. I can't remember."

"I would think, with dramatic news like that, you'd remember who told you." Mimi put her hand on her chin, and rested her elbow on the side of her chair. "Did they ever catch the guy who threatened her?"

Goulding's leg jiggled like a jackhammer. "Not as far as I know."

Mimi held her stare. "It must be very difficult to live with a secret like that."

Goulding's Adam's Apple bobbed. He started to answer. Then his body sagged. "All right. How did you know?"

"You said this is something *we're* still getting over," Mimi said. "And you have Wyllis Lowery's picture hanging up on your cubicle. I thought that was odd, because you didn't particularly like the guy."

Goulding's face sank. "You guessed it. I was the idiot who shot Wyllis Lowery. That's why I have his picture here. So I don't forget. Not that I ever have. It was the biggest mistake of my life. Why do you think I went from working from one of the top houses in the business, to working here?"

As much as Mimi had to pry that admission out of him, he

looked relieved to get it off his surgically-scarred chest. It was one hell of a secret to keep all those years.

"And you're in touch with Josephine?" Mimi said.

He nodded. "That started about a decade ago. I kept the money the old man gave me but I never spent it. I considered it blood money. I didn't know what to do with it.

"So I asked a mutual acquaintance for Josephine's address, and I sent her an anonymous letter asking if she wanted it, or maybe she had a place I should donate to. She wrote back this long response, telling me her thoughts about the situation. I sensed she wanted to talk about it. I did, too.

"We ended up speaking on the phone and having—I wouldn't say it was a nice conversation, because we both cried a lot. But it was an honest one. I apologized a million times, and she was nice about that. She said talking to me helped her. I hope so.

"She believes we're both victims of the Lowerys. But Wyllis didn't deserve what happened to him, and neither did his family. I can't imagine how his death messed up those two boys.

"I've been fortunate. Josephine kept my secret." He'd been staring at his shoes, but he brought his eyes up to her. "I'd like you to keep it, too. I can't force you to do that, but I hope you will."

"Of course," Mimi said.

"Not that I'm worried about word getting out. My lawyer said the worst they could charge me with is manslaughter, and the statute of limitations on that expired a long time ago.

"The Lowerys would never testify against me, considering they were implicated, too. Over the years, they've tried to bribe and threaten me into keeping quiet. I always ignored them. I want nothing to do with those people.

"Really, all I want is peace. I haven't had any since that night."

He rolled his chair back to his desk, and the projects stacked on it. "Anyway, enjoy the brooch. Sorry it's a fake. Hope you didn't pay too much for it."

"It's fine," Mimi said. "We only really paid for the diamond. How much do I owe you for fixing this?"

"Nothing," said Goulding. "It's on the house."

"But come on," Mimi said, rummaging through her purse. "You deserve some money for your work."

"No. Please. I don't want to take one cent for anything to do with that brooch." He paused. "I'm the one with the debt."

MIMI LEFT GOULDING'S OFFICE WITH THE BROOCH in her pocketbook. She checked her phone. There was a long string of texts from Rabinowitz. Mimi quickly called him.

"Where have you been?" he bellowed. "The Lowerys are dead-set on having you arrested. As your attorney, I strongly recommend you return that brooch, so I don't have to spend the night bailing you out of jail."

"Unfortunately, I can't give you that brooch," Mimi said.

"Oh God. What is it now?"

"No one has that brooch. The original was destroyed a long time ago. The one I have is a fake."

"Okay," said Rabinowitz. "But you should—"

"Don't you understand?" Mimi said as she sprinted down Forty-Seventh Street. "I always wondered why the Lowerys were so desperate to get their hands on this piece. And why they kept threatening and not following through. Now I know why. They don't want the world to find out one of their most famous pieces is a fake. This gives us tremendous leverage."

"It could, at some point," Rabinowitz mused. "But right now you have an arrest hanging over your head. Do you have any evidence for what you're saying?"

"Of course I do," Mimi said. "I've talked to the woman who designed it and a guy who worked on it. They both said, unequivocally, the brooch was fake."

"Okay. And will those two people swear affidavits to that effect?"

Mimi stopped walking. "Actually, I don't think either of them will. They told me those things to me in confidence."

Rabinowitz made a rumbling sound. "So let me explain. If I tell the Lowerys' attorneys that the brooch is a fake, they'll ask how I know that. And if I can't tell them anything, they'll laugh in my face. And then we're back to square one. What you're saying means nothing without evidence."

Mimi's phone buzzed. Darlene had finally answered Mimi's text. She proposed they meet at the same spot in Columbus Circle as last time.

"You're right," Mimi said. "I should gather more evidence. I need a little more time."

"No, no!" Rabinowitz yelled. "That is not what I'm saying! You don't have time! You need to—"

Mimi hung up, and went to meet Darlene.

CHAPTER TWENTY-NINE

M IMI STOOD IN FRONT OF THE COLUMBUS CIRCLE subway
station, until she spotted Darlene, a denim jacket draped
over her cleaner's uniform.

Darlene saw Mimi, then stopped, turned on her heel, and
crossed the street to Central Park. Mimi trailed her, several paces
behind.

Darlene trekked wordlessly through the park until they arrived
at an isolated gazebo by a lake. She sat down on the gazebo's sole
bench, but when Mimi sat next to her, Darlene told her to move as
far away as possible, so there would be less chance they'd be seen
together.

All of which made Mimi think: "Holy crap, Darlene is paranoid," and "Holy crap. Why is Darlene so paranoid?"

Darlene wasted little time getting down to business. "Remember,
I won't tell you anything, without you paying me."

"How much?" Mimi knew that was a terrible negotiating tactic,
but she'd never bribed a corporate spy before.

"Depends. What do you need to know?"

"A lot."

Darlene thought a bit, before declaring, "two hundred dollars
a question."

"That's a lot of money! I don't have that!"

"Then, I'm sorry," Darlene said. "Sorry I can't help you, and sorry I risked my job for nothing." She rose from her seat.

"Darlene, please. I'd love to pay you. But I don't have much money right now. Do you take Venmo?"

Darlene scowled. "Venmo?"

"Yes, it's an online payment—"

"I know what Venmo is!" Darlene yelled. "I'm not an idiot. That would create an online record the Lowerys could see. Do you think that's wise?" She raised her chin. "Cash only."

"But I have barely any money right now," Mimi pleaded. "I don't get paid until next week. How about I give you a down payment?" She rifled through her purse, and found a twenty-dollar bill. "Here's twenty dollars."

Darlene just stared at her.

Mimi searched more, and discovered a five. "Twenty-five."

"You're insulting me."

"I am not! Your rates are expensive!"

"Rosalyn paid me more! You're getting a discount." Darlene walked to the door. "Don't message me again."

Mimi ran after Darlene. "Please." She grabbed Darlene's jacket.

Darlene gave Mimi the evil eye. Mimi immediately let go.

"I just need you to answer one question," Mimi said. "Only one. Don't do it for me. Do it for Rosalyn."

Darlene turned around. "How would answering a question help Rosalyn? She's dead."

Mimi lightly touched Darlene's arm and looked her in the eye. "It helps Rosalyn, because she was killed, and whoever did it, hasn't been caught. This is about something more important than money."

Darlene's face stiffened. "That's easy for you to say. You don't have to break your back, emptying garbage for those people. Spend a few days doing that, and then talk to me about more important things than money."

Mimi took a rueful breath. "I'm sorry I said that." She moved closer to Darlene. "But you told me once, Rosalyn was your friend."

Darlene stayed stone-faced. "So?"

"You also told me that sometimes, when you go into Rosalyn's room, you feel her presence."

"Yeah. So what?"

"That's a big deal. I tried to feel her presence, but I couldn't."

Darlene turned away. "It doesn't matter."

"Yes, it does. All of this matters. Rosalyn mattered. Her memory matters." Mimi tried to catch Darlene's eye. "Do you know that I found Rosalyn's diary? And in it, she called you her closest friend."

Darlene's head swerved around, surprise washing over her face. "Really? She wrote that? She was a rich woman."

"That's what she said."

"But she was the lady of the house. I was just the cleaner."

Mimi tilted her head and smiled. "I guess she liked you."

Darlene looked to the lake. "We had fun sometimes. We'd laugh about the silly things Archibald or his mother said. That was nice."

"You told me that you miss her."

Tears formed in Darlene's eyes. "Sometimes." The wind blew a leaf into the gazebo, which landed at her feet.

Mimi stared straight at her. "Can you please help me? Whoever killed Rosalyn, needs to pay."

Darlene walked back and forth along the narrow length of the gazebo, until she sat down, defeated. "I will answer one question for you for free, in honor of Rosalyn."

Mimi searched her mind for her most pressing question. She settled on one.

"When I came to the Lowery estate, there was a man walking on the grounds. A tall brawny man, with a limp. Later, he attacked me. He said his name was George Morton. Do you know who that is?"

Darlene shook her head vigorously. "Never heard of him."

"The name's not important. But have you seen anyone who looks like that on the property?"

"No," Darlene said. "But I think that someone has moved into their third guest house."

"Why do you say that?"

"There's three guest houses on the estate. One is where Vanessa stays. The second is where I stay. And then there's a third house, which is usually empty. But I'm pretty sure I heard someone inside it last weekend. I also saw Claudia go in there, which I've never seen before."

"Do you have any idea who's staying there?"

"Beats me. It could be a workman. But do you think that has something to do with Rosalyn?"

"I believe it all connects in some way. I'm just not sure how. Can I ask one more question?"

Darlene was aghast. "I only promised you one."

"You didn't really answer the first."

"You get what you pay for." Darlene folded her arms.

"Please." Mimi said. "This will be the last one I ask, I promise. Do it for—"

"Don't mention Rosalyn again!" Darlene snapped. "Just ask the damn question. You can be very annoying, you know that?"

"Yes. People tell me that. Sorry." Mimi chewed the bottom of her lip. "Rosalyn said that she never had any contact with Shepherd in the year before she died. But then, why would Shepherd send her the Heartbrooch? I can't believe it was because of the curse."

Darlene was quiet for a moment. "That I can't tell you."

"Why not?"

"It's something that I was told in confidence." Darlene glanced at her watch. "I need to head back."

"All right. Thank you, though. Thanks for everything."

"Was I helpful?"

Mimi considered this. "I am not sure. Let's speak later." She checked her phone. "Vanessa just called."

"Talk to her," Darlene said. "She should be able to help you. Especially with that last question."

Darlene scurried out of the gazebo. When Mimi called Vanessa, she was surprisingly hostile.

"Mimi, I don't know what you are trying to pull," Vanessa said, a growl in her voice. "But I won't put up with it. When I told you I was tough, I meant it."

Mimi was baffled. "What are you talking about?"

"Let's meet in person. I'm in the city and I'm nervous my phone is bugged."

"Why would it be bugged?"

"I don't know," Vanessa said. "I don't trust anyone anymore." She sounded at the end of her rope. "Let's meet at the same diner we did last time, and hash this out face-to-face."

"What's there to hash out?"

"You know!"

"I don't!" Mimi insisted.

"I'll tell you when I see you."

"Fine." Mimi hung up, as confused as ever.

CHAPTER THIRTY

O N HER WAY TO MEET VANESSA, Mimi spotted the black sedan again. She'd been to three different places that afternoon, and she'd seen the black sedan at every one of them.

Nothing distinguished it from all the Ubers, Lyfts, and town cars that wander the streets of Manhattan. At first, she ignored it, figuring it couldn't be the same car. Yet, the more she saw it, the more she became convinced it was following her. With its polished black steel and tinted windows, it was both imposing and impenetrable. Mimi began to think of it as a person—grim, relentless, determined, always on her trail while hiding in plain sight.

Mimi jotted down its license plate, then hurried to the diner.

Vanessa was sitting against the wall. She appeared to have not slept. She greeted Mimi warily. A bowl of fruit sat in front of her. She hadn't touched it.

Mimi took her coat off, and hung it on the hook by the table. "So what's this about?" she asked, sitting down.

"You are trying to blackmail me," Vanessa said. "Don't think you're going to get away with it."

"I'm not blackmailing you!" Mimi exclaimed.

"Oh yeah? Then what's this?" Vanessa opened her purse and pulled out copies of two pages from Rosalyn's diary.

Mimi craned her neck to catch a glimpse of them. They were the sections where Rosalyn wondered why Shepherd had sent her the Heartbrooch.

"These were slipped under my door last night. They look like they were written by Rosalyn. You told me you read some of Rosalyn's old writings. Was this them?"

Mimi responded slowly, not wishing to anger this tightly-wound woman. "I found Rosalyn's diary at the estate, and those pages were part of it." She held up her hand to prevent Vanessa from interrupting. "But I lost the diary when I was running away from this fake Uber driver."

Vanessa looked puzzled. "You ran away from who?"

"It's a long story. But whoever gave you those pages, it wasn't me. I wasn't at the estate last night. Ask the Lowerys, they'll tell you."

"I'd rather not talk to them," Vanessa said.

"Why do you think you received those particular pages?" Mimi asked.

"That's none of your business. You swear you didn't put these under my door?"

"Of course not."

Vanessa scooped up the diary pages, folded them into neat little squares, and placed them in her purse. "And you think an Uber driver took them?"

"It's possible. But for what it's worth, I don't think that person really worked for Uber."

Creases formed in Vanessa's brow. "What did he look like?"

"I couldn't really see him. It was dark. He was tall and well-built."

Vanessa stared into space. "I need to get out of here." She was breathing fast.

"Vanessa, tell me. Do you think the Uber driver was someone you know?"

"Maybe," she said. "But it couldn't be him. It wouldn't make any sense."

"The person you're thinking of, did he have a limp? Because this person did."

"No." Vanessa took a deep breath. "He didn't have a limp. And it can't be him. Although—"

"I heard someone might be staying at the third guest house," Mimi said. "Have you seen anyone there?"

"No." She popped up from her seat. "I should get back to the estate."

"Don't go back there," Mimi said. "I think that's where the Uber driver is staying."

"Then I'll go somewhere else." Vanessa was in a daze, her face drained of color. "I don't know where." She removed her coat from its hanger, and stuffed her arms in it.

Beneath the fear, Mimi spotted an expression she recognized, because she'd just seen it on the face of Joey Goulding. It was a sad, haunted look, a look of infinite regret.

"Vanessa, tell me," Mimi said in an even tone. "It wasn't Rosalyn who asked Shepherd for the Heartbrooch, was it? It was you."

Vanessa stared at her.

"You pretended to be Rosalyn. I don't know exactly how you did it. But you did."

Vanessa's jaw fell. She stood immobile. "How did you know?"

"Those pages you received showed that Rosalyn never asked Shepherd for the Heartbrooch. I was trying to figure out why they unnerved you so much.

"Then it hit me. I'd always wondered: why did Shepherd send Rosalyn the brooch when they weren't even talking to each other? All the explanations I heard, about the curse, or how they were still having an affair, didn't make sense. But I now know the answer. Shepherd *thought* Rosalyn asked him for the brooch. But she didn't ask him for it, did she? It was you."

Vanessa gazed at her, in shock. "But how—"

"I'm good at figuring things out," Mimi said. "I've been on a roll lately."

Vanessa sat back in the diner booth, her coat still on. "You can't prove any of this."

"Maybe I can't," Mimi said. "But the police could, if I told them what to look for."

Vanessa bared her teeth. "Oh, so now we're back to blackmail?"

"No, we're not!" Mimi rapped the table. "That's not what this is about! I'm trying to find out the truth. It would be nice to finally hear it from you, or anyone, really."

Neither spoke for a minute after that.

"Why did you impersonate Rosalyn?" Mimi asked.

Vanessa shook her head slowly. "I was drunk."

"Drunk?"

"Yes." Vanessa rested her back against the seat. "It gets boring at the estate. Especially at night. There's nothing to do. And the place they have me staying in, it's so small. They call it a guest house, but it used to be the servant quarters. It's just one room and that's it. So sometimes, I drink. A lot. I was definitely drinking the night I sent Shepherd that email."

"You sent him an email?" Mimi's eyes narrowed.

"Yes, from a fake address. RosalynL95 or something. It was a joke, a goof. I never thought Shepherd would buy it. I was amazed when he did."

"But I still don't understand why you did it. What purpose did it serve?"

Vanessa looked deep into her fruit cup. "I had just spoken with Shepherd, and he kept talking about Rosalyn. He was obsessed with her. You know what a slap in the face that was? Hearing my husband—even my soon-to-be ex-husband—going on about his sister-in-law?

"My window looked up at Rosalyn's room, and sometimes I'd see her shadow through the shades. She had so many things I didn't. The Lowerys got her a nice job. She was living in the main house, while I was banished to a shed in the backyard. And, my stupid husband was more interested in her than me.

"So, I wrote to Shepherd pretending I was Rosalyn, asking him to send me the Heartbrooch. I thought I'd have him send the brooch to a post office box, then I'd sell it and finally get out of there. But I considered it a longshot. I never expected it to work. It was blatantly obvious it was fake, like a spam or something."

"What did you say?"

"I don't know. 'Hey, Shepherd. It's Rosalyn. I decided that I love you more than anything. I want to leave Archibald. Send me the Heartbrooch. I'll sell it, and we'll run away together.' That was a big thing with Shepherd. He loved the idea of running away with someone.

"He wrote back a minute later. He was so excited in his email, it made me physically sick. So I destroyed it and never answered him. I thought if I didn't respond, he'd forget about the whole thing. I didn't understand what a mess he was."

Vanessa's head sank. "A few days later, Darlene told me Shepherd sent the brooch to Rosalyn's office. And that's what got him killed."

"What do you mean?"

Vanessa rubbed her hands against her face. "He'd pledged the brooch as collateral to this loan shark. Once Shepherd gave it to Rosalyn, he no longer had anything to give that guy. I'm convinced his goons killed Shepherd. And I was responsible."

"I don't know about that," Mimi said. A thought occurred to her. "Let me check something."

She left her seat and snuck a glance out the diner's front window. The black sedan was waiting outside. She checked the license plate. It was a match.

Mimi sat back down. "Vanessa, I know you're not a bad person. I understand you made a mistake. Right now, I'm in danger. And I think you are, too."

Vanessa's eyes fluttered. "What do you mean?

Mimi motioned toward the window. "You see that car out there? It's been following me all afternoon. Have you seen it before?"

Vanessa stood up and looked at it. "I might have seen it at the Lowery's. I can't say for sure."

"I can't, either. I have a way to find out." Mimi pointed her eyes at Vanessa. "I need you to send another email."

SHORTLY AFTER THAT, VANESSA LEFT THE DINER.

Mimi ordered a cup of tea, which she periodically sipped while she mulled everything over. She felt she was on the cusp of a breakthrough. She remembered what Archibald said: "stories are how we make sense of life." *Don't try to solve this*, she told herself. *Make it a story.*

Mimi borrowed a pen from the waiter, and removed a stack of napkins from the dispenser. She wrote sketches of all the different players, all the facts she'd uncovered, everything she'd heard. She ripped them apart and put them together, like they were pieces of a jigsaw puzzle, until she developed a coherent narrative. Some stories didn't fit, and she knew why: they were lies. And when she understood the reason for those lies, that filled in other parts of the puzzle. After a while, she felt like she wasn't uncovering the truth, it was revealing itself to her.

She tried a number of counterfactuals. She couldn't think of any. The more she tried to disprove her theories, the more they made sense. The fake brooch, the fake email, the fake private investigator—it all added up. A tragic series of errors and misjudgments led to Rosalyn's murder, and could cause more if she didn't hurry. She spent another few minutes developing a plan to catch the culprit. It wasn't perfect, but it would have to do.

Mimi ran out of the diner. She left the waiter a big tip, since she'd littered the table with scribbled-on napkins. Then she called Rabinowitz.

He was happy to hear that Mimi wanted to give the brooch back—but far less pleased when he learned her plan. Ten minutes later, they were on a conference call with Michael and Detective Brill.

Mimi gave a rapid-fire version of her theory of the case, and how she hoped to reveal it. Neither answered, until Detective Brill, sounding both amused and impressed, said, "wow."

"Yeah," Michael said. "And let me add a word I never thought I'd utter. *Oy.*"

"Michael, I have to say, your girlfriend is really something," Detective Brill said.

"You're telling me," Michael said.

"I was trying to wrap my head around her theory," said Detective Brill, "and now I'm trying to wrap my head around her plan. And my main conclusion is they're both either brilliant or crackpot."

"Yes," Michael said. "Or both."

Mimi checked the time. "I am going to ask everyone to meet at Lowery headquarters at seven-thirty, just after it closes. That's about ninety minutes from now. I was hoping for some backup, in case things got hairy. Can you provide that?"

"How about this?" Michael said. "I won't go to the meeting. But I'll be in the neighborhood. Just in case. For boyfriend reasons. You don't have to go, Rita, if you don't want to."

Detective Brill took a long breath. "Oh no," she said. "I'll be around."

CHAPTER THIRTY-ONE

Ninety minutes later, Mimi arrived at Lowery head-quarters, accompanied by a skeptical, grumbling Elliot Rabinowitz.

After hours, the store had lost much of its majesty. Instead of classical music and hushed voices, the air was filled with the sound of vacuum cleaners. The lights on the giant chandelier were switched off, and it no longer resembled a sparkly colossus—more a giant cluster of saggy glass. A man stood on a ladder, silently dusting it.

Mimi and Rabinowitz were led to the Lowery conference room on the top floor. The walls were dotted with pictures of the company's former glories, including newspaper headlines, portraits of its founders, and photos of notable Lowery jewels—though, significantly, not the Heartbrooch.

At one end of the giant oak table sat Archibald, Claudia, and their attorney, who introduced himself as Brian Bombern of Wilton & DeVol. A young paralegal sat by his side, taking notes. Bombern was pug-nosed and white-haired, with a thick stomach and even thicker eyebrows. He handed Mimi his card. Archibald and Claudia sat stonily, not saying a word.

Rabinowitz set the fake Heartbrooch in the middle of the table, and for a few seconds, everyone stared at it.

Bombern cleared his throat, loud enough to be heard across the conference room.

"Let me say at the outset," he said, his fingers steepled beneath his chin, "that for the last week, my clients, the Lowery family and Lowery Incorporated, have been trying in good faith to negotiate an end to the various civil and criminal issues in this matter. Our offers have been exceptionally generous, but they have been met with stalling and delay tactics from your side. As I've warned Mr. Rabinowitz many times, my clients' patience is far from infinite.

"Fortunately, Elliot told us that you are finally ready to pursue a deal, which is why we agreed to this meeting. The Lowerys' sole aim has been to end the gamesmanship and resolve this case."

As he talked, butterflies danced in Mimi's stomach. She was ninety percent sure her plan would work, but she worried about the ten percent chance it wouldn't. If it failed, she might lose her freedom, her boyfriend, and who knows what else.

She'd be on much firmer ground if her three expected guests— the residents of the three Lowery guest houses—were there. But none had showed up yet, and she had no assurance any of them would.

"I'd like this over with, too," said Mimi, even as she devised ways to stall. She fingered the lawyer's card. "Mr. Bombern, it says you're one of the East Coast's Top 50 Superlawyers."

"Yes," he said. "It's a peer recognition I've received ten years in a row."

"Do you wear a cape?"

Mimi thought that was funny, but even Rabinowitz, who laughed at virtually everything, stayed mute.

"Just trying to lighten the mood." Mimi said. She figured her joke was no weirder than shaking hands with a lawyer who'd spent the day trying to put her in jail.

"We appreciate the effort," Bombern said, in what could only be termed a verbal eyeroll. "If comedy hour's over, we'll proceed."

"I'd like some tea," Mimi blurted.

"What?" asked Bombern.

"My mouth is dry," said Mimi. "I'm thirsty. I'd like some tea."

"That is outrageous," said Archibald.

"I agree," Claudia chimed in. "This woman has been quite rude. She does not deserve a beverage."

Bombern turned his head to his clients. "I strongly recommend that you not say anything for the remainder of this conference."

Claudia pantomimed a lip lock. Archibald folded his arms.

Rabinowitz turned to Mimi. "I advise you the same."

"Yeah, that's not happening," she shot back.

"If it will help move this along," Bombern said, "we'll get you tea." The paralegal jumped up from his seat and rushed out the door.

"I take milk and sugar," Mimi called after him.

An uneasy silence descended on the room, until Archibald received a buzz on his phone.

"What is this?" he asked. "It says Vanessa Lowery is coming up."

"Yes," Mimi said. "Given that Mrs. Lowery is still Shepherd's wife, and therefore has an arguable claim to the brooch, we'd like her to be part of any global settlement. Isn't that true, Elliot?"

Rabinowitz shrugged. "I guess."

"Fine," Bombern said. "Send her up. Now, I'd like—"

At that moment, Darlene entered, pushing a cart, topped with tea. She walked over to Mimi and placed the cup in front of her.

"Thank you, Darlene. Would you mind sitting with us? We might need your input."

"I'm sorry." Darlene's voice was barely above a whisper. "I can't."

Mimi gazed at her plaintively. She knew Darlene was worried about her job, but Mimi could really use her help.

"Please," Mimi said. "There may be things you could clear up."

"This is absurd!" Claudia yelled. "Darlene has no place at this table. She has work to do. The bathroom is a mess."

Darlene's fists tightened, and Mimi figured it was a good time to strike.

"We won't take long," Mimi said, pulling out a chair. "Mr. Bombern, can you assure Darlene that anything she says won't affect her employment with your clients?"

"Yeah, fine," he murmured.

Darlene sat down, careful not to look at the Lowerys.

"Can we start now?" Bombern said.

His words were cut off by Vanessa entering.

"Hi, everyone," said Vanessa, taking a seat, and glancing around the room nervously. "Sorry I'm late."

"Welcome, Miss Lowery," Bombern said, not hiding his annoyance. "And now that joke, tea, and guest time is over, can we proceed?"

"Actually," Mimi said, "there's one more person I was hoping would join us."

"Who now?" Claudia said. "The washroom attendant?"

"Claudia, please." Bombern's patience was wearing thin. "Miss Rosen, we don't need anyone else at this conference. You haven't explained why we need these people in the first place."

"To back up what I'm going to say," Mimi said. "The Lowerys asked me to research their family history. So I'm going to lay out what I found."

"That is outrageous," said Archibald.

"Mr. Lowery," Bombern said testily, "please stop calling things 'outrageous.'" He turned to Mimi. "Miss Rosen, we came here for a settlement, not a lecture. In my thirty years of practicing law, I've never seen such a spectacle. And Elliot—" He pivoted to Rabinowitz. "I am surprised that you, as a longtime member of the New York State bar, would allow your client to act in such an irresponsible—"

Mimi cut him off. "The Lowerys will want to hear what I have to say. I have new information on the death of Shepherd Lowery. They may want to dispute my findings. Otherwise, I can just present them to law enforcement."

Bombern and the Lowerys exchanged glances.

"Your choice, Brian," Rabinowitz said, chuckling.

"Make it quick," Bombern snarled.

Mimi walked to the head of the table. "Okay, let me begin by saying, when I had dinner at the Lowery estate, Claudia reminded me that she and her family are human beings that have had terrible things happen to them. And that was helpful, in terms of understanding what happened here.

"The death of Claudia's husband Wyllis was a terrible tragedy. Its repercussions are being felt to this day.

"Josephine Tomaso, the designer of the Heartbrooch, took the original piece with her to Italy, minus the black diamond, which she worried was cursed. After that, Tomaso decided to leave the business, and that brooch is now a valuable collector's item. So the Lowerys made a copy. Some might call it a forgery."

"Hold on," Bombern interrupted, aiming his finger at her. "That is an unsubstantiated accusation you have no proof of."

Rabinowitz looked up at her.

"Actually," Mimi said. "I *can* substantiate it. Rosalyn Lowery's diary mentioned she'd stored the original plan for the brooch in a safety deposit box. That shows the real brooch had the word 'loves' engraved between the two sets of initials. If you examine the brooch at the center of the table, you'll see that word has been completely erased. That's almost impossible to do without leaving any residue. That proves the piece I received is not the same as the original. If you want, we can check that safety deposit box when I'm done."

Archibald and Claudia both wore noticeable scowls.

"She has a pretty good point there, huh, Brian?" Rabinowitz said with a laugh.

"I'd like to continue," Mimi said, "if no one objects."

No one did. Mimi was in charge. She liked that feeling.

"So the Lowerys created this fake brooch, but they never sold or even displayed it, because they couldn't risk Jacqueline Tomaso emerging from retirement to declare it a fake. I'm also guessing that, since the Lowery company had cash flow issues, they used it as collateral to borrow against. Am I correct there?"

"This isn't a trial or deposition, and we have no intention of answering any of your questions," Bombern said.

"When I worked in newspapers, we'd call that a non-denial," Mimi said.

"It's true," Darlene piped up. "I heard them say that."

"Thank you," Mimi said. "Now, when Shepherd Lowery negotiated his exit package from the company, the family gave Shepherd this copy of the Heartbrooch, even though they knew it was a fake. Isn't that right?"

Darlene nodded. Archibald and Claudia shifted in their seats.

"I warn you, Miss Rosen," Bombern said, "these allegations are not well taken."

"I'm just getting started," Mimi said.

Archibald's phone buzzed. "That was security. They said someone came in through the back entrance."

"Is that unusual?" Bombern asked.

"That entrance is only accessible by family and top executives," Archibald said. "Security says they're working to identify the person."

Good, Mimi thought. That was the last, and most important, person she wanted at this conference, the resident of the third guest house.

"If I may continue," she declared, "at a wedding last year, Rosalyn Lowery slept with her brother-in-law, Shepherd. That was another painful moment for the family. It caused Shepherd's wife, Vanessa, to leave him, which in turn caused Shepherd's business to fall apart.

"Then Shepherd gave away his most valuable asset, the Heartbrooch, to Rosalyn. Why did he do that? Not because he wanted to saddle Rosalyn with a curse. Or because they were still having an affair. He did it because Rosalyn asked him to. Or at least that's what he thought. But Rosalyn didn't really ask him. Did she?"

"No." Vanessa hung her head. "I did. I impersonated her."

Archibald and Claudia both glared at Vanessa.

"Unfortunately, Shepherd Lowery had also pledged the brooch as collateral to a local loan shark. He was backed into a corner, and too proud to ask his family for help. So he had no other option but to—"

"Good God," Archibald cried. "Look at what security wrote back. That can't be true." He showed the phone to his mother.

Claudia glanced at it, but didn't react.

Mimi heard footsteps in the hall outside the conference room. "I think my final guest is here."

There was a knock on the door. A voice said, "Hey, it's me."

The man who once called himself George Morton opened the door and entered the conference room. His face registered instant alarm, as he'd only expected one person there. He certainly didn't expect a roomful.

Archibald turned white, like he'd just seen a ghost. Which, in a way, he had. "My God," he cried. "Shepherd!"

CHAPTER THIRTY-TWO

SHEPHERD LOWERY STOOD STARING AT THE GROUP gathered in the conference room. He was clad in the same baseball cap and dark shades he'd worn as a fake Uber driver. But underneath it all, he knew his cover had been blown.

"He's alive?" Archibald exclaimed.

"Sure looks like it," Mimi said.

"How did you know?" Shepherd asked, incredulous.

"I figured it out," Mimi said.

A table full of faces gazed up at Mimi, wondering how.

"First," Mimi said, "there was a guy roaming around the Lowery estate, and that would be extremely hard to do without the family knowing about it. I thought, how could this person be connected to the Lowerys, yet he didn't seem to be working for them, and he was careful not to be seen by Archibald. That didn't leave many people, but Shepherd was one of them.

"Number two, Shepherd sent Rosalyn the brooch because he believed she was going to run away with him. He couldn't do that if he was dead.

"Third, when Shepherd called me as George Morton, he talked about things, like whether Rosalyn was a corporate member of Lowery Inc., that only a family member would know or care about. He may have plausibly found out that information if he was an actual private detective. But, as we know, he wasn't.

"Fourth, George Morton left me notes, saying he was watching me. Shepherd did the same thing to Rosalyn. And Morton kept telling me that he was 'not stupid' and that he'd 'never give up.' Those were all things Shepherd used to say.

"Fifth, both Vanessa and Rosalyn believed that Shepherd would never kill himself. They were right. Sixth, someone slipped sections of Rosalyn's diary under Vanessa's door. In those sections, Rosalyn talked about how she didn't expect to receive the Heartbrooch. There was only one person, besides Vanessa, who would under-stand the significance of those pages: Shepherd. Seventh, Vanessa panicked when I described the man who chased me. That pretty much sealed the deal."

"But how is he alive?" Archibald asked. "He drove his car off a cliff."

"Yeah, it took me a while to figure that out," Mimi said. "Shepherd jumped out of the car before it went over the edge. Remember, he was a skateboarder. He owned all sorts of protec-tive gear. Though he probably hurt himself, considering he now walks with a limp.

"When I was in his fake Uber, he warned me how dangerous it would be if I jumped out. That was another clue, I guess. That's number, what, eight, nine?"

"Yes, yes," Claudia said. "But I don't understand what he's doing here."

"Why do you think I'm here?" Shepherd screamed at his mother. "You told me to come." His eyes bounced around the room, horri-fied. "Why are all these people here? You said it would just be me and you. I can't believe my own mother set me up!"

"I did nothing of the sort!" Claudia said. "I've been protecting you!"

"You have?" Archibald swerved to her.

"She's been sheltering him on your estate," Mimi said. "He's staying in the third guest house."

Archibald was horrified. "You never told me that."

"I am under no obligation to tell you everything," Claudia said. "It's my property, too."

Archibald grew visibly agitated. "I'm sorry. The fact that you're sheltering my brother after his fake suicide is information I should have been made aware of."

"Well, excuse me," Claudia said. "I was protecting my son."

"Yeah, right," Shepherd sneered. "How is inviting me here in front of a room full of people protecting me? I never should have believed your B.S. story, that you were gonna give me all this money."

"I didn't tell you that!" said Claudia.

"Oh yeah?" said Shepherd. "Then who did? I got an email from your personal address. I'll show you." He took out his phone and scrolled a bit. "Oh, hold it. Your address is a little different."

"Good Lord," said Claudia, burying her face in her palms.

Mimi shot a knowing glance at Vanessa.

"I'm out of here," Shepherd said.

"I wouldn't leave, Shepherd," Mimi called to him. "The police are downstairs."

Shepherd turned around. "What are you talking about?"

"There's police outside the store who will happily arrest you," Mimi said. "You faked your own death. That's a crime."

Shepherd stood at the door, ready to erupt.

"The best thing to do," Mimi said, "is sit down and listen. I have a few more things to say."

"I'm not interested in hearing any of your crap," Shepherd said.

"Actually, I think you will be," Mimi said. "I'm talking about you. It will clear up things you didn't know."

Shepherd stood in place. He looked puzzled.

"Shepherd, you'll want to hear this," Mimi said. "Sit down."

Shepherd took a seat, though he slouched and folded his arms, like a pouty child.

"Now that the gang's all here," Mimi said, "we can finish the story.

"When Rosalyn received the Heartbrooch, it felt totally out of the blue. She didn't know that Vanessa had impersonated her; she thought Shepherd had sent her the brooch to hurt her, because of the curse. She wanted to get rid of it as soon as possible.

"So she talked with a well-known expert on Lowery jewelry, who—I assume—told her the brooch was bogus and the diamond was real."

"So, hold it," Shepherd sat up. "The Heartbrooch I had was fake? That was *true*?"

"Yes," Mimi said, turning to him. "I went over that before you came. If you want, I'll catch you up on that part later.

"Now, it's safe to say, when Shepherd saw Rosalyn selling the Heartbrooch, he felt betrayed. Vanessa's email made him think Rosalyn was going to run away with him. Am I correct?"

"You need to shut up!" Shepherd shouted.

"I will when I'm done," Mimi said. "The story's not over. But we're close.

"When Rosalyn left my office, she was followed by the three guys who later attacked my friend Zeke. Those three guys were connected to the guy who loaned you money, correct?"

"Yeah," Shepherd said. "Those guys are a-holes."

"I'm not too fond of them either," Mimi said. "Rosalyn was so scared of them that, when she saw Shepherd drive up in his car, she was shocked, but even though she had a bad history with him, she jumped in, thinking Shepherd would protect her. Am I correct, Shepherd?"

Shepherd didn't respond.

"And then, I'm guessing, the two of them talked. As we just heard, Shepherd didn't know his Heartbrooch was a fake. So when Rosalyn told him, he didn't believe it. I would guess that Shepherd wasn't happy that Rosalyn only received twenty-five thousand dollars for the brooch, when he thought it was worth millions. Is that right?"

Shepherd just glared at her.

"I would also guess that Shepherd didn't like it when Rosalyn said she didn't want to run away with him. In fact, she pretty much considered him a creep. And Rosalyn wasn't the type to mince words. Was she, Shepherd?"

"Shut up," Shepherd yelled. "You think you're so clever, figuring all this out. You're loving this."

"No, I'm not," Mimi said. "Honestly, I hate it. This is the exact opposite of how the world should be. And this is the part I hate the most." She choked up and the entire room watched as she composed herself.

"Shepherd, intellectually, I know why you killed Rosalyn," Mimi said. "But I won't ever understand it. And I don't know how you lived with yourself afterward. Even as a dead man."

The room silently digested this.

"Surely," Archibald said, "you're not suggesting—"

"It's not a suggestion," Mimi said, trying to keep her feelings in check. "Right after Rosalyn visited my office, Shepherd, using the name George Morton, called my mobile and repeatedly referred to Rosalyn in the past tense. That was right after she was killed, before the police had even identified her. Also, my number's unlisted. The only way Shepherd could have gotten that number is by going through Rosalyn's things. And it's safe to say, Rosalyn wouldn't have allowed him to do that unless she was—" Mimi didn't want to finish that sentence. And she didn't need to.

Claudia's eyes turned red. "Shepherd, how could you?"

Shepherd stood up. "You believe what this crazy lady's saying? She has no evidence for any of this. You don't buy this crap, do you?"

He glanced around the room. It was obvious everyone did.

"By the way, Shepherd," Mimi said, "before I came here, I spoke to the police, and recommended they compare your DNA to the samples they found on Rosalyn. Needless to say, it was a perfect match."

Shepherd turned pale.

"Face it," Mimi said, "you're done."

Archibald rose from his seat and pointed at his brother. "I should kill you right now!" He reached into his pocket. Everyone flinched, expecting him to pull out a gun. But it was a handkerchief. He put it to his eyes and sat down. The room fell quiet except for his sobbing.

"Oh please," Shepherd said. "I can't believe my brother is suddenly broken up over the death of his gold-digger wife. You were ready to get rid of her. You hated her! She certainly hated you."

"I'm not proud of what I did," Shepherd said. "But I had no choice. Rosalyn was pissing me off. She threatened to tell people I was alive. That would have gotten me killed by that loan shark. It was either her or me. And I've been through way too much to—" He lost his patience. "Why am I explaining myself? I'm out of here." He stood up and marched to the door.

"Shepherd," Mimi said. "There's nowhere to run. The police are in the building. Elliot just sent them a text. They're coming upstairs. You can't escape."

"Oh yeah. Well, tell him to text I'm not going down without a fight." Veins throbbed on his forehead. "I've never given up in my life, and I won't start now."

He took out a pistol. The whole room shrieked.

Mimi was so stunned that she didn't think to resist when Shepherd yanked her arm and tugged her next to him. It was only when he pointed his gun at her head—burrowing it into her temple, like it was a drill—that she truly grasped what was happening.

"Let the cops come after me," Shepherd declared. "I'm getting out of here. And now I have a hostage. And if I just see one cop, and I mean just one, that hostage will die. Do you all understand that?"

No one said a word.

Mimi had learned to stay cool when she got in these situations—and she'd been in way too many for her liking. But she had to do something. Shepherd was so unhinged, he might kill her just for the hell of it.

"Shepherd, don't leave this room." Mimi struggled to keep her voice from quavering. "Everyone who's ever cared about you is here. Except for your kids."

"My kids don't care about me!" Shepherd snarled.

"Yes, they do," said Vanessa softly. "You should have seen their reaction when they heard you died."

"Please Shepherd," Mimi said. "I understand that you're mad at your family. From what I hear, they were not very good to you growing up. They called you stupid. They misunderstood you. They cut you out of the business. You never quite fit in. I get that. I've had similar issues."

He loosened his grip, ever so slightly.

"You've always tried to do things on your own, without your family. And that hasn't been easy. But not because you were dumb or incompetent. You're neither of those things. You were too ambitious. You were so desperate to prove yourself, you took on too much.

"It's like how you're planning to escape right now. It's not possible. You know that. The police will be looking for you everywhere and you don't move that fast. You hurt your leg when you jumped out of your car. If I can outrun you, you won't get past the cops. Face it, there's no way out of this. You're trapped.

"Luckily, you have a choice. You can either stay here, with people who care for you, and will try their best to get you the fairest shake possible. Or battle a bunch of cops ready to shoot you in the head.

"Shepherd, why did you spend the last week at Farrington Manor? Because that was your home. It was where you grew up. And when you were at your lowest point, that was where you went.

"You knew your mom would take care of you, no matter what. And she'll do the same now. Because she's your family. Maybe your family hurt you sometimes, but I believe they will always be there for you."

Mimi tilted her head up. "Shepherd, you're not stupid. You've never been stupid. People told you that, but they were wrong. Look at how you managed to convince so many people you were dead. You're very smart. And right now, there's only one smart thing to do."

Shepherd released a loud sad sigh. Then the man who never gave up, finally did. He let go of Mimi, dropped his gun to the floor, staggered to his chair, and cried.

His mother walked over, and put her well-manicured hands on her son's heaving shoulders. While Claudia generally stood ramrod straight, she now appeared unsteady. She teetered in her heels, leaning on Shepherd as much as consoling him.

She frequently snuck glances at her other son, who was crying too. She probably figured she'd have plenty of chances to comfort Archibald, but it wasn't clear what would happen to Shepherd. One could tell the difference between the sons by watching them weep: Archibald sobbed in small, controlled bursts, carefully expelling his tears into a monogrammed handkerchief; Shepherd's wails were loud and anguished—perhaps deliberately so, to drown out his brother. Yet, those were real tears falling down his face, which only occasionally landed in the crumpled tissue in his hand.

It was strange, seeing these two men sob, while portraits of their father and grandfather looked down on them, in this stately boardroom not meant for tears. Claudia didn't seem to possess much of a maternal instinct, but now, with her family in ruins, she was trying her best. Because, no matter how many times she patted Shepherd on the shoulder and told him things would be okay, everyone knew they wouldn't be—given what he'd done, and what he'd face for it. When the police came for Shepherd, he didn't put up his promised fight. He simply surrendered, his eyes dead, his gun lying impotently on the floor. As he was led out of the conference room, his body language was relaxed, like he was happy the whole thing was over with.

AFTERWARD, THE POLICE QUESTIONED EVERYONE, including Mimi. Considering Rabinowitz had taped the entire conference, they didn't need to hear everyone's version of events, but they quizzed them all anyway.

Detective Brill was amused that Mimi's twin bluffs had worked. Mimi had told Shepherd that faking his death was illegal. It turned out there's no specific law against that. *Who knew?*

Mimi had also told Shepherd that the police had matched his DNA with what they found on Rosalyn. They hadn't; Mimi had suggested they check that, but that process had barely begun. Yet, Shepherd believed her. It was a good story.

When it was time to go, Mimi made sure she said goodbye to Darlene. "Thanks for all your help," she told her. "I know you put your job at risk. That was really brave."

"It's okay," Darlene said, hoisting her purse on her shoulder. "Like you said, I did it for Rosalyn, and her memory."

"I'm sure she appreciates it, wherever she is," Mimi smiled.

Michael approached Mimi, his brow furrowed. "Hey, did you see the brooch anywhere?"

"The Heartbrooch?" Mimi asked. "Wasn't it put to the side with all the other stuff?"

"It was," he said. "But it's not there anymore. Someone must have snatched it. Rita doesn't know where it is either."

"But everyone left the conference room," Mimi asked. "Darlene, did you—?"

She turned around. Darlene was gone.

CHAPTER THIRTY-THREE

Mimi woke the next morning, having slept only in spurts, her head spinning from the night before. Her clock said nine a.m.—which meant she'd slept through three alarms. She quickly got dressed and hit the phone. She had one more thing to take care of.

When Mimi arrived at the office, Channah's face broke into a wild smile, and they shared a long hug.

"I'm so glad you're okay," Channah said. "I was worried about you."

"Yeah, I'm fine," Mimi said. "Sorry to be short with you, but I need to do something right now. And it involves you."

Mimi was surprised by how quickly the words tumbled from her mouth. She had way too many cups of coffee coursing through her veins; she felt both exhausted and ready to build a house. "Remember I asked you not to break it off with Zeke for twenty-four hours. You haven't done that, right?"

"No," Channah said. "I might do it later." She frowned, like she'd rather do anything else.

"And do you also remember I said I wasn't going to bug you about that?" Mimi responded before Channah had a chance to. "I lied. Well, it was a half-lie. I got someone to speak to you."

"Mimi!" Channah yelled. "I told you not to—"

"Yes, yes, yes," Mimi said, still in motormouth mode. "But it took a lot of work to get this person, and you won't want to disappoint him."

Channah crossed her arms. "Whoever it is, tell them I'm sorry, but—"

"It's Rabbi Hirschhorn, Yosef's old rabbi."

Channah emitted a long groan. She knew—as Mimi did—she couldn't blow off Rabbi Hirschhorn.

"Sorry," Mimi said with a shrug. "I had to bring out the heavy artillery."

Channah both feared and respected Rabbi Hirschhorn. He was a close confidant of Yosef, Channah's deceased fiancé. He'd helped Mimi solve Yosef's murder. If Hirschhorn talked, Channah would listen.

"This wasn't easy to arrange," Mimi said. "The Rabbi never uses computers. He hates them. He's only doing this because I convinced him time was of the essence. Zeke's at his office in Brooklyn, setting him up." She checked the time. "They should be ready now."

Mimi pulled her laptop from her bag and messaged Zeke, who pinged back the Zoom link. Mimi clicked it on it, and then angled the computer toward Channah—who eyed it suspiciously.

Zeke appeared on screen. He waved hello to Channah, then passed the computer to Rabbi Hirschhorn.

The Rabbi looked just as Mimi remembered. He wore the standard black hat and coat, and his long cottony beard stretched down his stomach. His impressive bulk filled his large wooden chair.

The Rabbi thanked Zeke for arranging things, and then, in his deep gravelly voice, ordered him to leave.

"Really?" Zeke replied.

"Yes," the Rabbi said. "We may discuss things that are improper for you to hear. Walk out the door and don't come back unless I call for you."

He said it with such authority that Zeke had no choice but to go. Mimi heard the door slam.

"Channah," the Rabbi intoned, "I consider computers a blight upon humanity. I've never video conferenced before, and I hope I never will again. The only reason I'm talking to you now is because Miss Rosen convinced me this was important." He stroked his beard. "Before we talk, have you spoken to anyone else about this issue? Like your Rabbi?"

"Yes," Channah answered dully.

"What did he say?"

"Not much," Channah said.

"I'll try to do better," Rabbi Hirschhorn said.

Even sitting away from the screen, Mimi could hear the Rabbi's heavy breathing. Yosef used to say that, as kids, they called him "Darth Rabbi."

"From what I understand," he said, "you don't want to marry Zeke because he proposed to you with a supposedly cursed diamond. Is that correct?"

"Yes," she said. While she couldn't ignore the Rabbi, her terse answers were a small stab at rebellion.

"Can you tell me why that bothers you?"

"It's hard to explain," Channah said.

"Please try. Even if you can't describe it exactly, sometimes it helps if you struggle with the words."

"Okay." Channah wrinkled her nose and sat up. She had no choice but to participate.

"I don't believe in curses," she said. "At least, not usually. I was all set to marry Zeke. Then he got attacked and I found out the diamond was cursed, and I put two and two together and now I'm scared to marry him. I'm sure that sounds silly."

"When you're talking about feelings," the Rabbi intoned, "there is no such thing as silly. Human beings are not rational creatures. Our emotions are who we are."

Channah's body shrank in her chair. "I'm just scared Zeke will get hurt. This time, he got beat up. Next time, who knows?"

"I see." The Rabbi tapped his finger on his chin. "It is normal to feel nervous before you get married. It is not normal to feel petrified. This situation is neither standard or healthy. You should not marry Zeke."

"Hold it," Mimi said.

"Do not interrupt, Miss Rosen," the Rabbi said. "I am not suggesting she should not marry him because of some so-called curse. I do not believe in such things. Our fate is in the hands of *Hashem*.

"I could say a few prayers and declare that the curse has been lifted. But I don't think that's the main issue here. Channah, if you really loved Zeke, you would not let a so-called curse stand in your way. Zeke seems like a nice young man and I'm sure he will make a fine husband. But you should not marry someone that you don't love. An unhappy marriage is not in either of your interests."

Mimi's face burned. This wasn't what she wanted him to say. "Um, Rabbi, can we talk in private?"

"No, we cannot," he thundered. "Channah, I understand you may be reluctant to break things off with Zeke, because you don't want to hurt his feelings. If you like, I can call him in and do it for you. It may not be pleasant, but it's for the best. With time, I'm sure you will both meet your rightful soul mates. While I don't believe in curses, I do believe certain things are not meant to be."

The Rabbi snapped his fingers at the young boy with *payis* sitting in the room with him. "Go get Zeke."

"No!" Channah cried, rising from her chair. "Do not get him. Don't tell him anything like that. I love Zeke. I swear!"

"You don't need to convince me," the Rabbi said. "You need to convince yourself. Are you sure?"

"Of course I'm sure. When I saw Zeke's face on screen just now, he looked so cute and sweet, I can't describe it."

The Rabbi nodded. "So, that brings us back to where we started. Because I assume you still have trepidations about marrying him."

"I do." Channah nodded. "I know it's—"

The Rabbi held up his hand. "Do not say silly!" The heavy breathing resumed. "Give me some time. I need to think." He closed his eyes, and rested his hands on his stomach. After about thirty seconds, his eyes popped open.

"Here is what I believe," he said. "You claim to be worried about Zeke. I don't think that's true. You know it's highly unlikely Zeke will be killed by a curse. You're actually worried about yourself. This isn't about him. It's about you."

"How could you say that?" Channah protested. "That sounds so selfish."

"It's not selfish at all," the Rabbi said. "It's human.

"Two years ago, you suffered a terrible loss. That pain doesn't go away. Sometimes, it may feel manageable, but it's something that is always with you. And if you marry Zeke, you worry that you'll lose Yosef for good."

Channah opened her mouth to speak, but no words came out.

"When Zeke was attacked, you became frightened you would lose him, too. That's why it set you back so much. Losing one person was bad enough. Losing two would be unbearable."

Channah had been keeping it together, but this broke her. "Of course it would be." Her eyes filled with tears. "That's not crazy, though."

"I didn't say it was," the Rabbi said. "Think about what you've been through. The first man you loved died tragically. The second got badly hurt. Then, you hear about a curse, and even if you don't totally believe it, you are unable to put it out of your mind. That's perfectly understandable."

Channah uncrossed her arms, put her head down, and started to cry.

"Let me ask you: even though your relationship with Yosef ended badly, are you sorry for the time you had with him?"

"No," Channah said. "I'm grateful for it. I wish it was longer, obviously. How could I not? But I cherish every second."

"And I believe that if—God forbid—something happened to Zeke, you will feel the same." For the first time, the Rabbi stared directly at the camera, his blue eyes like laser beams, piercing the screen. "Tell me: do you ever talk to Yosef, when you're by yourself?"

"Every day," Channah said through her tears.

"Have you talked to him about this?"

Channah studied her hands. "Not really. I'm afraid I'll hurt his feelings."

"Would you like to talk with him now?" the Rabbi asked. "Is there a place you can go where it's private?"

"I could go in the back, but Mr. Rosen is there."

Mimi sprang from her chair. "I can ask him to leave."

"If you want," Channah said quietly.

Mimi sprinted to the main office and her father's desk.

"Look who's here." Max smiled. "Public enemy number one. What happened last night? Rabinowitz said there was drama, and a gun."

"There was," Mimi said, "but that's not important right now."

"Someone put a gun to your head and it's not important?" Max said.

"Dad, I need you to leave the office and wait in the reception area," Mimi declared.

"I can't do that!" Max's mouth turned squiggly. "I have work to do!"

"You have to leave," Mimi insisted.

"Why? What insane reason could you have for ejecting me from my office?"

Mimi hitched in a breath. "Channah has to talk to Yosef."

Max stared at her. "Sorry I asked."

CHANNAH SAID SHE'D ONLY BE IN THE MAIN OFFICE for a few minutes, but as that stretched to more than ten, the mood grew tense. Max squirmed in Channah's chair, while Mimi sat on the floor of the "man trap," the small area between the two security doors at the front of the office. She had so much excess energy she kept standing and pacing until Max complained that drove him crazy. That made her sit down—for about thirty seconds, when she'd pop up again.

"Jeez," Max said. "What could those two be talking about? Or that one person? I'm not sure what's supposed to be happening back there."

"It's good they've kept talking," Mimi said. "Or whatever's going on. I'm not sure either."

The Rabbi didn't respond. He had turned away from the computer, and had his nose in a book.

When Channah came back into the reception area, her eyes were puffy and her cheeks wet. But she appeared at peace.

"How are you?" Mimi said.

"Fine," Channah said. "That was an interesting experience. It was mostly me talking, of course. Yosef didn't say much. But I didn't expect him to."

"So, you getting married?" Max asked.

"Dad, don't ask her that," Mimi scolded, though she wanted to know, too.

Channah took a second to answer, then smiled. "Of course, I'm getting married. Why wouldn't I?"

There was a brief moment of silence, then a big round of cheers. Mimi gave Channah a joyful hug.

Zeke was called back into the Rabbi's office. When he heard what happened, his smile not only filled his face, but the entire screen.

"Hi, Zeke, honey," Channah cooed.

"I guess we're engaged now," Zeke said.

"Yes, we are!" Channah's face lit up. "Sorry for making you wait so long. I'm sure it wasn't easy. But I love you and I can't wait to marry you."

"Channah, you've made me the happiest man in the world," Zeke said. "Though I also have an apology for you. We've gotten engaged and I don't have a diamond."

Channah laughed. "I'm fine without one."

As Mimi watched Channah merrily chat with Zeke, she wondered if she could ever be that happy with Michael. Mimi was glad she was back together with him. Yet, they were very different people, who led very different lives. They had some things in common, but she wondered if they were enough.

Ironically, the one thing they both had a passion for, the thing that brought them together—investigating crimes—was something that Michael had decreed they couldn't share. There were so many areas of Michael's life, so many areas of him, that she didn't have access to, that she didn't know.

Mimi decided she'd worry about that later. The Rabbi was ready to sign off, and Mimi wanted a quick chat with him. She whisked away the laptop so they could talk privately.

"Thank you so much for your help, Rabbi," Mimi said.

"My pleasure. I'm just glad I can stop staring at this screen. I feel dumber every second I look at it. And once again, I offer you an open invitation to worship at my *shul.*"

"Thanks," Mimi said. "I appreciate that."

"Something tells me we shouldn't save you a seat," he said.

"Probably not. But thank you again. The way you told Channah she should break up with Zeke was brilliant reverse psychology." Mimi paused. "I mean that's what it was, wasn't it?"

Hirschhorn's bushy eyebrows smushed together. "Not at all. I was ready to tell Zeke it was over. *Baruch Hashem,* she stopped me in time.

"My initial reading of the situation was completely incorrect." He shrugged his big shoulders. "It happens."

CHAPTER THIRTY-FOUR

Shortly after Shepherd Lowery confessed in the company boardroom, he pled guilty to the murder of his sister-in-law, Rosalyn Lowery—formerly known as Roz Ghinkert.

That made the Lowerys a big story. The family that once refused to have their pictures taken now had their photos splashed on the front page of every publication in America. Comedians ridiculed them on late-night TV; their every move was dissected on Twitter.

Several reporters tried to interview Mimi, but she turned them down. She didn't consider the Lowery story entertainment. She especially hated the articles that made snide comments about Rosalyn. When one social media know-it-all declared Rosalyn was as culpable as the rest of the family, Mimi almost threw her laptop across the room.

In an irony Wyllis Lowery could have predicted, all the drama turned the Lowery store into a mob scene—though it wasn't clear how many people were there to buy, and how many just came to gawk.

The boom in business wasn't enough to save the company. Once banks discovered their Lowery loans were backed by phony collateral, they pulled their credit lines. Soon afterward, Lowery Inc. declared Chapter 11. The brand was scooped up by one of those luxury conglomerates that Archibald always feared would sully its reputation. By then, there was little reputation left to sully.

During the Chapter 11 proceedings, the store's creditors sued the family, and as part of the settlement, Archibald and Claudia sold their treasured estate, Farrington Manor—which Mimi saw a certain justice in, since it was originally purchased under false pretenses. When Mimi expressed happiness about this to Michael, he said that whoever moved in would probably be just as crooked.

The Lowerys were never prosecuted for their financial misdeeds, despite abundant evidence of them. This didn't bother Mimi as much as she would have thought: their fancy lawyers probably would have gotten them off, while fattening their bankbooks. As her father might say, she had no desire to build their summer homes.

In the end, Mimi didn't wish the Lowerys ill. Both Archibald and Claudia had been betrayed by their spouses. Ordinarily, that would make them deserving of sympathy, but they both handled it so badly they inadvertently helped get those spouses killed. That was a lot to live with—and they'd been publicly humiliated on top of that. As far as Mimi was concerned, they'd suffered enough.

As for Shepherd, Mimi was sickened by what he'd done, but couldn't help feeling a certain sorrow at how badly he'd messed up his life. He really did have a lot going for him—and even more handed to him. What a shame he didn't see that.

Twitter was, naturally, not so understanding. Every day, there were regular calls for the Lowerys' heads. *It's different when you know the people*, Mimi thought. *Even when you know them, and don't like them.*

Maybe, Mimi figured, Archibald could use his newfound free time to become the writer he once dreamed. He had quite a tale to tell; not that Mimi would help him write it.

She did have the occasional vindictive thought. After she read that Claudia and Archibald had moved to New Jersey, she pictured them living in a low-rent apartment like hers, maybe the next town over. Perhaps, like her, they'd have to constantly complain to their landlord that their heat didn't work, or their toilet was clogged.

She doubted that would happen. The thought amused her just the same.

IN NOVEMBER, MAX CALLED MIMI TO HIS DESK. "I just got off the phone with Rabinowitz. That black diamond's turned up at an auction house."

"Really? Did they say who gave it to them?"

"No. They just said it was consigned by an anonymous person."

Mimi had a pretty good idea who that person was. Both Detective Brill and Michael believed that Darlene had swiped the brooch from the conference room. But there was only circumstantial evidence of that, and the police never pressed the matter, having plenty of loose ends from the case to deal with. Darlene soon dropped out of sight—though Mimi later found Facebook photos of her enjoying life with her family in Florida. Given the diamond's twisty history, Mimi couldn't get too upset about her taking it. According to the legend, it had been nicked from an Indian statue. Is it really theft if the gem was already stolen?

"Rabinowitz tells me," Max said, "that since we're the last listed owners of the diamond, we have a pretty good claim to it. And with all the nonsense about the curse and everything else, it could fetch a lot of money. I could make a nice profit on that thing. Finally."

"That's great."

"Yeah." Max took a sip of water. "But I'm not gonna do it. I'd have to bring a lawsuit and testify in court and pay Rabinowitz and you know how I hate doing that. I don't need the headache. I've heard enough about the diamond for ten lifetimes. Some things just aren't worth it.

"The insurance company reimbursed me the original twenty-five thousand dollars I paid, so as far as I'm concerned, I'm even. I mean, I'm not completely even. My premiums went up and I had to pay Rabinowitz's legal bills."

"Those were only twelve hundred dollars," Mimi said.

"That's plenty," Max said. "More than he deserves. Besides, I don't want that diamond, because—you know."

Mimi almost laughed at this. "What are you saying? That it's cursed?"

"No," Max said. "I'm not saying it's cursed. The only curse that diamond had was that it was owned by a lot of insane, greedy idiots."

He leaned back on his chair and wrapped his hands around his head. "But you look at all that happened, and hey, you never know."

NOW THAT THEY WERE BACK TOGETHER, Mimi and Michael fell into their familiar routine, like they'd never broken up. Yet, Mimi felt a certain wariness. She wondered if the two of them truly had a future.

Then, in December, Michael invited Mimi to celebrate Christmas with his family. It would be the first time she'd met Michael's mom and daughter, not to mention his siblings and their families.

Mimi had never been to a real Christmas celebration—except for things like office parties—but Michael assured her there was barely any religion involved, only "religious consumption of alcohol."

After all she'd been through, not many things made Mimi nervous. But meeting Michael's family did.

Thanks mostly to the aforementioned alcohol, Mimi had a good time. There were moments of awkwardness—as there were bound to be—and she often felt out of place, even as Michael diligently tried to include her in every conversation.

Mimi and Michael's daughter Catherine did bond over their shared love for Michael's dog, Louie. Of course, Mimi didn't have the same chemistry with either Catherine or Michael's mom that she did with Louie. Dogs aren't that picky. She figured she'd win them over eventually.

Mimi was particularly pleased that, at the end of the night, Catherine told her that it was "really really nice to finally meet" her.

"That was two reallys," Mimi enthused to Michael the next day at lunch, at Michael's favorite Mexican restaurant in Brooklyn.

"Not bad," he smiled. "I'm disappointed she didn't give you three."

As lunch went on, Mimi noticed Michael was fidgeting. Something was up.

"I want to talk to you," he said finally. "I've been thinking about what you said, that you have certain skills as a detective."

Mimi moaned. Not this again. She was thoroughly sick of this topic. "I told you a million times, I don't want to investigate anymore."

"If that's how you feel," Michael said, "I don't blame you. You've gotten into some hairy scrapes."

Mimi braced herself for another lecture.

"But after thinking about it—and talking with Rita—I realized that you do connect well with people. You did solve three murders. At this point, I'm willing to concede there may be something more than mere luck involved."

"Glad to hear you say that," Mimi said. "Finally." She took his beefy hand in hers.

If the conversation ended there, Mimi would have been happy. But there was more.

"As you know," Michael said, "I'm considering retiring from the force. I've been thinking about what I want my life to look like going forward. So, I have a proposal."

A shiver ran down Mimi's spine. She was shocked and a little disconcerted. "You don't mean—"

"No!" Michael recoiled. "I'm not talking about that. Come on. We broke up just two months ago."

"It's not such a crazy idea," Mimi said.

"It's not crazy, but—" He got flustered. "Can we not discuss that right now? Please listen to what I have to say." He tried to regroup. "Even though I'll get my full pension when I retire, I don't want to sit around the house all day, playing clarinet and walking the dog. Maybe I'll do that a bit. But not all the time. I'm way too young for that.

"One thing I'm thinking about is getting involved with security and private investigations. And, since my beat has always been the Diamond District, I figure I could set up something on Forty-Seventh Street. Lord knows there's enough issues there.

"So I figured," he said, "maybe you could help out a bit, particularly with questioning people and research. I've given up trying to stop you investigating. If you're going to keep at it, I might as well watch over you, make sure you stay out of trouble."

Mimi tried to wrap her head around this. "You want me to work with you? As a job?"

"It wouldn't be full time," Michael said. "At least not at first. It might be one day a week. Maybe two. It depends on how much business I get. You can still work for your father on your responsibly sourced diamond project. And later on, we'll see. This could turn into something.

"You have a lot of raw talent. It just needs to be molded in the right way." He removed an object from his coat pocket. "I bought you this book on how to be a private detective. I thought it might help."

Mimi examined it and put it down. "Thanks, but I read this already."

"You did? When?"

"I don't know," Mimi said. "In between one of the investigations. I can't remember."

Michael chuckled. "This will be interesting."

"So, just to be clear," Mimi said, "even though you told me a million times not to investigate, and even though we once broke up over this very issue, you're now asking me to work with you at your private detective firm? Are you sure? Do you really want to do this?"

Michael nodded. "I'll admit, there's a certain irony here. I apologize for those things I said. Well, most of them. Some, I stand by, but we don't have to discuss that now.

"Anyway, if this doesn't work out, fine. But I think we'll make a good team. It'll be nice having you around."

He nervously sipped his water. "Obviously, there are things for you to consider, like what your father might say. If you do less work for him, your income might take a hit. So my question to you is: do *you* really want to do this?"

Mimi didn't know how to respond. This was way more shocking than a marriage proposal.

CHAPTER THIRTY-FIVE

Michael groaned when he heard that, at religious weddings like Channah's and Zeke's, men danced with men, and women danced with women. "That sounds weird," he said. "Not that I'm homophobic or anything—"

"Don't worry," Mimi said. "I guarantee you'll have fun."

The ceremony was sex-segregated, which meant Michael sat next to Max during it, fidgeting and awkwardly wearing a *yarmulke*. It ended with the customary stepping on the glass and a chorus of *Mazel Tovs*. Mimi was the maid of honor and stood under the *chuppah* with Zeke and Channah. She winked at Michael when she saw him in the crowd.

As Mimi promised, Michael did have fun at the reception. While there was no inter-sex dancing—and the songs were all in Hebrew—it was a high-spirited affair, with all the men chanting and clasping arms and high-stepping and continually coming together, and breaking apart, in a joyous, sweaty scrum.

At first, Michael watched this, puzzled. At one point he jumped in, and soon he was dancing and kicking and jumping around with the rest.

When he returned to their table, he was out of breath and his hair was damp and his shirt clung to his chest. "This is awesome! I can't believe how wild this is. I gotta sit down. These guys have way more energy than I do. How long will this go on?"

"Oh, these go on for a while," Mimi said.

"Man," Michael marveled.

When Mimi first met Michael—and she viewed him as nothing more than an intimidating homicide detective—she suspected that he never smiled, except for smirks that expressed more disgust than happiness. Since then, she'd seen him smile, many times. But she'd never seen him show so much unguarded joy than at that moment. She couldn't believe a religious wedding brought it out in him.

The band began to play again, and he ran off to join the action.

Mimi started on her dessert, a non-dairy strawberry mousse, when her phone buzzed. It was her contact in the African Democratic Republic working on the socially responsible diamond project.

"Good news!" the message said. "After all these months of digging, we have finally found two diamonds on our patch of land. They're about a carat each. Color/clarity looks okay."

It was accompanied by a picture of two small gray rocks. Mimi showed it to her father, who peered at the picture through his glasses.

"Isn't that great?" Mimi asked.

"Eh," Max shrugged, getting back to his dessert. "If they say the color and clarity looks okay, that means it's terrible. But we'll get something for them. Not a lot. But something."

Mimi made a sour face. "Dad, this is a real breakthrough."

"I guess," Max said. "Now that they've actually found diamonds, maybe they'll have a better sense of where to look. So, who knows? We may start to actually make money on this thing."

"And," Mimi added, "do some good for the people over there."

Max nodded. "That, too."

Mimi leaned toward her dad, so no one else could hear. "If you don't want to keep working on this, you don't have to."

Max squinted at her. "What are you saying?"

"I know this is taking up a lot of your money and time, and it's not paying off."

"That's an understatement," Max said. "But it's interesting doing something new. You don't ordinarily learn new things at seventy-five years old."

Mimi drank a sip of water, steeling herself for what she was about to say. "I guess what I'm asking is, are you going to continue with your company?"

Max had just polished off a spoonful of his dessert, but when he heard her question, he put his spoon down and stared at her. "Why wouldn't I? I'm mentally with it. Right?"

"Of course you are."

"You better say that."

"You're fine. It's just that—" This required another breath. "Some of your friends in the business are retiring."

"Yes, and that's sad," Max said. "I'll miss Sol. But why would I pack it in? I just got two ugly diamonds from the African Democratic Republic. I'm rich!"

Mimi laughed. "I'm just asking—"

"Listen, despite all the headaches—most of which, I should note, are caused by you—I still enjoy this business. They'll have to carry me out feet first.

"Besides, I have two employees to take care of. I have Channah, at least until she has a baby, which, God willing, will be soon. And, of course, you."

Mimi gulped. The prior week, Michael had handed in his notice to the New York City Police Department and formally registered Michael Matthews Investigations LLC. Mimi had spent the last few nights designing its marketing. She'd told Michael she would happily join him in his new venture, even though they were also due for a trip to Belize. Michael said she should take scuba lessons first.

Mimi hadn't discussed working with Michael with her father. Not that it was the biggest deal in the world. She would only be working for her father four days a week instead of five, but since the office closed early most Fridays, it wasn't *that* much of a change. She didn't plan to quit anytime soon. But down the road, she might have to.

She knew how her father would react when she'd tell him. On the surface, he'd be all smiles, though he'd express reservations about what she was doing. (Just the word "investigation" was enough to set him off.) Yet, she worried how he'd feel deep down. Would he think his daughter was deserting him? She had worked at her father's office for two years. It had become her life. His, too.

"Dad," she said, "you know Michael is retiring. Police officers in New York can stop working at forty-two with a full pension."

"Really?" Max said. "Good for him." He wiped his chin. "I've been meaning to tell you, Michael's a good guy. If I have a daughter that's constantly getting into trouble, it's good that she's dating a cop."

"So it doesn't bother you that he's not Jewish?"

"Sure, it bugs me. A little. Not a lot. It helps there's not that many Jewish cops. And by the way, the reason I didn't like that first husband of yours wasn't because he wasn't Jewish. It was because he was a *schmuck*. And the world's full of those. They come in all religions."

Mimi laughed. "That's true."

"Besides, I learned a long time ago I can't tell you what you do. I've tried a million times, and you don't listen, so what's the point?"

God, Mimi thought. *Michael told me almost the exact same thing. Best not to think about that.*

"Anyway," Max continued. "I like Michael. I particularly like how he keeps telling you not to investigate."

"Yeah, Dad, about that—"

Before she could finish her sentence, Max shushed her. Channah's father was speaking.

Mr. Morgenstern opened with a religious benediction, then turned to the bride and groom.

"It's no secret that our family has known darkness," he said. "My daughter suffered a loss no person should ever have to endure, especially at such a young age. It's a loss that still lies heavily on our hearts.

"But Zeke, you are a special person. I will forever be grateful to you. You put the light back in my daughter's eyes."

Zeke beamed like he'd won the lottery.

The talk of loss made Mimi think about Rosalyn, which she'd been doing a lot lately. She remembered Rosalyn's last words to her: "It really seems like you're doing well." At the time Mimi considered that condescending, like Rosalyn was throwing her a bone.

Now, she thought, Rosalyn was being sincere. Yes, Mimi's life wasn't perfect. But whose is? When Rosalyn visited their office, she asked how Mimi was doing, but Mimi never asked the same about her. Mimi was so convinced that Rosalyn had it all, she couldn't see how little she had. Mimi wished she'd been there for her, and they could talk things over, like they did in the old days.

Mimi was feeling melancholy about her former friend, but she didn't want to ruin the wedding of her current one. The music began to play again, a particularly raucous version of *Hava Nagila*. Mimi succumbed to the lure of the dance floor. Channah's face glowed with sweat and when she saw Mimi join the crowd, she enveloped her in a big hug.

Mimi and three other women put Channah on a chair. They each took a leg and hoisted it in the air. Channah looked both terrified and thrilled. Mimi felt so happy for her, she almost cried.

Mimi knew from experience that life was indeed full of loss and darkness. But at that moment, she didn't feel cursed. She felt blessed.

GLOSSARY

of Yiddish/Hebrew/Diamond Industry Terms
(But Mostly Yiddish)

Baruch Hashem—Hebrew. Translates to "blessed be the name." Generally used as "thank God."

Bubbe-meise—Yiddish. "An old wives' tale." A fantasy.

Bubelah—Yiddish. Sweetheart, term of endearment.

Carat—Diamond industry. The unit that serves as a measurement for a diamond's weight. It is believed to have been derived from the carob bean. Also used for other gemstones.

Cert—Diamond industry. Short for "certificate." Trade slang for a report from a grading laboratory.

Chuppah—Hebrew. Translates to "covering." The traditional canopy under which a Jewish bride and groom get married.

Cleaving—Diamond industry. The process of separating a rough diamond into different pieces so it can be turned into a polished gem.

Frum—Yiddish. Devout, pious.

Hawker—Diamond industry. A person (generally a man) who stands on Forty-Seventh Street and tries to lure passers-by into a store, to either buy something or trade in their used jewelry.

Hashem—Hebrew. Translates to "the name." It is used by Orthodox Jews who don't wish to say the word *God.*

Hava Nagila—Hebrew. A Jewish folk song. Its title translates to "let us rejoice."

Hock—Yiddish. To bother, nag.

Internally flawless—Diamond industry. The second highest of the eleven clarity grades used to grade diamonds. (Flawless is the highest, but those diamonds are exceptionally rare.) An internally flawless diamond exhibits no visible inclusions under a ten-power loupe. However, it usually has surface blemishes, like graining or polish marks, that prevent it from attaining the top grade. These blemishes are usually extremely hard for the untrained eye to see. Sometimes even trained eyes have difficulty.

Karat—Jewelry industry. A unit used to measure gold, which indicates the proportion of gold, out of a total of 24. An 18-karat gold brooch consists of 18 parts gold, and six parts another alloy. Not to be confused with *carat* with a "c," which as, previously noted, is the weight measurement for gemstones.

Kishkes—Yiddish. A person's "guts."

Lashon hara—Hebrew. Negative speech about another person.

Loupe—Diamond industry. A small handheld magnifying glass that lets dealers examine diamonds at ten-power magnification.

Make—Diamond industry. A term that refers to a diamond's cut, specifically how well the diamond was cut. If a diamond has a "nice make," it was well-cut. If it has an "off make," not so much.

Man trap—Diamond industry. The small rectangular space

between double doors that's a standard security feature of diamond offices.

Mazal—*Hebrew/diamond industry.* Short for "*Mazal u' brucha*," which translates to "luck and blessings." Along with a handshake, it is used to seal deals in the diamond industry.

Maven—*Yiddish.* An expert—or sometimes, a self-described expert.

Mazal Tov—*Hebrew/Yiddish.* Translates to "good luck." It is uttered as a form of congratulations on happy occasions.

Meshuga—*Yiddish.* Crazy.

Meshugana—*Yiddish.* A crazy person. Noun form of above.

Naches—*Yiddish.* Something you derive pride or pleasure from.

Narishkeit—*Yiddish.* Foolishness.

Nebach—*Yiddish.* "What a pity."

Olav ha-shalom—*Hebrew.* Generally said after mentioning the name of a person who died. It translates to "may peace be upon" the departed one—i.e. "may they rest in peace."

Oy—*Yiddish.* An expression of dismay. Also: *oy vey.*

Payis—*Hebrew.* Sidecurls. Worn by some religious men and boys due to the Biblical injunction against shaving the "corners" of one's head.

Pear-shape—*Diamond industry.* A popular diamond cut that's shaped like—what else?—a pear. Some look more like teardrops.

Private—*Diamond industry.* Someone not in the industry that wants to buy a diamond.

Schmuck—Yiddish. A jerk. Kind of like a *putz.* As Max says, the world's full of them.

Shabbat—Hebrew. The traditional day of rest and prayer in Judaism. It starts Friday night at sundown and ends on sundown Saturday night.

Shul—Yiddish. Synagogue.

Table—Diamond industry. The flat facet on the top of a diamond that refracts light.

Tachlis—Yiddish. Bottom line.

Treatment—Diamond industry. An artificial process, which can be either temporary or permanent, that enhances a gem's color or clarity. As a rule, treated stones are worth less than others.

Tsuris—Yiddish. Problems, troubles, sources of aggravation.

Tuchus—Yiddish. Rear end.

Verkakte—Yiddish. Ridiculous.

VVS1—Diamond industry. VVS1 and VVS2 are the highest clarity grades next to internally flawless. VVS stands for "very very slightly included." It means the stone has flaws that are difficult for a skilled grader to see using ten-power magnification.

Yarmulke—Yiddish. A skullcap worn most times by Orthodox Jewish men, as well as by less observant Jews during visits to synagogues and other religious occasions. It is generally thought to signify that the wearer is always under God.

R OB BATES HAS WRITTEN ABOUT THE diamond industry for
three decades. He is currently the news director of *JCK*, the
leading publication in the jewelry industry. There, he has won 12
editorial awards, and been quoted as an industry authority in *The
New York Times*, *The Wall Street Journal*, and on National Public
Radio. He is also a comedy writer and performer, whose work has
appeared on FuseTV, comedycentral.com, and Mcsweeneys. He
lives in Manhattan with his wife and son.

Printed in the USA
CPSIA information can be obtained
at www.ICGtesting.com
LVHW030051230823
755984LV00015B/220